# Ain't No Sunshine

### By Tiona Pathenia Brown

This is a work of fiction. It is not meant to depict, portray or represent any particular persons. All the characters, incidents and dialogues are the products of the author's imagination and are not to be constructed as real. Any resemblance to actual events or person living or dead is purely coincidental.

ISBN-10: 0-615-31350-7

ISBN-13: 978-0-615-31350-4

*The truth is we're all messed up! I hope we get or keep the courage to face reality so we can deal with our truth, and start to heal our wounds. They run deep, so believe me when I say now is the time.* **You know who you are.**

**Alexis,**

*Each day I struggled to understand how I was going to be your mother. Why I had to be a mom? Was I going to be good enough for you, and would I have enough love in my heart to break a vicious cycle? I wasted my time wondering because you had enough love in your heart for the both of us. You never allowed me to hold back my love! I thank you for teaching me that children are not monsters and for opening my memory bank so I could remember I once was a child. I love you fat-butt!*

**Mom**

*Never doubt my love for you. I know you're not perfect and I know that because I have flaws. You taught me how to keep it real and you'll always be my big Sam.*
*I say to you...*
*Thanks for being my mother*

**Dad**

*You think you're always last and sometimes you are. But love doesn't have a place. I remember when you held me and that was enough.*
*Chicken Lady*

**Ten**

*We are so different but we remain family. A lot of times most of you get on my damn nerves and other times you touch a part of my heart that is difficult to penetrate. We will always be the one and only Brown's, with a touch of Cannon blood.*

**Jerry,**

*When you told me, I was stunned. How could he do this to you? I thought you would snap but like the pride and strength of one thousand black women, you said, "Hey, I still have to live!" The beauty in your words was that you meant them. You inspire me to judge not and educate first.*
*I love you ma.*

**Nyeisha**
*Sometimes you're lucky enough to get a sister and a best friend in one!*

**Tyisha**
*You know how we do. We ride, we take breaks, but at the end of the day, "I love you!"*
*Thanks for letting me be TB with an occasional P.*

**Keyona,**
*"Hello Sister" Do you know how much that greeting means to me?*
*You and I together make a mess but what would life be without a little drama!*

**Mom**
*When I don't know what to do or how I'll get through, you lift me up. I love you each day for teaching me how to love me!*

**Aunt Rene**
*I cannot thank you enough for your editing assistance, your encouragement, and your love; thanks a billion!*

*They say the Sun never sets,*
*that the Moon just hides it at times.*
*It seems the moon has permanently affixed itself to me,*
*cause I just can't seem to shine...*

"Bring that fucking anesthesiologist in here!" Monitors, blood, medical instruments, screaming, people, nurses, doctors, and a seventeen-year-old adolescent who is about to bring an innocent, precious life into this world. At this point, I still don't know where I went wrong. I was supposed to be in the honor society and pursuing my promising modeling career. Here I am, failing my junior year of high school, big as a house, and unsure if my baby's father is going to be here in time for our child's arrival. All I can do is scream for the lethal dose of drugs that will make this pain diminish. "Breathe and relax. The anesthesiologist will be back in a second to give you the epidural." These words from the nurse sounded comforting, but then a contraction comes and the pain takes over. "Any goddamn minute now!"

As far back as I can remember I always found myself in situations that I could not repair, or just didn't know how to fix. You would think I would have learned a lesson or two from my mother. She has ten children – her first at age sixteen and her youngest at thirty-six – and five baby fathers. But you know what they say about assuming.

My name is Sunshine. I am the third oldest of the ten, and I still couldn't retain the knowledge from the examples set in front of me. My journey has taken me through some tough times. I've learned some extremely difficult life lessons. Some still remain a mystery.

*Can all broken fixtures be repaired?*

## Chapter I

When I was born my mother already had two children – my oldest sister, Sandra, and my brother, Shawn – by two different men. My sister's dad stayed around until m y mom's eighth month of pregnancy, and then blatantly said that he was too young to be a father, so he took off. My brother's dad ran out the day she came home from the doctor's office with the positive pregnancy test in her hand.

When my dad came along, my mom was living in an efficiency in the ghetto of North Philly. He told me how he was going to the store one day when he first laid eyes on her. How she was so pretty that he didn't give a damn about her having children, or possibly having a man. He was staying with his mom at the time, and once he found out where she lived – which was only five blocks away – he made it his business to walk past her place daily. Equipped with her address, he waited one morning for her to come out and go to the store, or just open the door so he could say something to her. He didn't remember how long he had to wait (stalker tendencies, sure, but that's my dad), but he said when she did come out, she stared at him, he said hello, and then he ran some corny, broken down line on her that he couldn't even remember anymore. That was the beginning of their relationship. They had sex, she got pregnant, and I was born. What a fairytale, I know, but that's the story of my conception. Oh yeah, I had the enchanted palace to go along with it.

Our apartment was full of roaches and mice. We couldn't keep trash in the apartment because the rodents would eat through the trash bags. The place was so small that when you walked in, you were in. The bathroom, the stove, the bedroom… there were no surprises. It was just all there. The neighborhood wasn't any better. You could see crackheads and junkie prostitutes up and down 25th Street and Lehigh Avenue. The NA building (a.k.a. the recovery house) was just across the street from our place, and when they held meetings it sounded as if they were holding them in our apartment. Our walls were paper-thin and you could hear the slogan, 'One day at time', from all the recovering addicts at the opening and closing of every meeting. I always thought the meetings were a waste of time, because one day after the next they all seemed to relapse. My dad disapproved of the neighborhood because he was raised there, and he wanted better for us. Also taking into consideration his previous drug habit and knowing relapse was eminent, he had to leave the unfavorable environment. If that wasn't enough motivation, my mom was pregnant for the fourth time. We had truly outgrown the apartment. So when he landed a construction job he decided to move us out. The job was paying five hundred a week after taxes, so he knew he could afford to live in a better neighborhood. We moved into a three-bedroom duplex, in Germantown, with a monthly rent of six hundred and fifty dollars.

We hadn't really moved out of the city, but we moved just far enough to stop smelling the stench of crack. The neighborhood was great! There were beautiful big houses, huge green trees, and lawns full of grass everywhere. The streets were clean and there were no visible signs of crackheads or prostitutes anywhere. My mom was enthusiastic about the move, and when she found out our school was on the corner of the block, that only added to her joy. I was starting kindergarten, and my sister and brother were already in school, so she was thrilled with the fact that we could walk by ourselves. An added bonus to our move was our upstairs neighbors, Gloria, and her seventeen-year-old son, Ray, who were friendly and tolerant of inquiring children. Once my mom and dad became comfortable with them, they would let us go upstairs every so often after school.

Gloria was in the army, and she made it sound like the greatest job in the world. She never hesitated to tell us about her adventures. On occasion, Ray would tell us similar war stories, but he would reinvent them by adding characters, sound effects, and he even included us in the stories. Shawn and I would sit there for hours, entranced by their tales. Several times my mom told Ray to stop telling us about the army because she was tired of us asking her how we could join.

It was a feeling of glory to be at our neighbor's. We always wanted Sandra to come up, but she was too busy helping my mom with my younger sister, Stephanie. My mom had given birth almost immediately after we moved in, and she always wanted one of us to change a pamper or make a bottle. Since Sandra was the oldest she didn't catch any slack, and she did both our share. Sandra was only nine, but I swear she handled the baby just as well as my mom, some days even better. She often asked my mom why we didn't have to help, and my mom repeatedly told her we were too young. Shawn was six and I was five, (yeah, only nine months apart, so you know my mom didn't wait her six weeks) and we were very spoiled. My mom treated Shawn like a baby because he was her first boy, and being my dad's first born, he pampered me. My brother and I always prayed that we would skip being eight years old (babysitter's age), or that my mom didn't have any more children because we didn't want to help with them. We were never fond of crying babies or soiled diapers, and the smell made my stomach turn something awful.

By the end of my first school year, things started to change. My father became very distant and hardly stayed home. I would see him maybe three or four times a week, and even then it was only a glance of him. The only interaction he and my mom had was during the night. He would come in around midnight or later and I could hear them arguing. "What, you smoking that shit?!"

"If I am, don't worry about it. The rent paid, ain't it?"

"You fuckin' somebody?"

"As long as the rent paid, don't ask me shit!"

This went on for a month or so until I no longer saw my dad at all.

The absence of my father set my mom back on the bills. She was constantly late with the rent, and the utility bills were piling up. To make matters worse, the phone and the gas were in jeopardy of being shut off. Her welfare check wasn't enough to cover the living expenses for her four children and herself. She received two hundred seventy-three dollars twice a month in cash, and four hundred fifty-six dollars once a month in food stamps. My mom sold some of her food stamps at the Chinese store, which was around the corner from our block, to make ends meet. She got seven dollars in cash for every ten dollars of food stamps. Mr. Lee, the owner of the store, became so familiar with us, that he allowed us to cash in the food stamps on our mom's behalf. My mom cashed in a hefty portion, and she still came up short on some of the bills.

With money tight, she decided to get a job as a barmaid at the neighborhood bar. That was wise because they paid under the table. If welfare found out she was working a 9-5, 5-9, or working period, they would cut off her cash, her food stamps, and her health benefits. So working under the table was her only option unless she landed a professional job. Being a high school dropout her choices were limited, and since she didn't have to take the bar exam to work in this bar, she jumped at the opportunity. Not only was the job a good match for her, it was also good for the owner because she fit the description he was seeking. She was tall and slender, 5'8", light-skinned, curvy in all the right places with shoulder-length brown wavy hair, full luscious lips, and overall sex appeal.

My mom worked out arrangements for Gloria to keep an eye on us while she worked from 9 p.m. until 2:30 a.m. Sandra stayed downstairs with Stephanie, and Shawn and I went upstairs with Gloria and Ray. It was so much fun being upstairs because we got to stay up until all hours of the night. Ray had an Atari and we played Pac-Man until we played ourselves to sleep. We called Ray's place our summer camp, and since we couldn't afford to attend the camp in our area and all the free camps were full, Ray's place it was. Besides they offered extended hours. Some days when we ran out of things to do or when I got tired, I thought about my dad. However I started to become more accustomed to him not being around. I asked my mom twice where he was. Both times she instantaneously started crying, so I stopped asking.

The babysitting arrangements were working out well, and Gloria and my mom were getting along great. Gloria started leaving us in the house with Ray, and would hang out with my mom at the bar until she got off. They shared some of the same interests and problems (men and drinking), so it wasn't long before they became girlfriends. Although Gloria was a nice woman, it was somewhat strange to see my mom let her get close because she was such a loner. She always said, "Bitches have issues, and if you have the same gadgets as me, I don't need you." But I guess what they say is true: "You can't have your armor on every day."

My mom's new job brought a new aroma to our house. Every morning her room smelled like Jack Daniel's. I found miniature bottles of alcohol, and Shawn and I would lick the rim to get the taste of the liquor. We pretended to be drunk and staggered around the apartment. Sandra laughed at us because she knew we didn't get enough to be tipsy, let alone drunk. My mom never left as much as a swig in those bottles.

After about a month at the bar my mom was caught up on the rent and the bills, thanks to all the tips she made. She also had a few new guys in her life, and they would stop by or call frequently. Shawn hung up on them because he didn't want my mom to have a boyfriend, but it never bothered me much. When they called I told them she was asleep, which was true because she slept most of the day, like a vampire. She partied all night and slept all day. I didn't get to spend as much time with my mom as I used too, but we had food and the bills were paid, so I was happy.

Then out of the blue, when we were back on our feet, my dad started calling. He asked me a lot of questions, especially about my mom's job and about the new men in her life. But I knew what to say and what not to say because my mom had already quizzed me. I missed him and often asked when he was coming to see me, and he always said "soon". But I wasn't sure if he was telling the truth because my mom didn't want to see him, and when he called she said, "If that's your dad tell him I ain't here." As soon as I hung up she would say, "He ain't shit, he smoking that shit, and I don't want to be bothered with his broke ass!" I couldn't get angry because his drug addiction was real, and he had just gotten fired from his job. Their contract work was slow, and they were laying employees off left and right. His boss had warned him one time too many about being tardy, so when he showed up late for the umpteenth time, they fired him.

Two weeks or so after he started calling, like some kind of sick clockwork, my dad was back at home. He had lost weight and one of his front teeth was missing. His hands and nails looked dark, he slept most of the day, and when he was awake he always seemed paranoid. He went with my mom to work, and as long as Gloria was around everything ran smooth. With Gloria there, most men would slip her their numbers and tell her to pass them off to my mom. But the night she stayed home, my mom ended up getting fired because my dad got into a fist-fight with some guy who tried to slide my mom his number while my dad was at the jukebox.

Now that my dad was back home full time, money started missing, and our TV and VCR vanished. We all knew my dad had taken it. He started stealing my mom's food stamps and cashing them in for dope. It got so bad my mom slept with her pocketbook because he had found all of her hiding spots. Shawn and I spent all of our time upstairs to get away from the cursing and fighting. It was also our only chance to eat something other than Oodles of Noodles, because my dad's return resulted in us having an empty fridge and cabinets. Our refrigerator became a storage box for empty Government cheese containers, Similac, and powdered milk. The only person who was getting a complete meal was the baby, but soon Stephanie's formula was coming up short as well.

For me, things were the worst I'd ever seen, and going upstairs was my only refuge. Gloria had to go back to her army base for two weeks, and since Ray was of age, she allowed him to stay home by himself. We had really good times with Ray, so my mom said it was okay for us to continue to go upstairs. When Gloria was gone he let me play in her clothes and with her make-up, while Shawn played video games and watched movies all day. One day I broke a bottle of Gloria's perfume, and instead of telling Ray the truth, I told him I wanted to leave because I was bored. I knew my mom would be pissed because she couldn't afford to replace it, so I wanted to go. However before I could walk off he saw the broken bottle and my face clammed up. He assured me I didn't have to worry because he wasn't going to tell on me, and that he knew how we could have some real fun. Then he told Shawn to play the game, while he got me some of his mom's good clothes and jewelry to play with. He walked to the TV and turned the volume on the maximum setting, and then he took me into his mom's room and locked the door.

He sat me on the bed, kneeled on his knees, and asked me if I liked him. I told him yeah, and then he asked me why. I warily replied, "Because you're fun, and you let me play with your mom's stuff." Then he devilishly asked, "Since I'm being nice to you, can you be nice to me?" Unsure of his question or intentions, I said, "Yeah", and then he kissed me on my cheek. I didn't know what to feel or say, so I smiled. Then he put his finger in front of his mouth, signaling me to be quiet, and started to kiss me on my mouth. I pulled away from him when I felt his tongue in my mouth, but he gripped me tighter. Before I could think about leaving, my panties were off, his penis was out, and his fingers were in my vagina. He laid me back on the bed and started to lick and suck my vagina. All the while he was covering my mouth. Ray pulled my hands and told me to rub his head. I didn't want to, but even with tears pouring down my face he forced me to rub his head. "Do you like it?" I couldn't respond. I was dazed and unaware of what to say or why he thought this would be fun. Then he asked me if I wanted to taste it. Sobbing, I said, "Can I please go home?" He then pushed his penis in my mouth, and started moaning and asking me how it tasted. I didn't know how to escape and my mouth was hurting, and when I thought he was finished, the real pain began. "Ouch! Stop, please stop, THAT HURTS!" He covered my mouth with his hands and continued to penetrate my vagina. After he finished ejaculating in me, he pulled his dick out and lay beside me, while he caressed me. Then, as if nothing had happened, he got up and put my clothes back on. I was still crying so he wiped my face and said, "Don't tell nobody because you said you liked me. That's what people do when they like each other, so it's okay." He kissed me on my lips, unlocked the door, and went to the bathroom.

When I came out of the room Shawn was still consumed with playing the game, and he hadn't noticed that anything was wrong as Ray nonchalantly sat next to him and started playing the game too. I headed for the door because my vagina, and my mouth, were burning and throbbing with pain. When I reached for the doorknob he said, "Don't forget, we're friends." I went in our apartment and headed to the bathroom. I started crying again because my stomach was in so much pain. I didn't want my mom and dad to know what happened because me and Ray were friends. So I tried my best to silence my sobs, but when I tried to urinate I began screaming and yelling. My vagina was on fire, and I had never felt pain like that before. My mom ran into the bathroom to see what was going on. "What happened? What happened! Why are you bleeding?!?"

## Chapter II

When my dad came into the bathroom he started panicking and screamed at my mom, trying to figure out what happened. "Look at what that motherfucker did to my baby." He ran upstairs, not knowing that Shawn was still there, and he lost it. My dad stabbed Ray seven times. Once in the face, in the neck, twice in his abdomen, and three times in his chest. Shawn saw everything.

My dad was sent to Holmesburg Prison, awaiting trial for the attempted murder of Ray Edwards. Barely breathing and in a coma, Ray was listed in critical condition and placed in the Intensive Care Unit, at the Medical College of Pennsylvania. Immediately following surgery to stop his internal bleeding, he had to be placed on life support because his lungs collapsed. After receiving the tragic news from her sergeant, Gloria took the first flight home. She struggled to maintain her sanity as she watched him slip in and out of consciousness for a week. The doctor decided to take him off of life support because his condition wasn't improving and her insurance didn't cover the cost. After the plug was pulled, Ray never regained consciousness, and he silently passed away twenty minutes later.

The day after Ray died, my dad's public defender called my mom and said the charge was upgraded to murder. This was the last thing my mom needed because she was already on edge, because she was so worried about the condition of my fragile and youthful vagina. I was constantly spotting blood and having vaginal discharge, and whenever I urinated I cried and screamed. The doctor said I was lucky Ray wasn't a bigger fellow because he could have done some irreversible damage. Considering the fact that I had to get twenty-two stitches to repair my vaginal tear, I didn't feel so lucky. I had to get tested for STDs, and fortunately all tests came back negative. So when the call came, my mom was hysterical. She started throwing dishes, breaking lamps, and she started cutting.

"Oh my God, call 911! Mom, no! Mom! Shawn, call the cops! Sunshine, call the cops!" I couldn't move. My mom fell to the floor. She was holding herself and shaking, and there was blood all over her. Sandra had the baby and couldn't stop screaming.

"911. What is the emergency?"

"We need the cops here right away. My mom is dying!"

"What is your name?"

"Shawn! My mom is bleeding!"

"What's your address?"

"I don't know..."

"Shawn, are you there?... Shawn?"

The cops arrived and took us into our room while the paramedics helped my mom. Sandra looked the most stable so they asked her what happened, and where our father was. Since she didn't have an answer, they asked her if we had any family. She gave them the first number that popped in her head, and they told us not to worry, that our mom would be okay. After the paramedics took my mom to the hospital, the cops took us to the police headquarters to see how the Department of Human Services (DHS) would handle our situation. We spent a few hours at the police district until we saw the familiar face of our grandma, with the look of disgust on it. My mom's last encounter with our grandma ended on bad terms, and the tension between them remained thick. My mom never found a reason to forgive my grandma, after she put her out on the streets when she found out she was pregnant. My mom was sixteen with nowhere to go, and the memories of her struggle to find food and shelter never allowed her to heal their broken bond. So when my grandma bluntly and callously said, "It was only a matter of time" to the DHS worker, it came as no surprise to us.

My grandma and the DHS worker talked for about an hour before any decisions were made. They took us into a room and explained to us our mom had been 302'd, and she was unable to care for us. My grandma made it clear she only had room for two of us, and the other two would have to go live with our Uncle Carleton. Since Sandra was the oldest and could help her with the baby, she decided to take them; Shawn and I would have to live with our uncle. With the decision in place, they left the room and gave us less than an hour to say our goodbyes. Sandra kept assuring us we'd all be together again, and she reminded us to stay strong. I was unconvinced, and all I could do was blame myself. If I hadn't let Ray touch me, my dad wouldn't be in jail, and my mom wouldn't have tried to kill herself. I was standing in a room which felt as if the walls were closing in on me. A room filled with fear, guilt, and hopelessness. Then without warning the door swung open, and Shawn and I gave our sisters quick kisses and hugs. Then we left with our uncle.

## Chapter III

Living with my uncle wasn't too bad. He lived in a huge house in the suburbs of Elkins Park, not too far outside the city. He had so much backyard that it extended around to the front of the house – he actually had land! The interior was intriguing as well. He had a two-story home with three bedrooms, two bathrooms, a full kitchen, two dining areas, an enormous living room, an attic, a finished basement, and gigantic walk-in closets. The furniture looked and smelled expensive, like it had never been sat on. His house was better than any house I'd ever been in or even seen.

The first day we got there my uncle went over the ground rules and assigned us a list of chores. He showed us to our bedrooms, and told us our main goal was to keep them as clean as they were when we first saw them. He was very pleasant with us and said as long as we were courteous, neat, and honest, we'd get along well.

The trauma involving my mom and dad had really hit me, but since no one was talking about it, I just went along with the program. Soon school commenced, and we began our daily routine of breakfast at the small dining area table, along with brief discussions of what our day would entail. At the end of breakfast my uncle always gave us one dollar and five cents, because we had to pay for school lunch. He regularly joked with us about going from free lunch to paying for it. Sometimes he would sing, *"Well we're moving on up...to the east side"*. Shawn and I never paid it any serious attention because he provided us with everything, and we thought he was just joking. So after his brief comedy set, we were off to school.

I had always enjoyed school, but this school was a different story. We were a part of the 'I can't believe they're black' crew. There were only five African-American children in the entire school - Shawn and me, and the three sisters who lived across the street from us. Shawn was in second grade; I was in first. Being in different classes made things difficult for me. This kid in my class called me blackie and always asked if I was on welfare. Often he'd cause a scene in front of the other kids, and everyone would laugh at me. When we would go out for recess he'd ask me if I wanted a peanuckle sandwich, and although I never replied yes, he'd press his knuckles into my forehead anyway.

This went on for about a month until I got the courage to tell my brother. I was tired of being embarrassed, so one day at recess I told Shawn how David had been hitting me, and calling me blackie and welfare baby. My brother walked up to him and whooped his butt. He didn't ask any questions. Instead he started punching him in the face. Shawn did such a good job of beating David up that he looked like a professional boxer. His stance, his jab, and his uppercut all appeared as if he had professional training. I'd never seen my brother fight before, and I must say I was impressed, yet a bit scared he was going to seriously hurt David. By the time my teacher realized what was going on, Shawn had David in a headlock, and he was apologizing to me with blood dripping from his lips.

We were all sent to the principal's office. David and I were given a warning, but my brother was suspended for two days, and my uncle had to come in for a meeting with the principal. We had never gotten into trouble before and had no clue how my uncle would react. Shawn saw how nervous I was and told me not to worry because it wasn't my fault, but when we got home my uncle was pissed. He was shouting and asking us why we had to be the ones to start a ruckus in this neighborhood. "You can always move out the ghetto, but you can't take the ghetto out of you two! If I knew you guys were going to be ghetto, I would have bussed y'all back to your raggedy ass school." I was scared, but I'd been around so much screaming with my parents that I figured it would blow over.

At that moment my uncle did something that freaked Shawn and me out. He grabbed Shawn's wrist and started looking at his watch, then he walked over to me and did the same thing. "You did it! Your pulse is beating the fastest so you must be guilty." He sent Shawn upstairs to get the biggest belt he could find. I looked at my brother because I hadn't done anything, but he was given an order, so he walked to find the spanker. The belt he brought downstairs was bigger than both of our backsides combined, and I became upset because Shawn followed my uncle's directions too well. Just looking at the belt, I knew it was going to kill me or at least cause serious damage to my backside. "Sunshine, you think you can come up here and start this nonsense? I'll teach you to get your brother involved in your mess!"

That's when the beatings begin. After the first one, I thought I was paralyzed because I couldn't feel anything below my neck. I was so thin (35 pounds and only six years old), and with every swing of the belt my knees buckled, and I'd fall down. Each time I fell my uncle held me up and swung again. He continued spanking until I no longer cried, until he beat the cry out of me. And if I thought I had enough, I had to hold my arms straight out in front of me, while he put one phone book in each of my hands. "Each time you drop one you'll get a lick!" I tried to hold the books up but my weak arms gave out. But after four more hits he realized I would keep dropping them, so he instructed me to take my ghetto ass to bed.

From that day on I walked a very fine line and tried to stay out of my uncle's path, but regrettably for my backside, his belt had my name on it. My behind and back were tired of having purple contusions and welts. I went to school many times with no panties on, because I couldn't stand the pain of them rubbing against my bruised behind. I got so much relief from sitting my bare butt on those cold wooden chairs at school, that no panties after a beating became my new rule. My pulse always beat the fastest, so I got the bulk of the spankings. If something broke, if a dish was left in the sink, if Shawn left food in his room, if a phone message wasn't delivered, if I didn't do well on a test (less than 96%), it was more than likely, almost guaranteed, I'd get whooped.

## Chapter IV

By now we'd been staying with my uncle for two and a half years. I had adapted to the spankings and also to his occasional meltdowns. His breakdowns, which brought a smile to my heart, were brought on by the absence of his family. He had a rich man's family – a beautiful wife who gave him a son and then a daughter, but since his divorce he hadn't seen his children or his wife. They split because he spanked his daughter for leaving dishes in the sink, and the beating left black and purple marks on her backside. His wife moved out of state a year before we arrived, and she made it clear she didn't want any contact with him. Each time my uncle searched for them and was successful in getting their phone number, they'd have it changed within a day. One would think the loss of his family would have discouraged him from spanking anyone else, but that theory proved faulty because he showed no mercy on my behind.

Even though my uncle had a hardcore exterior, the lack of communication with his family really sent him through some devastating changes. When he thought we were asleep, he cried late at night. One night, although I risked getting my behind tore off (firstly for being up late, and secondly for spying on him), I peeked in his room and saw him holding a picture of his family and sobbing to no end. Sometimes I felt pity for my uncle, but the compassion easily dissolved, because how much sympathy can you have for someone who always found an illegitimate reason to beat you?

Somewhere between getting spanked, walking a straight line, maintaining straight A's, doing chores, and always feeling out of place and responsible for what happened to my family, I kept hold of hope. I prayed on my knees, on my back, in chairs, walking to school, at the dinner table (and not to bless my food), anywhere, and anytime I could. The only reasons I went to church were to pray to be rescued, and to uphold my uncle's reputation as a deacon. Members of the church should have done a thorough background check before selecting my uncle as a deacon, because I don't think they'd feel too comfortable knowing they had invited the devil's advocate into their holy sanctuary. Better yet, someone should have performed an exorcism on him to help him put the belt down. Instead they gave him a prestigious position in the church. My uncle had a lot of people fooled. He was one of those people who would do anything for you, take you anywhere, volunteer, and not only let you cry on his shoulder but offer a well thought-out solution. But don't luck up and be related or married to him because you stand a great chance of getting your backside spanked. Being kin was the only way you'd see his true colors. Not the handsome, middle-aged, stocky, muscular, brown-skinned, professional man, but his evil diabolical twin.

For the first year with my uncle, prayer was the only tool I had to keep my head and spirits up. Repeatedly I prayed for my mom to save me. However, time gave way to reality, and my faith in a rescue rapidly faded. In the beginning she tried calling us once they let her out of the mental hospital. But I think the guilt she felt from us crying, and pleading with her to come and get us became too much; so eventually she stopped calling. With the collapse of communication with my mom, I was even more thankful that we kept in steady contact with Sandra. Sandra called often to update us on my mom's progress and her whereabouts. She knew a lot more than we did. That credit was due to my grandma. She had a mouth on her, and it was no secret she disliked my mom, so she blurted out my mom's business like it was free lunch. One time Sandra told us our mom was smoked out, and in and out of rehab. Another month she said she was homeless and living in a women's shelter. What was I praying for? It was all overwhelming, but I felt any news was better than no news. However, after not receiving even an ounce of good news, I began to question the source and eventually tuned out all information.

Emotionally I was unable to handle the stress. I needed to vent. I knew my mom was having problems but I couldn't understand why she wasn't with us, and to make matters worse I had no one to talk to. Shawn was too angry with my mom for leaving us to talk to me, and I wouldn't dare tell my uncle my problems; he might have felt my pulse and beat me for that. Sandra, who I believed might have a deep, hidden love for my mom, proved to be the worst person to talk to because she had taken on the same attitude as my grandma. Some days I couldn't tell the difference in who I was talking to. She was pissed with my mom, but I felt this whole mess was my fault. I was left with no emotional outlet. So I kept my mouth shut and my pain bottled up.

While my uncle wouldn't talk to us about our mom, he was adamant that we see our sisters. As long as my grandma gave the okay, we spent the weekends at her house. Being at my grandma's was like being on vacation from a torture chamber. I didn't have to worry about all of those fine lines. I could just breathe easy. My grandma was sweet when she wanted to be, easier to get along with, and she didn't have any belts used for spanking in her closet. It was obvious she took a real liking to me because when I came over we spent most of our time together. She often talked to me about my life, and how not to grow up to be like my mother. I didn't care if she talked about my mom – and she did – because I loved my mom, and no negative descriptions or spankings would make me feel differently.

When the school year ended we visited my grandma more frequently, and each time I had to return to my uncle's I missed her more. As soon as I would get in my room, I'd call her and tell her how much I missed her, and how I loved being at her place. She loved having me over as well, and she asked me if I wanted to come live with her. I know she was confused with my decision to stay with my uncle, but I was scared to leave Shawn there. Maybe he would start beating him, and I couldn't handle that, so my only answer could be no. But my grandma had a better solution. When she called and said Shawn and I could stay the rest of the summer with her I was ecstatic. No spankings, no pulse readings, just love and fun. Then my face turned pale because I thought, "Is he going to spank me before I go?" It was the break I had been waiting for, and if I had to get one more spanking, who cared? By that time, I had lost count of how many I had received, and my behind was always purple anyway. Before my grandma hung up, she assured me     my uncle was okay with us staying with her for the summer, alleviating my anxiety.

Once my uncle confirmed our summer getaway I packed everything I owned. When he saw my bags, he said, "Leave some here because you'll be back." I wished I didn't have to go back to his house, but for now this vacation was good enough. We were packed, and waiting in the living room for my uncle to come downstairs and load the car, when the doorbell rang. I ran to the door and looked out the mail slot, because I wasn't tall enough to see out the peephole. I said, "Good day. Who is it?" No one responded, so I repeated myself, and then my uncle yelled, "Sunshine who is it?" "I'm not sure," I yelled back. All I could see was a pudgy belly. My uncle hurried down the stairs and opened the door. It was my mom and dad, and they were holding two large suitcases and a box of trash bags.

"I'm here for my kids!" my mom said. My uncle stood frozen and in shock for a few minutes, before he could get his words out.

"Let's talk inside." My dad appeared to be agitated with my uncle's reply, then he bluntly and aggressively said, "It ain't shit to talk about. You heard what she said! Give me my kids, and let me get their stuff!"

## Chapter V

It seemed as though we hadn't been in the car fifteen minutes before we were pulling up to my grandma's house. Shawn and I couldn't muster up the courage to say a word. We were so happy to see my mom that we just smiled and sat back. It was amazing how all of Shawn's anger simply flew out the window, and each time I looked at his face his smile got bigger and brighter. When we pulled into the driveway, the front door was already open because my uncle had called my grandma to let her know we were on our way. Sandra was standing in the doorway with a disappointed look on her face, and when we got out of the car she stared but didn't speak. When we begin walking towards her, she reluctantly strolled in the house to get her bags, without uttering a word.

Upon entering the house, there was a strange feeling in the air. My grandma came walking down the steps with Stephanie in one arm, and her clothes in the other. Instead of speaking she stared at my mom maliciously and rolled her eyes with disgust. When my grandma handed Stephanie to my mom, she started screaming and yelling for her mommy. Stephanie didn't know my mom, and she recognized my grandma as her mother. Instead of letting her scream, my grandma handed Stephanie to Sandra because she was more comfortable with her. Then she kissed both of them on their cheeks, and when I looked up at my grandma, tears were rolling down her face. I'd never seen my grandma cry before and she rarely showed emotions. I knew my grandma had allowed a layer of her defense to shed and had grown close to Sandra and Stephanie, but I didn't think she would care if they left. Our living arrangements were only temporary, and now it was time for us to go back with our family. My grandma walked to the door, as if to usher us out, and said, "Make sure you don't bring them back!" She didn't speak another word.

The car ride was filled with silence, uncertainties, and smiles from Shawn and me. We had no clue where we were going to live, how my father got out of jail, how many months pregnant my mom was, why Sandra was so pissed off, or why my mom and dad weren't talking to us. We finally arrived in North Philly. We were back in the old neighborhood, only five blocks from our old apartment. All of the drug addicts, trash, and rodents were exactly where we left them. The neighborhood felt gloomy and miserable. I had fallen in love with the fresh smelling grass, clean streets, and beautiful houses in Elkins Park, but this was our home now. If it meant giving up my large comfy room and beautiful scenery to be with my mom and dad, I was in.

Our new apartment was a one bedroom, but it was in fact bigger than our first apartment. Not big enough to adequately accommodate all of us, but we had a kitchen, living room, dining room, bathroom, and bedroom. All of us kids had to share the bedroom while my mom and dad slept on the sofa bed. Sharing a room wasn't the worst thing that could happen, but trying to share a twin mattress was. So Shawn and I quickly made floor plans with our pillow and blankets.

Within a few weeks of getting adjusted, things began to loosen up. My dad finally decided to sit us down and tell us how he got out of jail. The jury saw in his favor and decided to go with a lesser charge, which resulted in him spending two years behind bars. They weren't willing to let him off scot free, and he had to walk off the rest of his two-to-four-year manslaughter conviction on parole. As soon as he got out he found my mom, landed a job, got us an apartment, and came to get us. My mom came running into the room because she had to put her two cents in. "I found the apartment," she said, smiling. She told us she was going to have a baby girl in a few months, and she needed us to help her out while my dad was at work. We were excited and willing to help, but Sandra didn't share our enthusiasm.

Sandra and my mom were not on good terms. Sandra was incredibly distant and seldom talked to either my mom or my dad. She did talk to us and was particularly close to Stephanie. It was hard to tell who Stephanie's mom was because Sandra always had her. My mom tried vigorously to get Stephanie to open up to her, and she tried to teach her t o call her mommy, but she wouldn't. She'd just smile and then look at Sandra and call her mom. That hurt my mom a lot, and she cried about it sometimes. But instead of getting angry she let Sandra and Stephanie know how much she loved both of them, and how she hoped they'd forgive her. I wished Sandra could understand and let go of her hatred. I was thrilled that we were all together again, and I was especially excited at the return of my father.

My dad and I were really tight. He let me stay up late and sleep on the sofa bed, as long as no hanky-panky was going on. When I slept with my dad he held me so tight that I thought he would suffocate me. One night he woke me up at two in the morning and asked me if I remembered what happened to me. I looked to see if my mom was awake because I didn't want her to hear me. I was scared she might hurt herself again. When I saw she was sleep I said yes, and he started crying uncontrollably. He kept saying how sorry he was because he didn't protect me, and he'd rather die than allow anyone to hurt me again. He cried for almost two hours, while he held me close and apologized for not being there. I felt terrible and guilty. I never thought it was my dad's fault. I was responsible for the whole event. Ray was my friend, and I must have done something to trigger him. "Dad I love you, and you don't have to worry because I don't have any friends," I said in hopes of making him feel better. But then I began crying. The thought of my family being separated, Sandra's hatred towards my mom, the beatings, and the time my dad spent in jail – all because of me – was enough to cripple my mind. That night I fell asleep huddled in my dad's arms, and for the first time in a long time I felt safe enough to clear my mind and forget everything.

## Chapter VI

I fell asleep to a beautiful dream and awoke to a horrifying nightmare. My mom and dad were back on drugs, and my dad had lost yet another job. He didn't even wait for us to get totally settled in our new apartment before the drugs started calling his name. I was confused because I thought things were going good. We were a family again, and we were trying to move to a better neighborhood and live happily ever after. Two plus years clean, four months on the street and bam! Back on drugs. My dad returned to his old routines of stealing, scamming, and not coming around. My mom, who was seven months pregnant, had no business doing drugs. Her body was so skinny and frail looking, but her belly was plump. She looked like an Ethiopian kid from the Feed the Children campaign. I cried constantly because Sandra told us my mom was going to have a crack baby. Not that I knew exactly what that meant, but I was scared the baby would die.

Sandra kept in touch with my grandma (until our phone got cut off) who continued to reinforce her hatred towards my mom. Sandra wanted to leave us and go stay with her, but my grandma was afraid my mom would take her back at any given moment, and that was a pain she would rather not relive. Sandra had given up hope on our family and tried one of my old techniques of praying her way out. She suggested we join her and pray to get adopted. I never said that prayer because I loved my mom, but above all I loved my dad and didn't want to be with anyone but him. Even though I hadn't seen or heard from him in a while, I believed in my heart he was coming back. Besides, prayer, although it took longer than I would have liked, worked the last time. So when I did pray, it was for my mom and dad to kick their drug habit so we could stay together.

On top of my dad being on hiatus and my mom always missing or asleep, there was another important issue at h a n d – our landlord. He came through frequently looking for my mom or for his money. One morning I saw him when I was going to the store to get milk. He handed me an envelope.

My mom hadn't returned from her usual drug mission so I placed it on the kitchen table. When she got her check she'd get high all day and night, then show up a day or two later flat broke. Somebody forgot to inform my mom that she was supposed to raise us, so Sandra had to step up to the plate. She did the best for us with what we had, like a mother should. She taught Shawn and I how to make oodles of noodles and grilled cheese sandwiches which were our gourmet meals. We usually ate cereal for breakfast, lunch, and dinner (when we had milk), or peanut butter or jelly sandwiches (we never had both). When we didn't have oodles of noodles, cheese, milk (carnation or powdered), peanut butter, jelly, or cereal, she showed us how to make pretzels. She put butter in a heated pan, toasted both sides of the bread, sprinkled salt on one side of the bread, and then removed it from the pan and spread mustard on it. This was Shawn's favorite, and we all enjoyed making them. Hey, we had to create some joy in our life. If it was making pretzels, so be it.

When my mom finally returned from operation 'get high all night', she opened the eviction notice but treated it as a practical joke. She tore it up and went to sleep. The morning after she ripped up the letter, I asked her where we would stay if we were put out. She ignored me and continued eating her cheese sandwich. I was happy to see her eating because the baby had a better chance of surviving, so I just walked away.

A month had passed and we had forgotten about the landlord. He had sent several notices, and many of them read 'Urgent' on the envelope. I had also stopped crying when it came to my dad. He was nowhere to be found, and he never came by to see how I was doing. I felt betrayed. It was as if he had lied to me about everything, mainly about being my protector. We were all back in school, and Sandra's grades were definitely suffering because she spent most of her time at home with Stephanie. If my mom was out getting high, Sandra missed school. Sometimes my mom wouldn't come home until the next afternoon or days later. The school started sending letters in reference to Sandra's absences, but my mom didn't pay attention to them. When Sandra brought one of the letters home, my mom said to her, "You her mother, ain't you? You supposed to watch your baby." Sandra didn't bother crying. She just walked in our room and took Stephanie with her. She was her mother, and as far as I was concerned she was mom to Shawn and me also.

One weekend we were doing our daily routine of getting by. My mom was knocked out on the sofa, as usual, and it was time to make pretzels. But things were different this time. Our gas was shut off, and we had to use a hotplate to do everything. Cooking on a hotplate was just plain wrong; however Sandra didn't seem to mind. She actually liked them better than the stove because she could sit on the floor and use the hotplate. I hated that thing. We had to boil water to take baths, and it would take so many hotplates and so many pots to fill the tub, that I became comfortable with taking bird baths – washing only my face, pits, and private parts.

After we ate our pretzels, we lounged around the apartment and tried to entertain ourselves. Shawn played cards with Sandra, and I mostly read books. My reading was abruptly interrupted by a loud knock at the door. They kept banging and eventually woke my mom up. Two police officers and our landlord stood at the door. We were finally getting evicted! "Please get your stuff and go," one of the officers said. My mom was stunned, but I couldn't understand why. She knew she didn't pay the rent, so eviction was our only option. She had avoided the landlord and his letters. Now it was time for us to go. It was impossible for us to get all the items we had (mostly clothes because my dad had stolen anything valuable) out of the apartment in the allotted time the cops had given us, so we ended up leaving with what we could carry in our arms and what was on our backs.

## Chapter VII

When we got evicted from our apartment my mom borrowed bus fare from my dad's mom to take us to a place called OSHA. It was a placement center for homeless families. I was upset because we were walking through the streets with trash bags full of clothing, and we were indeed homeless. My dad's mom offered to let Stephanie and I stay with her since we were her grandchildren, but she said she didn't have room for the rest of us. My mom looked pissed off and asked, "Are you gonna give me the bus fare or not?" The thought of staying with my dad's mom didn't strike me as a great escape because I didn't know her that well, and I was scared she might beat me. I didn't feel like finding out if she was a beater or not, so when my mom said, "I'm keeping my family with me," I was relieved. Although my dad's mom was ticked off at her response, she gave us the money anyway.

OSHA looked like a thousand-year-old warehouse that hadn't been cleaned since it was built. The stench made it clear to me that some of the people there were living on the streets and hadn't taken a bath in quite some time. There were over one hundred women, children, and men and only ten chairs. For every twelve families, there was just one social worker. OSHA's staff offered no food, no juice, and no additional seats, just a long wait. We waited from 1:00 in the afternoon to 7:00 p.m. until our social worker called us.

Shawn and I tried to stand the entire time, but our legs began giving way. We had no choice but to join Sandra, Stephanie, and my mom who had set up camp on the floor. I knew we were taking a chance of catching some deadly strain of bacteria by sitting on that floor, but standing was no longer an option. When we were called, we all let out a sigh of relief and shuffled into a small office. The social worker was uncouth and nosey. He asked my mom if she had any money, where our fathers were, if we could we stay with anyone, how we ended up homeless, and how much welfare we got.

After my mom unenthusiastically answered his questions, he told us to go back in the waiting area until he called us again. People were coughing on us and pushing us out of their way. Most of the people were funky and just plain rude. An hour passed and my mom asked how much longer we had to wait. "If you didn't have so many children we would've had a place for you by now," he said without hesitation or regret. Our family was over their limit. The shelter's rooms were small and usually had two to three bunks or cots. They only had one to two large family rooms in every shelter, and they were always taken. You had to be put on a waiting list to get into one of those rooms. Because my mom had four children and one on the way, the availability of rooms was pretty scarce. Two same-sex children could share a bunk or a cot, but they wouldn't allow girls and boys to sleep together.

Around 10:00 p.m., our social worker finally handed my mom our assigned residential sheet and instructed her to wait for the shuttle. At 11:00 our ride arrived, and four other families had to squeeze on the shuttle with us. Someone thought they could do a magic trick by putting an OSHA bumper sticker on the back of a minivan, but that does not miraculously turn a minivan into a shuttle bus. Uncomfortable and cramped, we headed off to our new home.

## Chapter VIII

We were constantly moving from one shelter to the next. During that time my mom gave birth to her fifth child, Sandy. Each shelter we entered brought apparent friction between the women and my mom, but all the men seemed to love her. This was in part to my mom's beauty, which she regained because she stopped using drugs. She looked so youthful and beautiful, and her skin was clear, soft, and silky. It was as if she had never even done drugs. Her curves were back, and now her hair shined and blew through the wind with grace. It was almost expected that the counselors would hit on her. She was sexy when drug-free, and I gave many thanks to the shelter for her recovery. Our case manager did mandatory drug testing. If you came up positive twice after being in a drug program, you got the boot. Luckily my mom was more interested in us having a home, than in running the streets getting high. I was very proud of my mom's looks and I knew that was the reason many of the male counselors gave us special privileges. Eventually, that turned out to be not such a good thing.

The first shelter we got kicked out of was the Salvation Army. My mom had become friendly with a male counselor named Tyrone. He allowed me to spend a few nights at my dad's mom's house, which by shelter law was a definite no-no. No one living in the shelter could spend the night out. When one of the women found me sneaking in early one morning, she reported my mom and we were put out. There were so many rules to follow when we lived in the shelters: no company, no spending nights out, no food in your room, and most importantly no fun. If the rules didn't make you sick, the embarrassment of living in a shelter sure did. Many of my classmates made fun of me and threw things at me when they saw me walking home. They called me shelter girl, welfare baby, and made fun of my mom because she had more children than their families. One annoying, very popular punch line went: "Dang, ya mom pops out babies like she's building a football team!" I didn't think five children were excessive, but to homes with only two or three children, it was a circus. I cried through the jokes and the constant taunting, all the while keeping my spirits up by believing that one day we'd make it out of the s h e l t e r system.

The case manager at the shelter saved seventy-five percent of my mom's cash benefits. Yet when my mom told the DPA office that we were in a shelter, they cut off eighty percent of her food stamps because they knew the shelter fed us. So it was no more cashing them in for a little extra cash. My mom's case manager said when she saved enough money, and found a house with enough bedrooms for all of her children, we could leave. I kept waiting for that day, but houses with more rooms cost more money, and my mom's welfare check would only cover a portion of the rent. And hoping for the Philadelphia Housing Authority to save the day was a joke because their waiting list was numbered in the thousands.

We did a lot of moving around in the shelter system, but we never found a stable spot. Usually we slept in the gym (or recreation room) of shelters, which housed you until they found a permanent room for your family. On Christmas Eve we were in a shelter called Ogantz Manor, and they had the biggest gym I'd ever seen. They had plenty of cots, sleeping bags, and a few bunk beds. We grabbed two cots for my mom, Stephanie, Sandy and Sandra, but Shawn and I grabbed sleeping bags. Sleeping on the floor reminded us of the one fun time we had with Uncle Carl when he took us camping. We all set up shop in the back of the gym. Earlier that day, Shawn and I went to the dollar store to pick up some Christmas decorations for our ten-inch Christmas tree that we found while playing in the neighborhood trash. We couldn't find any defects with the tree, except that it was small, so we decided to put it up for our family. We also bought some presents to go under the tree. Nothing much - gum, nail polish, tissues, a few 99 cent toys, and some wrapping paper. With six dollars between us we made it work. While we were wrapping and placing our gifts under the tree, one of the counselors came over to admire our decorations. He was very impressed by our holiday spirit and promised to present us with something that would add to the festivities. Within minutes he returned to give us some left over Christmas presents, that he had in the office from the previous year's underprivileged children's party. With all the children in the shelter system you might wonder how anything would be left over, but miracles happen... I guess?

Christmas morning arrived, but the sun was not shining. My back ached from sleeping on the extremely hard gym floor, and I felt sick to my stomach. I tried to escape the gloomy morning with a jumpstart, so I went to the bathroom to wash my face and brush my teeth. When I came out I heard Shawn fussing. "Somebody took all our presents!" I looked at the tree; everything was gone. They didn't even leave the bubble gum. The counselors came in and searched the gym, but they never found the gifts. My mom said it would be alright, but that didn't place one tear back in my tear ducts. Shawn vented some of his anger by throwing the tree in the garbage. All the families were looking at us and some of them were saying, "That's a damn shame," but the enemy was under the same roof so they could've saved their pity. I didn't trust any of them. My siblings and I were outraged. We wanted justice, but our complaints to our mom were slightly disregarded. Instead of her getting frustrated she demonstrated great tolerance and began folding our cots and sleeping bags up. Then she said, "We'll be leaving here soon."

**Chapter IX**

We did leave soon. In March we moved into a two-bedroom house in Hunting Park. My mom thought up a plan, then convinced her worker to give back her savings. She knew if the housing authority couldn't find her a place, she had to do it on her own. My mom bought and typed up a lease, showing the place had more rooms than it truly did, and the worker fell for it. I was more than overjoyed – I actually started to breathe again. We could finally settle down and be proud of where we lived. No more missing countless days of school, and now I actually got grades instead of W's. The first time I saw a 'Withheld', meaning I wasn't observed enough to be provided with a grade, I had to question it. But during my shelter stay I became the queen of W's. It was a miracle I passed any of my classes. Moving around from shelter to shelter, we were always out of school. If we stayed up too late, if we helped my mom with the baby, if we had to go to another shelter, we wouldn't go to school. It just became the norm for us to miss days, but now we were settled and things would change.

Priscilla Street was snug, and we fit just fine. There were exactly sixteen houses on the block, eight on both sides, well nine if you counted the abandoned house on the right. Driving down our narrow street proved to be a tricky maneuver, and most car owners parked their cars on the back road to avoid taking the chance of getting their cars hit. Most of the houses were full of kids and ninety-nine percent were single parent homes. We hit the jackpot! My mom and Sandy shared the front room; Sandra, Stephanie, and I slept in the back room; Shawn took the basement. We girls were a little crowded, but it was our space and I felt free. We didn't have to sleep on a cot or on the floor, because my mom had just enough money from her savings to buy us mattresses and a few pieces of furniture. Nothing fancy, just the basics from a used furniture thrift store.

It took only a few weeks for us to become familiar with all the neighbors and the neighborhood. The back-road was the place to be when you got out of school or just needed a place to hangout. We started a club for all the children in the neighborhood, and we built clubhouses out of boxes. The club was a place to talk about our moms, jump on beds that we found in the trash, play cards, or play 'catch a girl, get a girl'. Truthfully, even if I wanted to play that game I wasn't allowed to because Sandra and Shawn were w a t c h d o g s . They remembered all too well the day I was molested and were scared it would happen again.

We loved the corner store. We didn't have to go far to get our snacks, and we stole chips and hugs every day because it was so easy. The owner was a thick, dark-complexioned woman who was in her late eighties from down south. Most days she sat in her chair and slept at the cash register. Other times she appeared delusional. Most adults on our block would wake her up when they bought items from the store; others would leave money on the counter if they had exact change. She rarely got that money because we would go in the store and take it. Some called it stealing - we called it free money. The only day we couldn't get our freebies was on the weekends when her daughter worked. She looked to be in her early thirties, and she was always alert. On occasion, she brought her son Ramon to help out, so if she was slipping he was watching.

Things really seemed to be working out for my family. Everyone was adjusting well, and my mom had found her a new man. His name was Bay, and he lived around the corner from us. In the looks department he was nothing to brag about, but he wasn't on drugs and he had a job. What started off as a date, quickly turned into something more. He began spending more time at our house and swiftly made every effort to befriend us. Bay gave us money and even tried to cook for us. He only knew how to make oodles of noodles - anything else he made was a complete taste catastrophe. It wasn't long before I woke up one morning and realized he had moved in.

## Chapter X

Cleveland Elementary was the school that now housed me. It was predominately black, and when I say predominantly, the only people who weren't black were the white teachers. I was now in the fifth grade and moving on the right track to graduation. For the first time that I could remember I had perfect attendance, and my grades were all A's and one B for every marking period. I couldn't get my math grade up to an A, and to be quite honest I don't even know how I pulled off a B as much as I hated (and still hate) the subject. As far as my behavior grades were concerned, they were perfect, and I received several certificates for outstanding conduct. In fact, I was a bit of a teacher's pet. I loved and enjoyed school, so it was second nature for me to study every day and complete the daily reading.

My teacher was very proud of me and often encouraged me to write and read whenever I could. Ms. Huntley was the type of teacher I needed because she pushed me to pursue my educational passions. Ms. Huntley was nice to me, but she showed a different side of herself to children who misbehaved. One would think her appearance alone would set all the children straight. She was a very tall and big-boned woman. She towered over all the male teachers at 6'0" and weighed more than all of the teachers at a solid 260 pounds. She reminded me of a big Russian man, just with long hair and breasts.

Jerome was our class clown, and Myeisha was our class bully. Jerome took his job seriously and never let a day pass without pulling pranks or telling jokes. He didn't care if he had to sit in the back of the class or stand in the hallway. He always managed to get his jokes in. Myeisha was more inconspicuous with her mischief. During recess she would bump into kids and dare them to hit her back. She'd take your lunch box and throw it in the trash, then wait for you to get it out so she could punch you in the face. Being on my own because Shawn was in middle school, I had to learn how to deal with Myeisha. I hid from her as long as I could until the day she approached me head on. Myeisha was about three to four inches taller than me and weighed about 20 pounds more than all the kids in the fifth grade. She looked like a bully. She was always ashy, had dirty nails, and what hair she did have she tried to slip it into a fan ponytail. Her ripped, dingy, and torn clothing only added to her bully fashion. I guess she started off as a tomboy because she lived with her dad and her three brothers, then some trauma or unresolved anger turned her into a bully. Rumor had it that her mom died during her birth, and that could've been the cause of her bullying, but I never had the guts to confirm the speculation.

Wednesday must have been my lucky day because during lunch Myeisha chose to pick on me. We were at recess, and I was sitting in the yard reading one of the books Ms. Huntley had given me earlier in the week. I was almost finished, with only two chapters left when she walked over. She snatched the book out of my hand and began ripping the pages out. As she continually and piercingly called me a nerd, along with some other choice words, all the kids in the yard encircled us. They started chanting "fight, fight, fight, fight," but I was scared, and I didn't want to fight her because she was so much bigger than me. Also I really hadn't fought before, besides the time Sandra kicked my butt because I didn't go to bed when she told me to. I didn't know if I knew how to fight, but after one jab to my head I quickly learned. I was fighting this big, ashy bully! I mean I was trying to kill her and it showed. I was punching, kicking, scratching. I even bit her. When it was all said and done, I hadn't won the fight, but I stood my ground. The kids in the yard saw it as a draw.

Once Ms. Huntley heard what happened she ran over and instructed us to follow her to the principal's office. She was hasty and irritated with Myeisha, yet consoling to me. She knew I wasn't a troublemaker so while we walked to the office Ms. Huntley told me not to worry. She told Myeisha, on the other hand, that she was getting suspended. She'd been in too many fights and started so much trouble that they didn't know what else to do with her. Graduation was only a few weeks away, and the principal debated if Myeisha would participate in the ceremonies. The principal never made mention about me being in the fight or about any punishment. He did ask me if I was okay and told me my mom was on her way to pick me up. Myeisha and I sat in the principal's office until our parents arrived. She knew I wasn't scared of her, and she never threatened me or even looked my way once while we waited. I had a devilish grin on my face because I knew if push came to shove, this little nerd could give her a run for her money.

My mom was the first parent to arrive, and when she saw how big Myeisha was she demanded to speak with the principal. He was currently in his office with another parent, so Ms. Huntley spoke with my mom in the hallway about Myeisha's disciplinary actions. When my mom came back in the office she asked me how I was. I could see the concern on her face. But I was fine and the only noticeable wounds I had were the few scratches on my face. My mom was still worried and from the look on her face she thought Myeisha whooped my butt. I guaranteed her I was okay and told her Myeisha wasn't stupid enough to try me again. She anxiously waited for Myeisha's dad, who took a long time to arrive because he was used to getting phone calls about his daughter misbehaving. When he got there they talked privately in the principal's office. The meeting lasted around twenty minutes. Then we went home.

When Sandra and Shawn came in the house I told them what happened and they couldn't stop laughing. My mom kept trying to tell them my fight story, even though she wasn't there, but she did describe Myeisha as the biggest fifth grader in the world and that impressed them. They started calling me Muhammad Ali and Shawn asked me to show him my boxing skills. After all, I was an obedient, shy bookworm, and for me to be excited about a fight, which I was in, was a bit out of character. It was the first time I actually had bragging rights and it felt good. Sandra and Shawn had their share of matches and I usually called on them if anyone picked on me, but now I was standing on my own two feet!

## Chapter XI

Middle school was the truth, and I was readily coming out of my shell. This time around I actually had friends. Ever since my fight I wasn't afraid to spark up a conversation, and I was very confident in myself. Now don't get me wrong, I wasn't arrogant or a troublemaker, but I wasn't this timid little girl anymore. I didn't just change on the inside, but I altered my outer appearance as well. Instead of wanting to wear loose, baggy, concealing clothing, I started to dress in a more stylish fashion. I borrowed (without permission) sweaters and shirts from Sandra and convinced my mom to get me jeans that actually fit my body. Even though I was thin with long legs, I was starting to get a little bump behind me so my new jeans enhanced my little booty.

My new confidence was great, but it certainly wasn't geared towards boys. I didn't feel like being bothered with them blowing kisses at me, or writing me love letters that asked me to check the yes or no box at the bottom if I liked them. Instead of throwing the letters in the trash, I checked "no" then sent them on their way until I received one from my classmate John. He was different and more mature than the other boys in my class. He was quiet (the sneaky, mischievous kind), handsome, and he had the cutest dimples. John was very popular among the kids in our grade, and all the girls in my class had a crush on him. He often smiled at me and sometimes gave me this look as if he was waiting for me to walk up and talk to him. So when he gave me the letter asking if I wanted to kiss him or not, I wasn't surprised that I couldn't respond. I wanted to send him my first "yes", but I wouldn't dare. I didn't have the nerve to talk to him, and I don't know if he thought I was weird or what because I never did answer his letter. Simply knowing he liked me made me feel good and that was enough for me.

Since boys weren't exactly my flavor, that left my best friends. We shared all of our classes and when we were at lunch or chilling in the halls, we were always together. The four of us rolled tough. Tanisha, who we called Lil Bitts because she was three inches shorter than all the kids in our entire school, Toya, who was the big girl in our click and had all the juicy grown-up stories because her mom told her everything, Tyisha, who looked older than all of us with her high school senior looking breasts and big butt, and me, the thin, smart, baby-faced, quiet one that was beginning to be turned on by mischief.

Gillespie Middle School was right next door to Gratz High School. That's where Sandra went, and every morning my friends and I would stand outside with my sister until the bell rang. Sandra was really cool because she d i d n ' t complain about her little sister and her friends sitting outside chilling with her and her friends. As long as I didn't talk too much and I did what she told me to, I was fine; and she typically had something for me to do or say. After school when Sandra and her friends wanted to start trouble or had beef with some girls, they'd walk down to my school and get me if I wasn't already up at her school. Usually they'd tell me to bump into a girl or say something smart to them, and if she reacted they'd beat her up. Not that they needed me to start trouble but Sandra knew I'd be a good alibi for her. There was no way my mom would get mad at her if she knew Sandra was fighting to protect me.

Why Sandra was such a fighter I didn't know. She was extremely pretty with very feminine features. Being sisters, we favored, but there were some noticeable differences. She looked mixed, as if she had Indian or Dominican in her blood. She must have gotten some of her looks from her father's side, even though we never met him, because many of her traits weren't visible on our mom's side. Sandra had a bronzed, brown-skinned complexion. She was short but not a dwarf, petite yet thick in all the right places (breast and butt), and she had the waviest hair I'd ever seen on a black girl. Her hair came all the way down to the middle of her back, and she never had to get perms. Once in a while she would straighten her hair to pull the waves out, but she wasn't big on doing her hair – ponytails usually sufficed. I always thought she was too pretty to be in fights, but my thoughts never left my mouth because I didn't want her snapping on me.

Sandra wasn't only good at fighting. She was just as good at dodging the repercussions of starting trouble. She didn't get suspended because before the NTA's (the school police) would get to the fight, she and her friends would disperse. And the girls she fought or jumped never told the principal or the NTA's, because they were scared the next beat-down would be worse. If my sister even thought a girl might go to the principal and tell, she didn't hesitate to initiate round two. So everyone kept their mouths shut, helping Sandra stay under the radar.

One day after school I was hanging out in front of my school with my friends, when Sandra ran up to me and told me to come on. She was with three of her friends. We followed them up to Gratz where five girls were standing, looking as if they knew what was about to happen. Sandra ordered me to go and punch the girl with the short haircut in the face. That girl was standing in the center of the five girls, and she appeared to be the ringleader of their group. Even though my sister, her friends, and my friends were going to follow up after I swung on the girl, I was a little nervous because I didn't want to get hit back by this high school girl.

While I hesitated everyone was staring and rolling their eyes back and forth, but after Sandra gave me the "get your ass over there before I hit you" look, I started walking up on the girl. All five of them looked me up and down because they thought I had a message to deliver from Sandra that was going to start some trouble. The girl in the center, the one I was supposed to hit, gave me the worst look ever. She was rolling her eyes, balling up her fists, and sucking her teeth before I even got within an arm's distance of her. At first I had chill bumps on my arms, and my stomach was in knots, but with each step I took, my sister, her friends, and my friends were walking up behind me. My adrenaline was pumping and without saying a word I just hit her! Everybody started swinging, but when she went to hit me I dipped it. My sister rushed up on the girl with the short haircut, got her on the ground, and started stumping her. My sister's friends, and my friends and I were fighting the other girls.

This time the NTA's came before my sister or I could get away. They broke it up and told us to stand against the wall. My sister was heated. She really wanted to finish fighting the girl. If you can call it a fight. After all, the girl was on the ground getting the living shit kicked out of her. So when one of the NTA's gripped her up she resisted, but his grip was nothing to laugh at, and eventually she eased up. I'd never seen Sandra fight with such hatred and intensity before. I don't know what that girl could've done to her, but I knew it had to be serious because this time she let herself get caught.

## Chapter XII

"You go to Gillespie!" We were sitting in the principal's office, and if no one else was anxious and afraid, I was. At first the principal treated the fight like business as usual until he found out four of us didn't go to Gratz. He was yelling at my sister, her friends, and the girls we were fighting, promising to expel them if he found out they had anything to do with us being involved. Sandra and her friends were cool, calm, and collected. Not one of them shed a tear. The principal was a tall, broad-shouldered man, and when he spoke the bass in his voice matched the roar of a full-grown lion. My eyes were filled to their maximum capacity with tears, and each time he looked at me or asked me a question, the tears started to fall and silence filled my lungs. I didn't have the courage to speak, and when I mustered up the strength to look at my friends I saw that they were crying too.

The phone calls had been placed to our parents, and the principal guaranteed us everyone would be suspended. I'd never been suspended. I was unsure of how the discipline procedures were going to work, especially since we weren't in our own school. My mind was filled with thoughts of being expelled, and I had flashbacks of Uncle Carl's belt. I didn't want to get a beating – even though I felt the crime warranted a spanking – but I was sure I'd receive some form of punishment. My mom was the first parent on the scene. She was irate. She walked directly past us and went to speak privately with the principal. While they were talking, Sandra started to show signs of fear, and her gangster facial expression quickly converted to that of a cold stone punk. I could understand her fear because my mom and Sandra had gotten into it before, and my mom was never too shy to pop Sandra in her mouth or up against her head – closed fist or open hand pimp slap.

After the ins and outs of parents in the principal's office, it was finally settled. Sandra, all of her friends, and the five girls were to be suspended for five days. They couldn't be in or outside of school grounds while on suspension.

Thankfully Sandra didn't get expelled because no one confessed to the principal why we were at the high school, and without proof they couldn't get rid of her. As for the four of us, we had to return to our school for discipline. My mom told Sandra to go home and wait for her, and then we walked with Lil Bitts, Tyisha, Toya, and their parents down to Gillespie.

Being in our principal's office didn't feel so good. Mrs. Archie was a paddle type of principal. She sent a note home to parents explaining the disciplinary rules and the options they had if they didn't want their children paddled – which was to send your child to a different school. She didn't take any crap from her students, and we knew she wasn't going to show any mercy on us for being in a high school acting a fool. Mrs. Archie was obviously disappointed when she saw I was involved. My grades and behavior were excellent, and I frequently volunteered in her office as a student office monitor. When she saw Lil Bitts there was no shock factor because she was looking at a repeat offender. Lil Bitts had been paddled more than three times before, and Mrs. Archie struggled to get her behavior to an acceptable level. Toya and Tyisha never had any run-ins with Mrs. Archie so I expected their punishment to be moderate.

Deliberations were brief. Our parents were in Mrs. Archie's office maybe five minutes before leaving with our disciplinary sheets. Our sentences were as follows: Lil Bitts got three days out-house suspension with two weeks in- house suspension; I got one day out-house suspension, because the fight involved my sister, with a week in-house suspension, and Toya and Tyisha both received one week in- house suspension with a warning. I didn't mind in-house suspension, but to have an out-house suspension on my record was upsetting. I was through with going up to Gratz, and Mrs. Archie made it crystal clear that we were not to be loitering in front of the high school anymore. The sentences were effective immediately.

On the walk home my mom was mostly silent. I knew I had disappointed her. When she asked why I got involved all I could do was swallow air. I didn't know if I got involved to look cool in front of my friends or to impress Sandra, but I had done it, and I didn't want to get Sandra into any more trouble by blaming her. The walk home was leading up to a conversation that I wanted to dodge, but it was impossible.

"You know you have to be on punishment for a while."

"Yes."

"Do you know why?"

"Yes I do, and I am sorry."

"Sorry doesn't get good grades or make you a better person. You're not sorry; you're in recovery. Now get your shit together, Sunshine."

I had received harsher lashings, and when she said I was in recovery I wanted to laugh because she was using NA lines on me, but I knew better and held my giggles in. As long as I didn't have to get spanked, I felt the punishment would be just. After my mom stopped at the store she pulled me close to her, looked me directly in my eyes, and said, "You can make it. No, you're gonna make it, so don't let this experience be your downfall." My mom always told me I was smart and said I'd get into college if I kept my grades up and stayed on the right track. I was frustrated for being involved in the whole mess, and it hurt me to see my mom so dissatisfied with me. The rest of the way home I walked with my head down, tears falling, with my mouth shut.

When we walked in the house, Sandra had the nerve to be in the living room watching TV. I heard of being stupid, but that was plain dumb. I went straight to our room and left the door open because I wanted to hear the inevitable. My mom immediately started yelling at Sandra for getting me involved. She wanted to know why Sandra thought it was okay to come home and watch TV. Sandra wasn't saying much. My mom was doing most of the talking, and then I heard it. Sandra had gotten slapped. She must have said something to piss my mom off and got popped for it. Sandra started crying, and my mom told her to go down in the basement. Then she shouted, "Don't bring your ass out of there because I don't want to see your face!" After that my mom yelled for me to wash the dishes.

By the next morning my mom had prepared a list of chores for me to do while I was at home. I only had one day off, but she had given me enough to do that by the time Shawn came home from school I was still cleaning. I was scrubbing the bathroom when he walked in yelling, "Stupid dumb dummy!" I wanted to ignore him, but he was getting under my skin with that stupid dumb dummy line.

"Who you talking to?"

"You. See what happens when you follow instead of lead?"

"Now you're a genius?"

"Well I sure ain't on punishment. You want me to help you?"

"Yes… For real?"

"Yeah. On second thought, I would help you, but you're a stupid dumb dummy. Now run my bathwater when you're done." I wanted to slap him but he was right. I sure could see what following the leader got me – punished! Sandra didn't have any chores, just restrictions. No TV, no phone, no outside contact, no going to the store, no playing cards or games, no company, no nothing. To make matters worse Sandra wasn't talking to me, but I knew once she cooled down she would. Besides, it wasn't like I snitched so she shouldn't have been mad at me anyway.

## Chapter XIII

In-house suspension was a breeze. All that was missing were the rotating classes and my classmates. There were five students who had in-house suspension. The four of us and some boy I'd never seen before, and I didn't care if I ever saw him again because he spent all day picking his nose. I just wanted to do my bid and get out. Each day we had the same teacher, and each morning he gave us a pile of work to be completed before the end of the day. He was aware that we were close friends so he had us sit far apart. The classroom was set up with five rows of six chairs. He made us sit one to a row, and we couldn't sit directly behind one another. Recess on the school's gated roof was eliminated, and instead of going to the lunchroom, they brought us our lunch. We had thirty minutes to eat, and we couldn't talk to each other during lunch or anytime for that matter. Considering the possibilities, I felt we got off easy. The week actually went by pretty fast.

Lil Bitts still had a week and three days to go, and she called me every night to tell me how lonely she was. When Toya, Tyisha, and I went back to class everyone had heard our story. They thought it was funny and decent, but I wasn't impressed. All I wanted to do was to stay out of trouble. I didn't need to worry because Mrs. Archie implemented a tool to make sure we did. She left out one little detail on those disciplinary sheets – daily monitoring. Each one of our teachers had to sign our daily report. If we got out of line, we would automatically be suspended.

When Lil Bitts got released back into population, it was the first time we all had a chance to sit down at the lunch table and talk about what happened. She was the first to burst out, "I got my ass whooped! My mom tore the skin off my butt, and I'm on punishment for a month."

"You're always in trouble so that's why you got a beating," Toya said. "And by the way, keep your bad ass away from me before you get me into any more trouble."

"Toya, I know you ain't talking. This is all S u n s h i n e ' s fault!" Lil Bitts said.

"Y'all don't have to worry about me doing nothing else."

"Why, what happened to you?" Tyisha asked.

"Nothing really. I'm on punishment, but I don't want any more suspensions on my record. And you?" I asked.

"My mom told me to keep away from Lil Bitts and that was it." We all started laughing after Tyisha said that. Lil Bitts was trouble, but she didn't start this.

"Well, what do we do now?" Lil Bitts asked.

"The same thing we do every night, Pinky," Tyisha replied. Again we all burst out laughing. I know what we did was wrong, but it felt good and it was fun. It was just a shame we got caught. At least now we were back together, but I definitely was going to steer clear of trouble.

At home Sandra was still on the outs with me, and she was being a bitch about everything. I told her I didn't tell, but she still treated me like an invisible family member. I'd rather have her say why she was so upset with me and get it off her chest, instead of ignoring me. It was disappointing because I looked up to her, and I wanted at the very least a complete sentence if we couldn't hold a conversation. The best I got was "excuse me" or even better "move". My mom should have kept her in the basement if she was going to act like that, but Shawn needed his room back. Sandra and my mom weren't exactly the best of friends either. If my mom was in a room, Sandra avoided it, and now she spent most of her time in our room. They just existed in the same house without ever really saying much to one another.

One friendship in the house was on the rise. Bay and Shawn were tight as ice, and they went everywhere together. Bay was a movie man and always wanted to see the new releases, so he'd take Shawn to the movies weekly. He tried to be friends with the rest of us too, but the sparks never ignited. I didn't dislike the guy, but he was my mom's boyfriend and I didn't care to know anything else about him. Besides, Shawn knew his background well enough for all of us. He knew where he went to school, how much money he made (not the real amount, but what Bay told him), his favorite car, favorite movie, and everything and anything concerning Bay. Another favorite hobby they shared was fixing cars. Bay was an auto-mechanic, and he taught Shawn tons about cars. He taught him how to change tires, find and seal leaks, change oil and brakes, spot bad transmissions, and other car stuff like that. Whenever Shawn wasn't in school, he'd walk to Bay's job to help out. At times it was funny, because when they had a tough job they'd both come home greasy. That grease was tough to wash off, and sometimes Shawn's fingertips would still look dirty even after he had washed his hands four times. My mom was happy that Shawn was taking an interest in something other than the streets, and she encouraged him to hang out with Bay as much as possible. He was a good role model for my brother, and though I didn't care for him much, I respected him for that.

I tried to find a way to get back on my mom's good side, and school looked like my best resource. She was so proud of my brother, and I wanted her to have the same feelings towards me. So I did everything I could to stay out of trouble.

Each time I received honor roll or perfect attendance for the marking period, she took me out to eat. I got to pick the restaurant, and I always chose the Ten Dollar buffet. I loved to eat. I could eat more than anyone in my family! Once my mom even got me tested for a tapeworm because it seemed like the more I ate the smaller I got. When we went out to eat I felt good because my mom and I spent one-on-one time together. The closeness I was seeking was there, and I definitely felt I was regaining her trust.

## Chapter XIV

With my improved behavior, Mrs. Archie took me off of daily reporting and I was back to being an office assistant. My main objectives were to keep my grades up and to stay out of trouble, so I had to make a few changes in the friend department. The four of us were still friends, but I had to give Lil Bitts a break. Every other week she was in a fight and she had received in-house suspension twice since we got off. Toya and Tyisha were still lying low where trouble was concerned so I kept them close. The school year felt as if it was breezing by because we only had one more marking period before the summer break. It wouldn't be too much longer before I could put the whole suspension behind me and start the next school semester off fresh.

Things around the house were in a bit of disarray because Sandra and my mom were always at it. My mom yelled at her constantly, but I don't think Sandra was listening because her facial expressions suggested "in one ear and out the other". Sandra had gotten her period when she was nine, and my mom said that was part of the problem. She said girls shouldn't get their monthly so young because they can't handle the hormones, and that's why Sandra was such a "B" (my mom's shortcut for calling someone a bitch). I got tired of the whole arguing thing and the day school let out, so did I. With my mom's permission, I spent a few weeks at Toya's and Tyisha's houses. She called and checked on me but most of the time she left me alone. I tried to hook up with Lil Bitts, but as usual, she was either on punishment or in the middle of getting her butt whooped for doing something wrong. Every time we made plans she did something to force a cancellation.

In August, my mom got tired of me being away and requested I come home and spend time with my family. I wasn't delighted but I figured my friends could come over. I wanted Tyisha and Toya to stay at my house for the last month of break, but with all the arguing and the crowded conditions I didn't bother asking. I tried to hang out with my family and enjoy them as much as I could. Bay and Shawn spent most of their time at his job; Sandra was always gone; and my mom was busy with the younger kids, so I really didn't understand why she wanted me to come home. To keep myself busy I helped out with the kids a bit and cleaned up the house, but still ended up bored. I didn't want to do much reading; I just wanted to go over to my friend's house. Not that they had better families, but they did have more room. It was like having to share your room with only one person. Tyisha and Toya didn't have sisters or brothers, which in my neighborhood was rare, so that made staying with them that much better. However, I was stuck at home, forced to deal with my reality. And that's what I did.

One bright summer morning my mom left early to go food shopping and asked if I could keep an eye on the kids. There was no fun in babysitting, and those kids got on my nerves. I made silly faces and drew pictures with them, and they were still unhappy. I was just about to die from frustration when my mom walked in the door and said, "We got a hooptie!" Bay had bought my mom a car. It was a mustard-colored, two-door, matchbox car. It was small, but that didn't take away from my mom's happiness. She needed a car and since she never had one, you would have thought she had just won a brand new Lexus or a Saab. Bay had surprised her with it. He even put a red bow on the front. I thought it was embarrassing and ghetto to put a bow on a used car, but he thought it was cute. Shawn told me Bay went to the auction to buy it, but he wouldn't tell me how much he spent. Bay and Shawn fixed cars they bought from the auction and told us the cheap cars sold for as little as fifty dollars. The body of this car looked like a fifty-dollar find, but its true value was in its smooth and quiet engine.

Now that my mom had a car I started to have fun because we drove everywhere. We went to the market, the corner store, the crab-shack, Caldor's, past our old neighborhood, to my grandma's (my dad's mom), to the thrift shop (my personal favorite), to all the parks in the suburbs, and anywhere else my mom could find. We all couldn't ride at the same time comfortably, but our tiny car did manage to fit five, even six if we lapped it; but it was a tight squeeze.

Sandra showed no enthusiasm about the new car. She and my mom rarely went anywhere together, but I was like a suction cup to those seats. When it came time for us to take a ride, I was the first person in the car and the last person out. It became my summer camp. To me, it was the life.

Shawn's attitude towards riding in the car was whatever because he had bigger aspirations. He wanted to drive the car. He swore he knew how to drive, but the most driving he'd ever done was the one time Bay let him drive the car on the back road. Since then he acted like he was a professional, when he really only drove half a block. The entire five seconds he was driving Bay had his foot so close to the brake; you might as well say Bay drove for him. But Shawn was persistent, and he pestered my mom so much she finally let him drive on the back road by himself. He did a good job and I'll admit I was impressed, but he didn't have a driver's license and wasn't old enough to get his driving permit. So my mom firmly placed his desire to hit the streets on the back burner.

Because we all enjoyed riding in the car so much, as a special treat Bay rented us a van so all of us could go to an amusement park. Shawn wasn't feeling well and wanted to stay home, and Sandra, who just wasn't feeling a family trip, decided not to go with us. The rest of us went to Dorney Park and Wild Water Kingdom because they had water rides and rollercoaster's. My mom hated rollercoasters and since Stephanie and Sandy were too small to ride most of the rides, they could all have a good time at the Water Park. Bay and I were left to master the rides. We rode every rollercoaster – big, small, fast, medium, even the kid rollercoasters.

After we had our stint in Dorney Park we headed to the water park to find my mom. When I spotted her I noticed her bathing suit was snug and she looked chubby in the waistline. This was the first time in a minute I had a chance to look at my mom's stomach because she had been wearing Bay's baggy t-shirts lately. I noticed that her stomach was poking out so either she had an ulcer or she was pregnant. As I walked up to her she could tell I was about to ask her, so she asked Bay to look after the girls while she took me to get some funnel cake. I was steaming.

"Yes. I'm pregnant. I didn't know how to tell you, but I was going to tell you soon."

"When Mom?"

"Soon."

"How far are you?"

"Four months, but I haven't gotten that big," she said with a faint smile. I couldn't believe Bay had gotten my mom pregnant. Disgusted is a fraction of what I felt and hurt wasn't too far behind. Why did she deceive me, and why was Bay acting like we were friends when he knew he got my mom pregnant? My mom paid for the funnel cake and handed it to me, but if she thought I was hungry or even had a sweet tooth, she was dead wrong. I couldn't believe my mom was going to have another baby. We barely had room in the car and we had absolutely no room in the house! A few tears fell down my face onto my funnel cake, and when my mom realized that I was crying she said, "It's gonna be okay, and you know I have enough love for all of y'all."

The pregnancy news ended my day at the park. I didn't say another word to Bay. I hesitantly walked behind him and my mom for the rest of the afternoon. They tried to encourage me to ride the water rides or at a minimum converse with them, but there was absolutely nothing to say. I was my mother's child, and she didn't let me know she was expecting. How could she keep such a secret from me, from us? We weren't the closest family, but this was privileged information for everyone under our roof. Even if she told me not to tell any of our neighbors or friends that would have been fine, but keeping such a secret depleted a huge portion of my respect for her. When they realized the day was ruined they decided we'd head home.

Needless to say, the radio rode us home because no one said a word to each other. Stephanie and Sandy both fell asleep, and I sat in the back of the van with my head down. When we pulled up to our block I lifted my head up because I heard sirens. All the neighbors were focused on our house, and the cops were at our front door talking to Sandra. My mom jumped out of the car and tried to figure out what was going on. When I looked at the corner of the block, towards the back road, I saw my mom's car crashed into the utility pole. Bay took the girls out of the car, and we all headed for the front door. My mom was crying. She wanted to know what happened to her car. The first name I heard come out of Sandra's mouth was Shawn. He was sitting in the back of one of the cop cars, crying, and holding his head down. Shawn had taken my mom's keys and took her car for a joy ride. No wonder he wanted to stay home. This fool had driven the car right into a utility pole at the corner of our block. Luckily no one was hurt, including stupid Shawn, but the cops were taking him to the Juvenile Detention Center.

Bay was at the cop car cursing Shawn out through the slightly cracked window, but he didn't peep out a word. When Bay started pounding on the window because Shawn wouldn't tell him why he took the car, the cops escorted Bay into the house. I knew Bay was heated with Shawn because he took to him like he was his son. After the cops reassured my mom that Shawn was fine and allowed her to take a closer look at him, they took him away. "He has to be processed and that can take a while, so you don't have to rush down to get him. Somebody will call you from the center once he's processed," one of the officers said. Bay took my mom into the living room and tried to comfort her, but nothing seemed to work. He asked her to calm down so she wouldn't hurt the baby. Just as he realized what he had said, Sandra glared at him. She understood. She walked upstairs and slammed our bedroom door.

When the time came, Bay took my mom down to the detention center to pick up Shawn. She was terrified he could've been killed but angry because he stole her car. She didn't know how to react. Bay was truly disappointed, and they both looked lost as to what to do with him. Even though my mom wasn't pressing charges he had to face the judge, because he was underage and had no business behind the wheel. Shawn was issued a counselor who he had to report to on a daily basis via telephone, and he was placed on a nightly 8 o' clock curfew. But his final punishment wouldn't be known until he had his hearing. Once Shawn came home he was ordered to stay in the basement every second of the day. He could only leave to use the bathroom, and my mom sat his meals on a serving tray at the top of the basement steps. Shawn followed my mom's instructions precisely and never said a word about his apparent discomfort.

With Shawn currently dealt with, Bay and my mom went to deal with the car. The left side was dented, but it wasn't totaled or critically damaged. It still drove, and Bay managed to pull the dents out. It ran quietly so my mom continued to drive it, and she made it clear that if anyone else touched her car, they should start looking for a new place to live. The last few days of August were quiet. Everyone stayed away from each other. We all knew my mom was pregnant (I told Shawn one day when he was coming out of the basement to use the bathroom), and no one was pleased about it. I started thinking of how bland the month of August started out, and in an instant, everything had changed. My mother and Bay had deceived me, Shawn was potentially on his way to jail, and Sandra was still acting like a B. If this was summer fun, I'd had enough.

## Chapter XV

I was glad to go to school because I needed to get away from home. Five and a half months after school resumed my mom had a baby girl, Syreeta, making our house terribly crowded. My mom, Sandra, Shawn, Stephanie, Sandy, Bay, the new baby, and I were too many for our two-bedroom house. We had to create new sleeping arrangements. My mom, Bay, and Syreeta took the front room. Sandra, Stephanie, and Sandy took the back room; while Shawn and I shared the basement.

Our family was growing, but instead of growing closer we started growing apart. Sandra, now a sophomore in high school, was fed up with babysitting and our family. She spent most of her time at her friends' houses or running the streets. One night Bay and my mom were going out when my mom told Sandra to watch us. She had been babysitting us since she was six, and it had taken a toll on her. Instead of her usual go-with-the-flow attitude, out of nowhere Sandra said, "No, I'm not watchin' them no more." My mom slapped her so hard she left a hand imprint on Sandra's right cheek. Bay tried to comfort Sandra, but with tears rolling down her face she shrugged him off and ran out the house. My mom was cursing up a storm while she waited for her to come back. Before we knew it, midnight rolled around and Sandra still hadn't returned. My mom called the cops, but they said if she hadn't been gone for twenty-four hours she wasn't considered missing. Bay went out looking for her in the neighborhood, and I called the few numbers I found in her phonebook, but we had no luck.

Sandra came back in the morning. She walked right up to my mom and said, "I ain't watchin' them no more!" I saw my mom's arm rise up, and for a moment I thought she was going to slap Sandra on her other check, but instead she hugged and kissed her. My mom was more concerned with seeing her unharmed and alive than about her babysitting the kids. Fortunately for Sandra, her babysitting days were now behind her. Unfortunately for me, my days had just begun. My previous life of going to school and spending the early evenings with my friends was suddenly converted to feeding a crying baby, along with catering to two other brats.

Why couldn't my mom just slap Sandra back into babysitting? I needed help, and when I looked around the house my options were limited. Since Shawn was the only boy his domestic duties were limited – all he did was take out the trash. They still spoiled him even though he stole the car and crashed it, but that was just how they treated Shawn. Bay, who worked most of the time, always wanted to take my mom out when he got home. His game plan was no help for my needed solution to find an alternative babysitter. I had to accept that I was stuck with a job I didn't apply for.

After school, even if I was studying, my mom and Bay ran errands, and they'd tell me to look after Syreeta, Sandy, and Stephanie. Sandy and Stephanie were not as much trouble as Syreeta. They were both manageable and went to sleep once they had dinner and a bath. Syreeta was a story of a different color. She cried for fun, cried for pity, cried for food, cried to be changed, cried instead of laughing, and cried every time she saw me. I didn't have much experience with cry-babies or raising babies at all, so I didn't know how to shut her up. This new arrangement brewed up some ill feelings in me towards my mom, Bay, Sandra, and all the kids for that matter.

On the weekends my mom and Bay partied all night, so the cycle continued with me on babysitter duty. I got no help from Sandra who was also always out, and Shawn was too busy playing Nintendo from dusk to dawn. Okay, my mom let Sandra off the hook. She needed a break. But why was I being punished? So if Toya called and asked me what I was doing – Me? What was I doing? Babysitting! I didn't even get an interview for the job, and now if my mom went anywhere she called upon me to babysit. I couldn't deal with Syreeta. She cried so much when my mom wasn't there. It was obvious the problem would be solved if my mom stayed home or took the cry-baby with her. Something had to be done, and if my mom had to play pitty-pat on my cheeks, so be it. I wrote her a letter saying I could no longer watch Syreeta.

Dear Mom,

Please don't be mad at me and kick me out but I can't watch Syreeta by myself. She always cries and poops a lot. I try to make her hush and I rock her back and forth, but she still cries. I know that Sandra doesn't want to watch the kids anymore, but I can't do it either. Please don't be mad at me. I can help change pampers and make bottles. I just don't want to watch Syreeta by myself because I don't know how to make her stop crying.

Love,
Sunshine

I left the letter on my mom's bed and when she came in that night she read it. She woke me up and said, "I'm not mad at you, baby. You can tell me anything." I was smiling on the inside because if I smiled in her face she may have thought I was trying to pull one over on her. I didn't want to do anything that might have gotten me slapped. Then she kissed me on my cheek and said, "Love you, good night." I had been exonerated for whatever crime I did to get me the punishment of babysitting, and I was relieved and excited. Now I could enjoy the smell of the outdoors and be a kid again.

## Chapter XVI

Sandra definitely didn't have to worry about babysitting my mom's kids anymore because soon she would be watching her own. Yes, she was pregnant. My mom had first become suspicious due to Sandra's increased and frequent eating and sleeping habits. Her body also began to change. My sister, who was always thick in the right places, was now pudgy in her tummy area. Her energy around the house weakened, and apparently she put the same amount of effort into her schoolwork because she was failing. More than likely she'd have to repeat the tenth grade. Sandra was a mess. Her attitude was funky, and she developed a potty mouth whenever she talked to Shawn or me.

Though Sandra hated our family, she found someone to love – her boyfriend, Jermaine. He lived just a few blocks from our house, and the entire school year, when she was supposedly at her girlfriend's, she was with him. Jermaine was twenty-one, tall, and slender, with a smooth, semi-glossed, dark skinned complexion. He was a street hustler (petty drugs), but he made enough to take care of himself. We didn't see him much but we all knew they were messing around. At first my mom didn't know how old he was because he had a baby face, but when she found out she hit the roof. My mom put Sandra on punishment, but nothing worked, not even slapping her up against her head or cursing her out. Finally my mom threw up her hands because she knew nothing she did would stop Sandra from seeing Jermaine.

Back to the pregnancy. My mom was washing clothes, and when she did her usual routine of checking our pants for gum or trash, she came across a letter from the clinic in Sandra's jeans. It stated that she was two to three months pregnant and gave her an expected due date. My mom was furious. She stormed into the living room and confronted Sandra with the letter. My mom stood crying and screaming, "Why, Sandra, why?" Sandra never answered, but my mom kept going. "So where you gonna live? I think you're    smart enough to know the only one havin' babies and living under my roof is me!" Sandra looked blank. I don't think she considered the possibility of being put out or where she would go, especially if we're talking about living with family. She didn't know her dad, and the only other family connection was our grandma (my mom's mom). For a second it looked like she had an answer for my mom, but my mom shouted, "You want to be grown Sandra?! Do you? Oh now you ain't got nothin' to say. I'll say it for you then. You gotta go!" My mom told Sandra to get her stuff and get out, and when she didn't move fast enough, my mom suggested she get help and call a ride. Sandra realized my mom was serious and she needed to call somebody, but who? She was too embarrassed to call our grandma, but she did call someone.

Jermaine came knocking on our door and was greeted with motherfuckers and fuck you's. My mom was yelling at the top of her lungs, and if the neighbors didn't know why she had been screaming at Sandra earlier, they sure heard this time. Sandra tried to pack her clothes, but my mom wanted her out immediately. She left with tears racing down her cheeks, her hands sheltering her face, and with Jermaine by her side. All the yelling caused such a ruckus that the neighbors came outside. Not to the windows - these nosey folks came out their doors and onto their porches and steps. I never imagined Sandra pregnant. Even though she got on my nerves, I hadn't envisioned living without her. She had been a mother to us. When she became distant, I just chalked it up to her being a teenager. Now she was about to be a mom. Shawn didn't share my sympathy. He was upset and showed no mercy. He called her a stupid bitch so many times that it replaced the use of her name.

Sandra now lived on 19th & Erie in an apartment building called the Taj-Mahal. It was a horrible name choice because it looked nothing like the Taj-Mahal in Atlantic City. It looked more like an abandoned house with working electricity. To be fair, some houses can look tacky outside with the insides of a palace, but not the Taj-Mahal. It was a three-story building with six apartments inside, and almost everything was raggedy. Jermaine had an efficiency on the first floor and managed to make it look livable. You could tell he recently painted the place. He even went a step further by getting a cheap furniture set off the Avenue and some fake plants to give his place some life. He didn't have much room but he was determined to make space for Sandra.

It took my mom a while, but she finally allowed Sandra to come and get her stuff, and then they sat down and talked. They discussed how she was going to support the baby and where she was getting prenatal care. My mom told Sandra she'd take her off her welfare check and allow her to get her own cash, food stamps, and healthcare benefits. Sandra looked relieved because my mom was finally speaking to her without using profanity, and she needed the money from the welfare check to give her some independence and an extremely small sense of security.

With Sandra's pregnancy, my mom went into clinic counselor mode. She gave Shawn and me the speech on having protected sex and what to do if you think you're pregnant. The speech was geared more towards me, and my mom was uncomfortable with giving up too much information, so she deliberately forgot to fill in some spaces. The speech was simply: "If you mess with boys or girls you will get pregnant or get them pregnant. So to save yourself lots of trouble, don't deal with them privately, unless you want to get put out." Not only did my mom give out daily speeches, she also made us go to church. We were forced to attend a Seventh Day Adventist Church. I thought I was Baptist, even though I didn't attend church regularly. I knew I was baptized as a Baptist. Now we had to stop eating pork, attend church on Saturday, and we couldn't violate the Sabbath. This meant when the sun set on Friday night we couldn't clean up, support any stores or businesses, or take public transportation until the sun set on Saturday evening.

The church itself wasn't bad, but the rules were aggravating. Every time the Sabbath came I would get hungry and not for my mom's cooking, but for a bag of chips or some other junk food. It seemed as though my mom didn't have junk food on Friday nights on purpose, like she was tempting me to break the Sabbath. And I wasn't alone in my suffering. Shawn hated the church and he hated the rules even more. He'd sneak to the store and ride the bus, not because he had somewhere to go, but to intentionally break the Sabbath. I was hoping we could vote out my mom's Seventh Day Adventist religion and I could go back to being Baptist, but we needed another vote (and the kids didn't count). The joke was on me because Bay was so wrapped around my mom's finger that he loved our new lifestyle. He said he felt empowered and was finally in touch with God. However he wasn't too in touch because when I last checked fornicating was still a sin. What a hypocrite.

My mom was extremely active in the church, which meant that we had to follow along. We went to church on the weekdays and on the weekends. If the church had an all-night revival, we had to go. How do adults expect children to stay up all night and listen to a pastor's monotonous voice without falling asleep? However it didn't matter to Shawn or me what they expected because we never stayed awake. The moment I sat in my seat I was asleep within thirty minutes tops, and Shawn, please, he fell asleep instantly. If the pastor knew how to change the pitch of his voice and if the choir wasn't made up of three 87-year-old women with no vocal skills whatsoever, I might have stayed awake longer.

The only reason we had to go to this boring church was because Sandra decided to get pregnant. My mom must have taken that into consideration and decided to invite her. Maybe Sandra was trying to maintain what relationship they had, or she was scared to be on her own with no family support; whatever the reason, she showed up with Jermaine and her round basketball belly. Surprisingly they appeared to be interested in the sermon and her attendance did wonders for her relationship with our mom. Now Sandra and Jermaine were more than welcomed in our house, and she and my mom talked and hung out on a regular basis. They talked about baby names, what she wanted to have, boy or girl, who was going to be her labor coach (my mom, of course, she was a pro), and where she wanted to have the baby shower. When my mom suggested she have the baby shower at the church, I was irked. What was she thinking?

Sandra's presence back around the house brought a time of happiness for me, and although she was pregnant her attitude was shifting to a much softer, more pleasant side. She talked to me about being pregnant and the consequences of having a hard head. She also said she wished she had listened to my mom's advice on abstinence and safe sex because she only wanted the best for her. Then she told me how important it was for me to go to church (whatever) and be respectful. Sandra also asked me about boys and if I thought about having sex, but I was only in the seventh grade so she had to be tripping. I laughed at her. Even if I did want a boyfriend, I wouldn't want him to see me with my clothes off. My breasts looked like my back, I was straight up and down, except for my little butt-butt. Honestly I just wasn't into boys, and all I wanted to do was hang out with my friends and do seventh grade stuff.

But Sandra's questioning made me feel good. I didn't mind answering her because now I had my big sister back, and besides I had a few questions of my own. I wanted to know why she had sex, why she had an attitude towards me, was she going to stop being nice to me, was she going to marry Jermaine, did she tell grandma, but before I could get all my questions out, she stopped and said, "Motor, I'm sleepy. I love you. We'll talk later." Sometimes I would go on and on, hence the nickname "Motor-mouth", and my family knew I would never stop asking questions, so they'd stop me in my tracks. To bottom line it, I talked too much some days.

I was enjoying my family. Things were calm, and we were all getting along. Even with Sandra moved out of the house, we were still crowded, but we made it work and somehow let the attitudes go. But I just couldn't get over going to church, and then my mom began hinting and suggesting we get baptized into the faith. She was already gaining ranks within the church, and she was entrusted with their donations, paying bills, arranging revivals, and assisting the pastor in any way she could. He was grateful for my mom's participation – so much that he often sent us food donations, movie passes, museum tickets, and occasional small monetary donations.

Our church, New Life, started to gain members thanks to my mom and the other women who went out recruiting. Now recruiting was something I just didn't do. I wasn't about to walk up to someone and ask them if they had found Jesus. Because if finding Jesus meant sitting and listening to our monotone pastor Jordon on Saturdays, neither one of us would ever find him. My mom knew I'd rather get spanked or punished before I would recruit. She was reluctant but gave in to my non-participation. The majority of the door-knockers and field agents were women. The men of the congregation usually worked, and when they had time off, they didn't spend it recruiting. Bay tried his hand at it one day and soon realized he'd rather be working or relaxing, than having strangers look at him like he was crazy. Should I even bring up Shawn because you know my mom let her prince skip out on recruiting.

Being good at recruiting and being active in the church meant we only saw my mom's shadow around the house. We all pitched in with the kids when she wasn't home, but it was starting to show that we needed our mom back. Bay was trying to be daddy and mommy. I respected him because when Syreeta was born he didn't treat any of us different, and he really tried to spread his love around. But one acting parent can only do so much. Bay looked lonely most of the time. And I don't know if the other kids thought it, but I felt my mom loved the church more than us. I talked to my mom about it when she decided to come home, and her reply was, "God's work doesn't have a time schedule, and if you want to come to church more often, you're welcome." Bay tried a different approach. He cried. He asked my mom to spend more time at home, with him, with the kids, but his tears were ignored and my mom told him the same thing she told me.

In response to our pleas, my mom stepped up her church attendance into full gear. She spent the weekends at church revivals, being a bible study teacher, recruiting, and she also traveled to other congregations with the pastor to worship. They traveled out of state on the train or sometimes h e drove. Bay was irritated at this because he wanted to know if they shared a room or had separate beds. He was also concerned as to why my mom was the only one traveling out of state with the pastor. But my mom ignored Bay and said, "Love isn't jealous. Just open your bible. I love you, Bay, but no man is going to interfere with God's work." That was the end of the discussion. My mom continued to see the pastor and the church more than her family.

We decided to be the best family we could without her. If we kept the kids in check while he was at work, Bay rewarded us with trips to amusement parks, to the carnival, the library, swimming at the YMCA, and he even took me to the thrift shop. One weekend when I came back from going to the thrift shop on the avenue, I saw Jermaine's car in front of our door. Jermaine had accumulated a few dollars and bought a 92 four-door Buick Sable. When I reached the steps I could see Sandra sitting in the car. She was in pain. Her water had broken, and she needed to get to the hospital. They stopped past on their way to the hospital to pick my mom up. It was around 4:00, but my mom didn't come home from church until six or seven. However, Sandra wasn't going to the hospital without her because she was scared. So Sandra, Jermaine, Bay, and I rode to the church to pick her up there.

It was a five-minute ride, but with Sandra trying to breathe through contractions and yelling at Jermaine for driving too fast, it seemed much longer. When we reached the church it appeared empty. Church let out at 1:00. After services everyone chatted and said their goodbyes, so it was clear around 2:30, 2:45. We spotted my mom's car and assumed she was either in the basement counting the collection or cleaning as she often did. I decided to go in and get her. No one was in the worship hall so I went down into the basement to check the kitchen and the treasury's office. Both were empty. I turned to go back to the car when I heard some noises coming out of the pastor's office. I tried to open the door, but it was locked. I saw an opening through the keyhole and looked through it. The pastor had my mom on top of his desk and they were... I saw Bay's foot, and the next thing I knew he had kicked open the door. "What the fuck is this?" Bay said. The pastor and my mom were naked, fucking on top of his desk. Bay started beating the crap out of Pastor Jordon. Either the punches had dazed him or he felt guilty, but he wasn't fighting back. When Bay finished almost killing the pastor, he gripped my mom up and started slapping and choking her. She was pleading and crying, but Bay was too far gone to show leniency on her. Jermaine came running in. He would soon wish he had pulled off and went to the hospital instead. He grabbed Bay and told him to stop, but the man had a death grip on my mother's neck, so it took Jermaine a while to pry his hands lose. The scene was vicious and repulsive. I never made a peep nor did I try to help my mom. How gross is it to sleep with the pastor? He was monotone but obviously not limp. My mom was screwing the pastor, and I felt embarrassed and dirty.

Bay walked off. My mom was crying and trying to aid Pastor Jordon so we left her. When we got in the car Sandra was sweaty and had lost control of her breathing. She said she felt like pushing and asked for our mom. Then Jermaine really put the pedal to the metal and got us to Temple Hospital in less than three minutes. Jermaine and I didn't say a word when Sandra asked us what took so long, and where my mom and Bay were. I knew our faces told a story, but she was in too much pain to probe us for details. We pulled into the emergency department, and I jumped out to get someone to help us. A nurse brought out a wheelchair and took us straight up to labor and delivery. By now Sandra was screaming and her contractions were less than a minute apart. They rushed to get Sandra undressed, on the labor table, and examined. "She's completely dilated and the baby's head is crowning. This baby is coming," the doctor said. "Push, Sandra, and don't forget your breathing," the nurse told her. Jermaine and I pushed the pastor's experience out of our heads. We were both excited and scared at the same time. I was going to be an aunt, and I couldn't wait. The nurse told Jermaine and me we could hold her legs apart while she pushed if we wanted. Sandra had already made the decision for Jermaine because she told him not to let go of her hand. I went down to the end of the bed to hold one of her legs, while the nurse held the other. Each time Sandra pushed for a count of ten seconds we were closer to meeting the new baby. I saw the head and started to get nauseous because this was the first time I'd ever seen such a thing, but I maintained my balance and my lunch. As I continued to hold her leg, my blood was rushing and my adrenaline was pumping. The view was amazing, and at the same time i t was X-rated because this was my sister's vagina I was intensely looking at. The doctor shouted, "One more push Sandra!" And the baby's slippery body popped out with a head full of hair. He was a chubby thing. "Dad, we have a boy," the doctor said. Jermaine's facial expression immediately went from anxious to ecstasy. He wanted a boy and that's what he got. Sandra was excited too, but she wanted to rest because she was beat. The nurse said she could hold the baby for a stint but after they got his weight and prints, he had to go to the nursery for routine observations. Jermaine hogged the baby until the nurse came and took him, and then he stepped out to get cigars for his soon arriving family and friends. He was a proud pappy.

When it was just Sandra and me, the questions began: "What happened at the church? What took y'all so long?"

"I don't want to say."

"Why not?"

"Because it's embarrassing and it makes me sick. I hate Mommy."

"What happened? Sunshine, you better tell me right now!"

"She was having you-know-what with Pastor Jordon, and Bay caught them. He beat up the pastor and Mommy."

"Call Shawn and make sure everything is okay and…I can't believe this shit! Why would she do that?" I started crying and went to the payphone to call Shawn because the room phone wasn't set up for outgoing calls. He didn't know what happened, and I didn't want to trigger his anger so I sucked up my tears and made myself laugh before I called him. "Sandra had the baby! It's a boy."

"Who he look like?"

"Like a baby."

"Real smart."

"Well, where's Bay and Mommy?"

"They're not here. What, they on their way?"

"No, they got into a fight, but I'll be there soon."

"Well hurry up because you know I don't do domestics."

"Whatever boy."

## Chapter XVII

Our house burned down! Bay torched the place. After he finished, he walked to the corner and called the cops from a payphone. The fire spread rapidly, and by the time the fire department arrived two other houses had caught fire. When Jermaine came back to the hospital, Sandra asked him to drop me off at home so I could help Shawn with the girls. As we got closer to the house I could see gray smoke clouds, and within a few blocks the smoke began to choke me. We had to park three blocks away, and the top of our block was taped off with yellow police tape. I knew something bad happened but had no idea it was this bad. I could see our house was one of the houses on fire, and I tried to run to it but an officer told me I couldn't go down there. But I had to get down there, down there was where I needed to be, so I started screaming at him. "My sisters and brother are in there. I live in that house! Oh my God…Get the hell off of me! I have to save my brother!" The officers weren't listening to me. Nobody was listening to me. They wouldn't let me past the yellow tape. I started hyperventilating. Jermaine tried to calm me down, but I couldn't get a hold of myself. I was cursing up a storm and fighting the cops because they wouldn't let me get to my family. The paramedics put me into an ambulance and had to put restraints on me. To say tears were coming down my face was an understatement. I had the Mississippi river beat. I cried my soul out and every part of me went numb. The house was so badly burned that there was no way anyone could have survived the horrific blaze. Fire was coming out of every window and every door. The blaze was so strong it melted openings through the brick walls. I'd lost my brother, Stephanie, Sandy, and Syreeta. At that moment I saw my brother's and my sisters' faces. I could see their pain, and they were on fire, burnt to a crisp…

"Sunshine, Sunshine, wake up! Come on girl, get up." The voice was so familiar, but I couldn't react to the commands. My eyes were so heavy, and my vision was blurred. I waited a few minutes before I tried to open my eyes, but the voice continued to call to me. The light from the room was overpowering. I squinted for a while before becoming conscious of two things. I was lying in a hospital bed, and the voice belonged to Sandra. When I opened my eyes and began to focus, I saw my mom and Jermaine sitting in the room. It was all coming back to me. My mom had caused the death of my sisters and my brother, and I wanted to hit her. "I hate you! Get out now!"

"Sunshine, calm down. Everything is all right."

"Sandra, how can you say that? She killed our family! I want all y'all to get out!" My weeping began again, my head started spinning, and I could feel myself blacking o u t. Sandra looked at me like I was crazy, and I started wondering if the whole thing was a dream.

"Shawn and the girls are okay. They weren't in the house when it caught fire. They're at Bay's mom's house," Sandra said. I burst into tears of relief and started screaming hallelujahs and thank you to God.

"I want to see them now! Sandra, get me out of here and take me to see Shawn." I needed proof. My mom stood up out of her chair and said she would take me shortly. My moment of happiness was short lived because I became so angry that she opened her mouth, trying to sound like a concerned mother. I was five seconds away from calling her a bitch and telling her to go jump off a bridge, but I knew Sandra would have slapped me. So I kept my mouth shut and let my anger show through my facial expressions and the heat coming out my eyes. The doctor came into my room and told my mom they wanted to keep me overnight for observations because my blood pressure was still too high. All I wanted to do was see my brother and sisters so I could believe the news, but it seemed I would have to wait until I got released. With Sandra only three floors up on the maternity ward, I was willing to wait because she was close by. With all the deception I encountered I was skeptical about taking anybody's word for face value. I wasn't in the mood for my mom's company so I asked the doctor if everyone could leave so I could rest. He replied, "That was going to be my next request because I heard some commotion coming   from this room, and that's not good for my patient. So if you'll all say, see you later to Sunshine, I must ask everyone to leave." When my mom started to walk out, she looked back at me. I smiled, rolled my eyes and lay down in the bed. If she thought she was off the hook, the joke was on her and I wouldn't soon forget she caused this whole disaster. As the room emptied my body began to reveal what the doctor had suggested – I needed to rest. I felt fragile, and my eyes, although I tried to keep them open, had gone on automatic shutdown. I was out of it, and there was no fighting it.

Later on that night Jermaine brought Shawn to my room. I had not fully awakened, but the moment I heard his voice I started tearing up. Shawn also had tears in his eyes. We hugged and told each other "I love you". I wanted to talk to Shawn in private, but there were too many people in the room. I had to do something about that.

"Jermaine, can you hit the road?"

"Sure, no problem. I'll be upstairs. If you need me, call up."

As soon as Jermaine walked out of the room, my eyes went straight to my brother, and he knew the questioning would begin. "Shawn, what happened?"

"Sunshine you need to rest."

"Shawn…"

"Don't worry about all this stuff right now."

"This stuff is my family! I don't know where we're going to live, or if I am ever going to talk to your mother, or what I would do if something happened to y'all…"

"Shhh. Don't worry about that because we're okay."

"Where are the girls?"

"They're still at Bay's mom house."

"Is he in trouble?"

"Sunshine you didn't hear?"

"Hear what?"

"The old lady next door to us died in the fire."

"Mrs. Renee?"

"Yeah. She couldn't get out in time."

"Oh my God Shawn… Why didn't anyone tell me?"

"Cause they figured you was too messed up."

"What's gonna happen to Bay?" That question sent Shawn to the brink of no return. His nose and tear ducts started running like a river with a broken dam. I couldn't comfort him. Bay was his father, and now he was going to lose him. Through his sobbing and muffled speech I found out Bay had turned himself into the cops. They were going to charge him with Mrs. Renee's murder and three counts of arson.

We never called Jermaine that night. Instead we lay in that hospital bed and tried to be each other's rock. Shawn had told me his bad news, and now I had to tell him mine. It was obvious he knew Bay set the fire, but he didn't know why. With both of us confused and disoriented, telling him about my mother and the pastor seemed to spill out effortlessly. When I closed my lips I was concerned about his reaction and wasn't sure how I would handle it. But Shawn didn't comment on how he felt about our mother. His only remark was, "That's why he did it."

## Chapter XVIII

The Red Cross contacted my mother and tried to assist her with housing. They offered her a three-day stay at a hotel, free of charge, and said they would pay her security deposit fees should she find another house or apartment to move in to. If my mother couldn't find a house or an apartment, her other option would be staying with friends or family members, of which she had none, or going back to the dreaded shelter. Not surprisingly, she opted to stay with Pastor Jordon, the only choice I would never have considered. Her decision let me know right away I had to make alternative plans. I talked to Sandra and pleaded with her to let me live with her. I knew there would be hesitations due to space limitations, but I explained to her I would sleep on the floor if I had to. She was okay with me staying, but of course she had to run it past my mom first. However, if she had any problems with it I was going to run away. There was no way in hell I was going to live with the Devil and his whore. They had broken up my family, and if Bay wasn't so in love with Shawn and the girls, when he set the fire he could have taken them away from me.

The day I was released from the hospital I moved in with Sandra and disowned my mother.

Things were crunched in the Taj-Mahal, but I had to be there. I slept on the couch while Sandra, Jermaine, and Jermaine Jr. shared the makeshift room. Sandra got me excused from school for two weeks so I could deal with everything that happened and try to regroup. My mini- vacation went faster than a hurried wind, and the moment I returned to school the gossiping began and the regrouping dismantled. Every kid who lived in my neighborhood had heard the story and passed it on. I was embarrassed and when asked about the ordeal I kept my mouth shut. I thought I would find comfort in my friends, but Tyisha and Toya had different plans. They ignored me and made smart comments when I walked past them. Unexpectedly, Lil Bitts was the one person who I could count on even though I had shunned her. We had drifted apart because of her behavior, but now she was there for me. If anyone made a smart remark, sucked their teeth, or even looked at me funny, Lil Bitts was all up in their face. Normally I would have stood up for myself, but I was too weak to fight. Every time I saw Shawn in the halls or in the lunchroom I grew weaker. Knowing I couldn't save Shawn from Pastor Jordon's home, I grew even more disgusted with my mother and her sweet ole pastor.

Outside of school Shawn and I rarely spoke, and this crushed my heart. If he didn't call me, I certainly wouldn't call him because calling Pastor Jordon's house was off limits. Whenever my mother called my house, I hung up on her. Sometimes when Shawn did call, my mother would take the phone from him and try to talk to me so now I hung up on the both of them. When we saw each other at school we tried to talk between classes and at lunch, but with all the stares and every kid and teacher in our business, we never really had a chance to speak openly about our feelings. It looked like a dead end. When I tried to find a loophole my mother put up another road block. For whatever reason she didn't want Shawn over at Sandra's so she took away a great opportunity for us to communicate. I don't know why, but I gave up. I was tired of hearing my mother's name or saying it for that matter. Now Shawn and I, although I loved him more than words could tell, spoke occasionally, and instead of having the chance to speak candidly about Bay, Pastor Jordon, the fire, or my mother, I grew to enjoy and appreciate our brief run-ins.

As the school year progressed, the kids found other things to talk about. My story became a thing of the past, and now I had bigger fish to fry. Next year I would be graduating, and I wanted to make the best of it. Mrs. Archie kept a close watch on me because of everything going on in my life. She had gone from principal to therapist. I used to eat lunch in the cafeteria, but now she forced me to have lunch in her office. She even tried to bring Shawn in, but when she saw he wouldn't open up to her, she stopped calling him down. I wished he would've opened up because we could have spent more time together, but I didn't blame him for wanting his privacy. In my eyes, he had lost a father and now he had to live with the man who was responsible for his loss.

During my visits, Mrs. Archie praised my strength, and towards the end of the school year she entered me into an honors program. When I graduated the eighth grade I would spend my summer attending Temple University. The college offered a program for eighth through twelfth graders in which you could experience college life by actually taking college courses and getting college credits. The most exciting benefit to the program was once you completed the ninth grade you could live on campus during the summer and take your classes, as long as you maintained your grades and attendance. The program's goal was to help inner-city children with excellent academic performance and attendance to receive scholarships to Temple. They were willing to give up a full scholarship, as long as you stayed in the program from the eighth grade until your high school graduation. I was psyched! I wanted a college education, and this was my chance to get it. Since I wasn't born with a silver spoon, let alone a silver dollar, I knew this was the best offer I could get. Besides I wasn't speaking to my mother, and I had no idea what her plans were in regards to my college education or my college fund or if there even was one; and I wasn't about to ask her either. So this was an opportunity I definitely couldn't sleep on.

## Chapter XIX

"The award for Perfect Attendance for the year, Honor Roll for the year, and Outstanding Academic and Social Performance goes to Sunshine Cannon!" When I walked onto the stage all you could see were my teeth. Mrs. Archie couldn't stop smiling either, and a tear rolled down m y cheek as she handed me my trophy. She was so proud of me, and a big portion of my getting here was in part to her. I saw Sandra, Big and Lil Jermaine, and Shawn when I looked into the audience. They were front and center, full of smiles, and applause, and Shawn got in a big, ghetto, "Yeah that's my sister. You go girl!" I couldn't have been happier or prouder of myself. I was graduating from the eighth grade with honors, and I knew if I continued on this path it would only be a matter of time before I had that full scholarship, including room and board to Temple University.

Prior to my graduation I spent several weekends and weekdays with Mrs. Archie and her family. Truth be told those several weekends and weekdays were more like a year and a half. I was with Mrs. Archie more than I was with Sandra. She took a real liking to me, and she invested plenty of her time sharing her educational and life knowledge with me. Maybe she felt sorry for me because I told her about all the crap my mother had put me through, but whatever the reason it was to my benefit. In the year and a half leading up to my graduation she had taken me to places I had never seen before, in and out of the city. I met tons of professionals and learned professional etiquette. She showed me how to dress professionally and how to sit with a skirt on, how to hold a conversation without saying um, like, ya know, and how to feel confident in a room full of established, successful people. I used to irk Sandra's nerve when I came home speaking in my professional tone, using proper grammar, with my new suits (that Mrs. Archie bought) and my dress shoes on. I felt really good about myself and even though I sometimes got on her nerve, Sandra always encouraged me to learn as much as I could from Mrs. Archie and to respect her.

Being that Sandra was busy with the baby and her man, Mrs. Archie's presence was more than welcomed. There was so much going on in my sister's life because Big Jermaine had turned from Pac-man to Brick-man. When his former boss was murdered, the Connect remembered Big Jermaine as being loyal and ready to make moves. In no time he was selling weight to the big timers and all the small timers wanted to work for him. As soon as he came up on some paper he started to make changes in our lives. We all had new wardrobes, and Sandra was surprised with a brand new Saab. He bought himself a BMW. It was used, but it could have passed as new, and both cars had automatic this and automatic that. I loved riding with Sandra and everyone in the neighborhood envied us. When we rode past, being sure we had our privileged looks on our faces, you could feel the stares and the hatred coming through the windows.

After he bought the cars, clothes, and some jewelry, he decided (although I felt he should have done this first) we needed to exit the neighborhood. He asked us where we wanted to live and how far away from the neighborhood we wanted to go. Sandra wanted to move out of the city, but not out of the state, and I wanted to live where I didn't have to change schools but far enough that I had to catch a bus or two. It was sweet of him to give us a say, but I knew he would have the final word. With a hefty down payment and two months' worth of made-up pay stubs for Sandra, she was pre-approved for a mortgage and the search began. Within a week Jermaine and the realtor called us to meet at a house they thought we might like. It was an instant hit. We purchased a roomy, two-story, three bedroom home, with walk-in closets, hardwood floors, carpeted bedrooms, a fenced backyard, driveway, and a finished basement in Oxford Circle. It was extremely beautiful inside and out. Our block was quiet and although our house was a row home, our neighborhood had more of a single home feel to it. And the neighbors were cool, even though many of them weren't used to having black people living on their block.

Seeing that Jermaine got us here on drug money, we had to be cautious about what we did, who visited us, and it was the law that we never told anyone where we lived! That rule was so strict my own mother was not invited over for quite some time because Jermaine had to be sure she could keep her mouth shut. Also he knew how much I disliked her and he didn't want me to feel uncomfortable. My mother rarely visited and when she did, she didn't bring Shawn or the girls. So why did she bother showing up? The first time she came over, Sandra gave her the grand tour with a smile from ear to ear. I could hear my mother through my door saying, "Hallelujah, praise the Lord for this blessing." I hated the sound of her voice and stayed in my room the entire visit. The second time she came over I was in my room playing with Lil Jermaine. She called for me to come downstairs, but I ignored her. Sandra came up and told me to "go see Mommy". My face was filled with instant heat, but Sandra told me to do something so I did it. When I came into the living room, my mother asked me how was school, and how I felt now that my graduation was right around the corner. I kept my answers short and sweet and they went something like, "I'm fine" and "okay". I started to walk back upstairs when she said, "Where you going? You don't have time to talk to your own mother?" I decided that telling her the truth would have been better because she was a Christian, so I said, "I have plenty of time. I just don't want to talk to you!" She wasn't quick to respond, but I knew she would. "Sunshine, you're gonna have to forgive me. I never meant to hurt you or any of my children."

"You got Bay locked up, and you could have gotten my brother and sisters killed. Now you want to sit here and play the sainthood card. I don't have anything else to say to you and if we're done here I'd like to be excused to the confinement of my room."

I ran upstairs to my room because I was through and I also didn't want her to see me crying. I wasn't crying because I cared about her only because I was so angry with her. Have you ever wanted to hit somebody but because you had some common sense, respect, or morals, you kept your fist hidden and your tears leaking? At times I felt guilty about wanting to hit her because she was my mother, but too many times it felt impossible for her to be my mother. She wasn't committed to her role as my mother. Sometimes she had a sub, and why she felt she could just show up and demand respect or forgiveness didn't register with me.

Sandra came upstairs and I knew she was going to give me a speech. "Sunshine, why are you still angry with her? She is trying to mend fences, so why not give a little?" "Because I don't want to. You don't understand how I feel, and I want to be left alone, please." Why was she being so forgiving after everything that happened? I just couldn't let go of the memories. No one knew how many nights I wet myself when I had nightmares of my brother and sisters being burned to a crisp. Every night I slept on top of a towel, which was on top of a large garbage bag, so I wouldn't wet my sheets or my mattress. When I did have an accident I washed the towel out and hung it up, but if Sandra or Jermaine were awake when I tried to sneak to the bathroom, I threw away my soiled items. I'd put my towel and my pajamas in a bag at the bottom of the trash can, and I poured laundry detergent in the bag so it wouldn't smell. Sandra often said the washing machine was eating up our towels because they kept disappearing. So to keep the focus on the towels and not my pajamas, I slept naked. I wrapped myself in a towel on top of the garbage bag, because if I had an accident I wouldn't have to throw my pajamas out. Thankfully no one knew my secret, and now wasn't the time to talk.

After Sandra went back downstairs she began comforting my mother. I heard my mother saying she couldn't take it and wouldn't come back over. Sandra decided from now on she and Lil Jermaine would go over to Pastor Jordon's house and visit her there. This was fine with me because I knew instantly I wouldn't be asked to go. I did want to see Shawn and the girls, but if that meant seeing Pastor Jordon or my mother, they would be missed.

Sandra began visiting my mother quite frequently. With Jermaine in the streets most of the day and night, she needed someone to communicate with. She wasn't allowed to bring any of her friends to the house, and she didn't have too many friends to visit. And since most of our neighbors were white, middle-aged couples or senior citizens, she saw no friendships there. Sandra could have made friends but she lacked the confidence I saw in Mrs. Archie. She didn't care about your color or your background, how much money you had or who you knew, because when she was in front of you, you were no more than a human being, and best believe she always felt she had one up on you, even if she didn't. Luckily people skills were a part of my DNA and I was able to make many friends on the block. The neighbors were always inviting me over for dinner, and two of the elderly women wanted me to help them in their garden. Mrs. Archie found it funny because she had given me two plants and I killed them in seven days or less. She said the plants were strong and could maintain themselves, but someone should have told the plants that because they died before I had a chance to repot them.

I liked my new senior friends and wanted to impress them, so to learn more about having a green thumb I decided to spend the weekend at Mrs. Archie's house for intense training. I can't say for sure why but in the middle of my mission I was prompted to come home early. It was a good thing too because Shawn was at my house. I couldn't believe my mom had let him come over. Sandra saw how excited I was and left the two of us alone in the living room. However Shawn wasn't talking to me. Instead he sat on the couch with an annoyed expression upon his face. I asked him what was wrong, but he wouldn't respond. Then I asked again and still nothing. We both sat on the couch for a good while before he decided to open up. "They're giving Bay fifteen to life, and he can't apply for parole until he's done his mandatory fifteen years."

"Who told you that?"

"Sunshine, it doesn't matter, he don't deserve this... He's the only father I had... Man, why is this happenin' to me?" Shawn didn't shed a tear, and I was at the point where I saw tears as pointless. I would either deal with a situation and move on, or not deal with a situation but leave the tears out of the equation.

After Shawn realized there was nothing he could do to bring his father back, he began to ease up. Sandra had to pick him up because he spazzed out. He was yelling at my mother and saying how much he hated her and Pastor Jordon. He had thrown and broken dishes, and then he went outside and broke Pastor Jordon's car windows out. When Pastor Jordon ran up on him and asked why, Shawn balled up his fists and began to swing, but my mother jumped dead center in front of the Pastor to protect him. It was just like her to take sides with the devil. Shawn was sent over to our house until he cooled off. But how could he calm down when he was forced to live with the two people that were at the root of his pain? I went upstairs to talk with Sandra. "Sunshine, I don't want you to say anything bad about Mommy or Pastor Jordon to Shawn. I just want him to cool down so he can go back home."

"If I was him, I would never cool off and just stay here with us." She gave me a "This ain't your damn house to be making no decisions" look, so I agreed to her unfair demands.

Shawn ended up staying with us for two weeks until he decided he was going back. Pastor Jordon, my mother, and Shawn had a talk. I don't know what was said, but Shawn told me he didn't want to talk about it and that he was ready to go home. Sandra and I were disappointed. We had both fallen in love with him being at our house. He catered to us. He cleaned like a British Butler and someone taught him how to cook! Shawn cooked like a five star chef and was more than willing to put his thing down in the kitchen. Sandra loved this because she was so busy with Lil Jermaine that she rarely ever felt like cooking. Although I didn't want him to leave, my new motto was, "No More Tears, Just Deal with It", so I dealt with Shawn's decision.

When he left I had to get back to the business of school and graduation. Mrs. Archie was pressing me to apply to Central and Girls High School. They both had excellent academic curriculums and a high percentage of their students went on to college, but I wasn't sure if I wanted to go to either school. I brought up the suggestion that I    attend

Dobbins A.V.T.S High School because I wanted to experience a trade school before going to college. Mrs. Archie wasn't thrilled with the idea at all, and she didn't think Dobbins was the school for me. She was more interested in a strict, academically-motivated school, and thought trade schools were for students who weren't interested in college. Dobbins offered classes in Cosmetology, Auto Mechanics, Dentistry, Architecture, Culinary Arts, and Fashion Design. I was interested in fashion and hair. Especially since my little bones were developing, and my clothes looked great on me. I was 5'5", weighed 115 pounds, and my breasts had grown from knots to a full 34 B, pushing towards a small C. Mrs. Archie said I was very mature for thirteen, so she made sure I had the right bras (the ones that covered up everything) and the right clothing to keep away the stares of men and boys. She was skeptical about my developing body, but she assured me we could handle it because my head was in the right place. And yes, I noticed my body, but I didn't spend too much time worrying about it. I hadn't started dating boys yet, and Mrs. Archie kept me so involved in my activities and my schoolwork that I didn't have the time. In addition to not having time, Mrs. Archie and Sandra were always stalking me, and Big Jermaine was protective as well. Whenever I did get a chance to see him he made every effort to check on me and to see what was going on in the boy department.

Boys aside, I applied to Central, Girls High, Engineering and Science, and Dobbins. They all had placement tests so Mrs. Archie spent hours upon hours trying to prepare me. She also made it clear she didn't want me to attend Dobbins and that I need not prepare for their simple test. I took the tests, and to me they were all passable, but Central's test proved to be the most challenging. Each school gave all applying students a grand tour. Out of all the schools I toured, Dobbins impressed me the most. Their Cosmetology and Fashion Design classrooms reeled me in because they were set up like the actual working arena. Inside of the Fashion Design class, they had body mannequins, measuring tapes, sewing machines, thread upon thread, exotic and local fabrics, and everything a young designer would need. The instructor for the fashion curriculum told us how excited and dedicated all the current participants were, and she showed us the prom dresses the top designers made. They were beautiful. They looked similar, if not identical, to the dresses seen in fashion magazines. The Cosmetology instructor was just as alluring. Their classrooms were filled with mannequin heads, shampoo sinks, pedicure stands, tons of mirrors, curlers, dye kits, perms, relaxers, rollers, pin clips, bobby pins, combs in all shapes and sizes, blow-dryers, hair gel, hair sprays, clippers, smocks, scissors, and lockers (to place your supplies in). All the students had their own stations with a full-length mirror and a working barber/beauty chair. Both curriculums were equally attractive. It was a challenging decision.

Just about a month and a half before I was set to graduate, Mrs. Archie called my teacher and asked her to send me to the office. I knew she was calling me to tell me which schools had accepted me, but my mind was already set on one school in particular. After the Dobbins tour, that was all I talked about. I was sure I aced the entrance exam because my mind never tensed up or second guessed any of my answers. With Central's test I had broken too many sweats and had erased so many of my answers that my answer sheet looked like a piece of scrap paper. Girls High and Engineering & Science tests, I was sure I scored at least in the ninetieth percentile, But no more guessing games, now was the moment of truth.

"Hey girl, how are you feeling?"

"Just tell me because I know why you called me in here."

"Okay, I won't hold out any longer. They all want you."

"They all who?"

"Stop being silly. Each school you applied to has accepted your intelligent, sophisticated, trend-setting... Oh girl, you the bomb!" I started cracking up laughing because Mrs. Archie seldom said anything that was considered ghetto or slang, and when she did it sounded so funny.

"I can't believe it! Dobbins wants me too?"

"Yes, but we don't want them, do we?"

"Um…"

"You know better than to use 'um'! Sunshine, I'm not going to make this decision hard for you, and I won't be disappointed either way, but I want you to think long and hard about the academic rewards for each school. I want you to go home and talk this over with Sandra and then make your decision. You don't have to reply right away, but they need an answer in a week, two at the most."

The decision was mine to make but I wanted to get my big sister's opinion. Sandra and Big Jermaine were both in the house when I came home. I ran into their bedroom to tell them about my acceptance letters, but something was wrong. They were sitting on the bed and Big Jermaine had tears in his eyes while Sandra was comforting him.

"What's the matter?"

"Sunshine, you know better than to run in here without knocking!"

"I know. I'm just excited about the high schools that accepted me."

"Sunshine, we need some time to ourselves. Take Lil Jermaine outside, and I'll talk to you in a minute." Sandra just brushed me off. I would have gotten pissed, but I knew something was going on so I took my nephew and went outside. When it got too dark and cold for Lil Jermaine to be outside, we waited in my room.

A minute had turned into 11:00 at night, and I woke up when I heard Big Jermaine slam the front door. Sandra came into my room and found Lil Jermaine asleep, and I was just lying there. I could sense that she was nervous. She told me Big Jermaine's best friend had gotten shot in a drive-by. I wanted to know the details but Sandra didn't want to talk any further. When I asked her where Big Jermaine went she started to tear up. "He is…he'll be back," she said in an unconvinced tone. Sandra took Lil Jermaine with her to put him in his room. "Sunshine, you know to keep this between us so don't go telling Mrs. Archie."

"I know."

"Oh by the way, which school accepted you?"

"All of them."

"Which one you goin' to?"

"Dobbins!"

"Okay. Well, you know whatever you do we got ya back."

After the shooting, the vibe through the house was fearful. Sandra was worried something could or would happen to Big Jermaine. Immediately new rules were implemented, and we stopped going by the old neighborhood because Big Jermaine felt safer if we stayed closer to home. As far as school was concerned, I was to go straight there and come straight home. Big Jermaine said if I felt I was being followed I should go to the police district (which was in walking distance from my school) and give Sandra or him a call. I usually got a ride home with Mrs. Archie and I didn't think anyone was following us, but he insisted I be cautious, especially on the days I had to take the bus.

Big Jermaine started paying more money on the mortgage, and our house was about eleven thousand dollars shy of being paid off. Because he didn't want the FBI to become suspicious of the large amount of money being spent, he didn't outright pay it off. Instead he made bi- monthly payments of eight thousand dollars. Now I don't know how paying eight thousand every two months on a mortgage wouldn't be suspicious, but I heard him telling Sandra any one time payment over ten thousand dollars, and they'd call in the Feds. The house was in Sandra's name, and honestly how she could afford to pay the majority of the mortgage off on a modest, made-up, housewife's salary may have been hard to prove. Luckily the Feds never gave us a call.

In the following weeks we were still on Red Alert, but Jermaine was becoming more relaxed. I needed to start shopping for my graduation dress because it was only two weeks away, and I wanted to be the best dressed eighth grader the school had ever seen. Big Jermaine told me he was going to have someone make my graduation dress and not to worry about the cost. I wanted an all-white, soft fabric, fitting, long dress, a pair of white sandals, and a nice clutch purse to match. Big Jermaine took me down to 4$^{th}$ and South to get what I needed. When we entered the shop, the owner,

Moyo, came running up to us. He was very excited to see Big Jermaine and treated him like he was the mayor of our city. The first thing I blurted out of my mouth was, "Why are you acting like we're famous?" He kindly responded, "No baby, you sure ain't famous, but ya uncle spends enough money in here ta get the royal treatment, o-tay?" He knew how to suck up, and apparently his flattery had gotten Big Jermaine to spend plenty of dollars at his shop. But he wasn't all talk. He had a good sense of style. You could s e e it in his shop's interior design and from his attire, head to toe. Moyo showed me all types of fabric. Silky, cotton, rayon, polyester, Gucci, Armani, the list was on go in g. Trying to explain and sketch the dress I wanted was frustrating and a waste of time because when I stood up to take a deep breath and to clear my head, I saw the dress I wanted in one of the photos on his wall. This dress was perfect. I had to have it. It was strapless, form-fitting, perfect coverage of the boobies, long and lean, sophisticated, and soon mine. The fabric was Gucci. It put me in the minds et of a prom gown, but it could be worn as a graduation dress. My dress would be almost identical to the picture, but I had to have spaghetti straps, Jermaine's orders. I was fitted for my gown and looked through a few more pictures before selecting my clutch bag. Jermaine left Moyo $480, and I didn't know if that was a down payment or the final payment. I only needed about two yards to make my gown, and I had no clue how much a yard cost, but I knew I was going to look fabulous. I started thinking about the limited time Moyo had to make my dress and without me uttering a word he said, "You ain't got nothang to worry 'bout. It'll be ready by the end of the week." The only thing I had to do now was get my shoes.

Big Jermaine said he did clothing but not women's shoes so Mrs. Archie met me at my house to take me shoe shopping. This would give Mrs. Archie and me a chance to talk about her disappointment with my school selection. We were running about an hour late. Big Jermaine wanted to make a stop for some food, and we got caught up in the thrills of South Street – which is famous for its Philly cheese steaks, art deco, the water view, fabric row, and the many exotic and expensive stores that line the street. It was the only place to be when the weather was great.

When we pulled up to our house, she was in front of the door waiting patiently. As I got into the car Mrs. Archie asked, "Where do you want to go?" She may have thought I was joking, but I was so serious when I told her I wanted to go to Payless. I had seen a pair of white string sandals that would go perfect with my dress. Mrs. Archie wanted to take me to Strawbridge's or to the King of Prussia Mall, but I wasn't feeling the long ride. But she didn't mind the drive so I chose the mall because they had a Payless there. I started to bring up my high school selection, but Mrs. Archie wouldn't hear a peep. She said I had made my decision and she was backing me. Therefore I let it alone. If she was really behind me, only time and her actions would tell.

After the graduation ceremony ended, I was ready to come out of my blue with gold trim, cap and gown. My family, Mrs. Archie, Lil Bitts, and I were headed out to dinner. Mrs. Archie picked out a restaurant in New Jersey, and Big Jermaine was treating. I took off my cap and gown and went outside to take pictures in front of the school. Sandra had bought a new camera and wasn't afraid to use it. Before she started clicking my mother came up to me and gave me a hug. She had a nerve to show up with Pastor Jordon, and if that wasn't enough she was pregnant. In my mind I started thinking, did she get married, how could she be pregnant by the pastor and not be married, and why was she trying to ruin my day? Sandra walked up to me and whispered, "Play nice", so I played along and took the photos. We started taking pictures, and I must say my dress was worth every penny, but I started to get agonizing cramps. Standing became a tough task, so I bent over until I could get the cramps under control. Mrs. Archie asked if I was okay, and I said, "Sure, I just feel a little pain in my stomach." I wish it was only pain, but then I felt a gush of fluids rush out of me into my panties. I tried to play it off, but Sandra came running over to me with her sweater. I looked down at my dress and saw blood all over my new, white, Gucci graduation gown.

## Chapter XX

My graduation was ruined and all plans were off. Everybody wanted me to go home and change clothes, and then pretend as if nothing had happened. But something had happened. This was as embarrassing as it was dreadful. People were whispering, and some of my classmates were laughing. I wasn't sure how to stop the bleeding, and I was too embarrassed to talk about anything. I rode home in the backseat of Jermaine's car, sitting on top of an old phone book he had in the trunk. When we got home Sandra talked to me about my period and introduced me to a maxi-pad, and a beautiful gift I like to call the tampon. Then she took me into the bathroom and showed me how to use both of them. I had never shown her my vagina or even looked at it much myself, but I felt comfortable with her looking because I wanted to learn the proper way to use a tampon. But when Sandra noticed I had developed a full head of hair down there, she laughed, and I instantly went from feeling comfortable to uneasy. I wanted to shy away, but I didn't because I needed to know how to stop this traitor. I found the tampon to be more useful than the pad because it held things inside. After having my graduation gown destroyed, I didn't want to take any chances with a maxi pad. I refused to allow even a tiny spot to devastate my life again. Sandra told me I should be on my monthly for about three to five days, and based on my weight, the flow should be light to moderate. She also suggested I mark this dreadful event on my calendar, so I could keep track of when this unwanted visitor would appear again. I took it a step further and gave it a name; Mom.

Two weeks later, when I started to feel normal again, I decided to return Mrs. Archie's calls. She was all excited about me getting my period, and she still wanted to take Lil Bitts and me out to make up for our graduation. Since my monthly was off, I agreed. She took us shopping at the mall and then out to eat. I had a great time at the mall and dinner was delicious, but as soon as Mrs. Archie dropped me off, I was back to my thoughts. My mother had shown up to my graduation pregnant. Was she married? I went into Sandra's room to get some answers. "Did you know she was pregnant?"

"I thought she was but I wasn't sure."

"Did you know she was coming to my graduation?"

"Maybe."

"Well why didn't you tell me?"

"I didn't know for sure, and I didn't tell you about the pregnancy because I didn't want you to be upset before your graduation."

"So you wanted me to be upset after graduation... And look what happened to me. My period only came on because she showed up with that pastor!"

"Sunshine go take a walk and get yaself together." I walked away for five minutes but came back to talk some more. I knew my mother and the pastor had nothing to do with my period coming on, but I wanted to blame them. "Are you okay now?"

"Yeah."

"Okay, to keep it real – I knew she was pregnant, but I knew you would react negatively about any news involving Mommy so I didn't tell. She's having twins if you want to know."

"Is she married?"

"No."

"Who's the father?"

"The pastor, of course."

"You sure?"

"See the negativity." She was right. Nothing about that woman made me think or feel positive, so I went in my room. I was done talking about her.

However, when I was in my room my nerves and my anger got the best of me, so I went in the living room to give my mother a call. She answered the phone on the first ring. "Why did you have to ruin my graduation?"

"Excuse me."

"I never asked you to show up." She got quiet so I waited for a response but when nothing came I opened my mouth.

"Why would you embarrass me by showing up with a belly full of devil twins?"

"Let me speak with Sandra!"

"She's not here!"

"Where is she?"

"Not here."

"Sunshine you need to get under control."

"I am under control! I am just tired of you interfering in my life. I have to deal with enough, and every time I think I have some of the nonsense cleared up, you show up with more bags full of crap. Oh, by the way, how are my sisters I never get to see?"

"Sunshine, you can see them anytime."

"How? By coming into the devil's pit. You know I hate him, and I am not too far from feeling the same way about you!" She hung up on me.

I went back into my room and lay down in my bed. My head was pounding. I started to feel bad for speaking to my mother in such a rude and disrespectful manner. At one time in my life, all I wanted was to be with her, but now she had chosen the pastor over her own child. I started to fall asleep, but some fool was banging on our door like a m a n i a c. Sandra ran downstairs to see who it was. The steps echoed of stampeding feet and I knew it was my mother. She came in my room and told me to get my things. I lifted my head up and laughed in her face. Not pleased by my reaction she slapped me. And I slapped her back. Then she started choking me, and in that moment I realized I had hit my mother. Sandra tried to pull her off of me, but she had a kung-fu grip around my neck. She was trying to kill me. Wanting to get her hands off of me I hit her again, but this time I hit her with all the force inside my body. She was dazed by the punch I threw and began to loosen her grip. Sandra took my mom downstairs in the living room and tried to calm her down. But she kept shouting, "That little bitch. I'm gonna kill her." At first I didn't panic until she said, "She's coming with me." I sat in my room and started to think of a plan. I wasn't going to live with her or the pastor. I didn't mean to hit her, but what was I supposed to do? She would have choked the life out of me. Sandra came upstairs while my mother screamed obscenities up at me. "Why did you hit her?" she asked me.

"Because she was hitting me! Why are you taking her side? She came over here to kill me and you just stood there and let her."

"Sunshine don't play that bullshit with me. I tried to help you!"

"I'm not going to live with her."

"She's just angry right now. Let me talk to her and see what I can do. Everything should be alright."

"Be alright…she's crazy Sandra! I'm never going to respect her, and if I have to go with her I'll run away. I don't want to stay with her! Oh my God, please, please Sandra, I don't wanna leave. Please Sandra don't make me!"

Sandra and my mother were downstairs for some time. Lil Jermaine had awakened so I went to Sandra's room to get him. My mother caught one glance of me, and the cursing and screaming started again. I went in my room and closed the door. In my mind it was settled, and if Sandra made me leave she would be added to my "I hate you" list. Through the screaming I could hear another knock at the door, it was Pastor Jordon. I wanted to go down and slap him, but my instincts told me to keep my butt grounded and keep an ear out. Listening through my door provided me with little news because it was hard to hear what Pastor Jordon was saying to my mother. I was headed downstairs to get my nephew something to eat, but when Sandra saw me coming down the steps she ran up to see what I wanted. She quickly instructed me to go back in my room and said she would bring the food upstairs. My mother looked at me with hatred and disbelief, and I returned the favor. One look at Pastor Jordon and I wanted to leap off the steps and make a permanent dent in his forehead.

It was decision time. I sat on my bed as Sandra walked in my room. "You're staying, but you need to apologize. If you can't apologize, you can't stay."

"Are you serious? I didn't do anything. If I hit you, wouldn't you hit me back? It was a reflex."

"Sunshine, go apologize so we can get past this."

I went downstairs and stood in front of the devil and my mother. I looked at the floor and callously said, "I apologize for hitting you and for speaking to you in that manner. I didn't mean to hit you. It was just a reflex, and the second time I was trying to defend my life." She may have wanted a heartfelt apology, but she received the watered-down version.

## Chapter XXI

Temple's Upward Bound program was a way for me to clear my mind because my mother and all her threats had me on pins and needles. She told Sandra if I ever disrespected her again, I would have to move back in with them. After Sandra gave me that piece of information I straightened up my act and learned how to curb my tongue. Now that I was taking college courses I didn't want any drama to interfere with my education.

The Upward Bound program was excellent and it came with benefits. They provided us with tokens for transportation and paid us a weekly stipend of sixty dollars. Temple also had a fully stocked cafeteria, and they provided us with breakfast, lunch, snacks, and dinner, free of charge. Our initial meeting was held in Anderson hall where we met all the participants. The program was comprised of thirty students – eighth through twelfth graders – who were handpicked by their principals and teachers from several Philadelphia public schools. Mrs. Archie was the head of the program, and on the first day of class she gave us a list of do's and don'ts. The rules were pretty simple. The main three were: never miss a day (unless it was a medical emergency, such as death); don't misbehave; and do not interfere with the current college students, specifically – if you were dating, you should think twice before trying to date the college students. Challenging the rules meant termination from the program.

All of the participants knew how extraordinary the program was, and while they didn't want to risk getting kicked out, many of the girls couldn't get the boys off of their brains. Even though it would have been safer for them to like the guys in our program, they were fascinated by the college guys and had some stimulating stories to tell about them. And I must admit they seemed much more interesting than the boys in our program. Some of them not only went to school but they held down jobs, many of them had great bodies, and you could see they were doing something positive with their lives. Being a newbie, I was jealous because I wasn't allowed to stay on campus, but I was determined to make the best of this once in a lifetime opportunity.

I took two college courses that summer. Newbies went part time while the varsity kids took three classes. Both of my classes were two hours each, and there was an hour after each class that was to be spent in the library devoted to studying, but these hours weren't monitored. Many students spent them wandering the campus, but I thought it was a good idea to study. Spanish 101 and Computer Science Information (CSI) were my assigned courses. Spanish was a language of love and an excellent language to learn with our growing Latin community. I seriously considered being a translator and took great interest in the course. In our first class, we started out with the basics – numbers, days of the week, months, colors, times, family members, and to add a nice bonus to it all, we had to learn all of that information by the end of the week. Now I knew Mrs. Gonzales was kidding, but when Friday came, she pulled out a stack of quizzes and said, "You want a taste of college life? Well, you kids got it!" I couldn't believe it. Everything she taught us was on the quiz, and she didn't leave one thing out.

When we got our grades back, what was more embarrassing than my 62% (ranking in the top 10 percentile) was the grade our Spanish counterpart received – a whopping 22%! How in the hell can you fail horribly when you have a Spanish name and were born in Puerto Rico? If the class didn't understand why Sabrina Sanchez failed, neither did Mrs. Gonzales. She screamed at her and demanded to know why she had forgotten her heritage and their beautiful language. To be fair Sabrina was raised in Philadelphia, and her parents never taught her. But that wasn't a good enough explanation for Mrs. Gonzales. So she told Sabrina to hand in a ten-page typed essay on Puerto Rico by the next day or she would fail her class. I thought the punishment was too harsh. I wanted to say something, but I wasn't going to help her type the paper nor was I willing to fail, so I kept my mouth shut. Everyone who thought Spanish was an easy A quickly realized the games were over and that they had a rough summer ahead of them. We needed a minimum of a C in each class to stay in the program, and it was going to be a struggle, if not nearly impossible to get a low C from Mrs. Gonzales.

Fortunately my CSI class was a breeze. Our instructor was too preoccupied grading papers to give us assignments, so he gave us busy work instead. He told us to play on the computer and see how much we could learn by the end of the week. Our systems were loaded with computer games so we played them. Common sense told me I should study Spanish during this period, but after playing Tetris for a while my common sense faded.

The computer lab was full of students working on important papers and projects. When they weren't sitting down they were always in a rush. They walked so fast to get from point A to point B it was like watching people board a New York subway. There was this one student who made sure he took his time, particularly when he saw me. He was always eyeing me, and he was cute, but the fear of being kicked out of the program kept my eyes in my sockets, as much as possible.

When we actually received a project from our instructor it was challenging, and now I really needed help. I guess all that time I spent playing games came back to bite me in the "you-know-what". I had to do a presentation on public schools vs. private schools. My title came easy: "The Good, the Bad, and the One You Can't Afford!" I needed a five-page, typed essay with graphics and charts. The writing portion was effortless because I knew from the beginning to the last period what I was going to say, but when it came to the graphics and charts I needed more help than the entire class. When I asked the instructor for help, he directed me to one of the offices in the back of the computer lab. The door was open but the guy had his back turned to me, so I knocked on the door and said, "Hi. Professor Reid said you could help me with my assignment." It was the guy who had been eyeing me. He worked as a Computer Lab assistant. All this time I could have pretended to need help just to get a little closer, and now that I had a solid alibi I was off. He looked up at me like he hadn't heard me the first time so I spoke again. "Hello and how do you do?

"What are you...a Southern Bell?"

"No, just being polite. My name is Sunshine. Will you be able to help me with my project?"

"Well, don't take this the wrong way..."

"What?"

"You have a beautiful smile."

"Thank you."

"Did anyone ever tell you you're going to be a heartbreaker?"

"No, but it sounds good coming out of your mouth."

"Um, feisty and all grown up?"

"No, I'm not, but I tend to speak the language spoken to me."

"Okay, what can I help you with?" I handed him my paper and showed him what I had so far. He started making adjustments and corrections, as if it was his own. When class ended he handed me my project and asked if I knew his name. With a flirtatious look and smile I said, "Mr. Assistant of the Computer Lab". He giggled, and I walked away.

I was into the program, but I was feeling Andre (Mr. Assistant of the Computer Lab) a lot more. I kicked my family and Mrs. Archie to the curb and spent more time with him than with anyone else. I felt like I was falling in love with him, but since I'd never loved anyone in a boyfriend capacity before, I wasn't sure I would know it when it happened. Andre was twenty, a junior pursuing a BA in Computer Science, 6-feet, brown-skinned with a well-built frame, a head full of locks, and he had them LL Cool J lips. They were stunning, and each time he spoke, the words would vibrate off his lips into my mouth. I definitely had a thing for him, but I knew my lies would get me into trouble someday. I told him I was sixteen because I figured the plumpness of my full C's and my round behind wouldn't give way to my fourteen-year-old identity. Even though sixteen wasn't legal age, it was much closer to eighteen than fourteen was.

Andre invited me over to his dorm on the weekend, but I had to decline in order to stay clear of any Upward Bound students. He didn't accept my answer and said he would pick me up Saturday afternoon. I really wanted to go, but I knew I needed a quick alibi so I called up Lil Bitts. "If Sandra calls, I'm at your house."

"Okay."

"Is your mom there?"

"No."

"Good!" Sandra never questioned me; I never gave her any reason too, but just to be on the safe side I wanted everything straight. Now that my story was set I told Andre to meet me at Broad and Erie. I wanted to get as far away from the house as possible but close enough for him to find me. Since this was the first time I was going to see Andre outside of Temple, I wanted to show off my sexiness. I wore the shortest jean skirt I had with the tightest t-shirt I could find. My breast print and nipples could be seen through my shirt, so I decided not to wear a bra. I let my hair down and bumped it straight, and for the final touch I added clear, glossy lip gloss to my lips.

On my way to Broad and Erie I received more attention than I needed and some of it came before I left the house. Based on Sandra's look she wasn't pleased with my style of dress, but she didn't make me change so I was a happy camper. The other attention came from the jealous stares of women and from the gawking and calls of men. It didn't bother me though because I was dressed for Andre, and I wanted to make an impression. I was standing next to the pizza shop, and when he pulled up his eyes almost ran off his face. He jumped out of the car and opened the door for me and said, "I never saw you like this before."

"That's because we always see each other when I'm in school. You're disappointed?"

"Shit no, you look good!"

"Okay. Where are we going?"

"To my place." I was nervous, but I didn't want to seem immature so I went along with the program.

When we arrived at his dorm, he told the guard at the desk that I was his little sister. Either the guard was an idiot or he knew they brought their girlfriends up to the room frequently, because he never took his eyes off my breasts or asked for my name or for I.D. When Andre opened his door, I saw two of his roommates and two of their friends in the living room. They were playing video games. When I entered they looked at me and smiled. He walked me into his room and told me he would be right back. After five minutes, I heard the television shut off and the front door close. Then Andre came into the room and said, "We're alone." Immediately I felt so much better because I had been longing to kiss him, but I didn't want to with all those guys sitting in the living room. When he sat on the bed I went straight for his lips. I wanted to enjoy every moment of them, so I sucked them slowly, but firmly enough to let him know I knew what I was doing, and I could tell he was enjoying it. He began to suck my neck and began kissing on my breasts through my t-shirt. When he went to pull up my shirt, I pulled it down because all I wanted to do was kiss. But he kept at it until eventually he had it off and my nipples were in his mouth. His lips weren't for show at all. He had definitely brought them out to play.

My body started releasing juices into my panties. He pulled them off, and although I wasn't ready for that I let him continue. Next he took his fingers and gently parted my lips. Slowly he laid me back onto the bed and started to kiss my clitoris as he gently slid two of his fingers inside of me. He had me sounding like the women off of those 900 lines when they were coming, but I wasn't faking and I had the juices to prove it. When he removed his fingers they were dripping wet and he looked me in the eye as he cleaned them with his mouth. He headed back down and kissed, licked and sucked my pussy while all of these juices kept coming out of my body. I wanted to explode, I wanted to scream, but instead I grabbed his locks as hard as I could without hurting him. But that wasn't helping, so I begged him, "Oh my God, please stop. I can't take it, Andre, please stop."

"Call me big daddy."

116

"Daddy, please stop, I can't take it, please."

"I said Big Daddy!"

"Big Daddy, please stop. I can't take it anymore, please!" He said his tongue wasn't through playing a game with my clit, and I would have to take it. I'd never had a guy down there, with my consent, and I didn't know he could make me feel powerless by gyrating my clitoris.

To my surprise, he stopped, but my vagina was panting for his touch. I was like a cat in heat that kept lifting her tail and pushing her pussy in your face. He had taken off all of my clothing and his, except for his boxers. Then he smiled at me, stood up, and pulled them off. It was enormous! This was the first time I had freely seen a penis, and I never knew they were that big. I panicked. "Andre, I want to go home."

"Why?"

"I just do so please take me home!"

"Sunshine, calm down. I'm not going to make you do anything you don't want to."

"Okay, then take me home!" He grabbed my face and started kissing all over me, right down to my nipples. Each time he sucked on them, my body would submit to any position he wanted me in. He laid me back on the bed and started massaging his penis up against my vagina. I was anxious to know what it felt like, but I just didn't feel ready. So I tightened up my legs and shut him out. "Sunshine, why are you being like this? I want you to stop playing games."

"You're not even my boyfriend."

"Baby don't do this. I want to feel inside of you."

"But I never did this before."

"Straight?"

"Yeah." He was quiet for a moment. Then a smirk came across his face. "Do you want to suck it?"

"No. Suck what?"

"Come on now. Don't act like you don't know what I'm talking about."

"I don't."

"My dick."

"NO!"

"Why you acting like a baby? You'll still be a virgin."

117

"I know that, I wasn't born yesterday."

"So you gonna do it?"

"Why should I?"

"It's not like its bad. I did it for you, didn't I?"

"Yeah..."

"Didn't you like it?"

"Yes."

Nervous, but wanting him to like me, I let him talk me into it. I wasn't sure if I would do it right, but I decided to model it after the way he did me. He made sure he took his time, and he was gentle but not scared. I started to lick the tip, just like he told me. Then I made sure my mouth was soaking wet and started to slide my mouth down his penis, from top to bottom. I was surprised at how much I could fit in my mouth without gagging. He stroked my face and hair, and then he started to move my head faster and faster, up and down his penis. He pulled it out and showed me how to masturbate his penis with my hands, and then he told me to put it back in my mouth and continue doing what I was doing. I started to twirl my tongue to the rhythm, and this seemed to really turn him on. He grabbed my head and again moved it down and up his penis, faster and faster. "I'm 'bout to cum... Oh fuck... I can't believe this... oh shit here it comes. You want me to cum in ya mouth?" I didn't know what to say, so I just kept sucking, slurping up and down, faster and faster. His penis was rock hard, and with one jolt and a "Here it come!" I could feel his liquids in my mouth. I wanted to push his penis out of my mouth because the cum didn't taste good, and I wanted to spit it out, but he held his dick in my mouth until all of it came out. When he let me go I ran into the bathroom to spit the cum in the toilet.

When I looked in the mirror, I looked rough though I hadn't had sex. I needed to fix my hair, shower, and brush my teeth. As I cut on the water to take a shower, he walked in the bathroom. He was smiling and jumped in the shower with me. Andre washed my body from hair to feet, and he even sucked my toes after he washed them. I washed him too but stayed away from his penis because I didn't want him to get any ideas. He kept smiling and wasn't saying anything, but I decided to get a conversation going. "So did you like it?"

"You know I did."

"How am I supposed to know? I never did that before."

"You're trying to tell me you never sucked anyone off before?"

"I said no!"

"Don't get mad. Shit, it felt so good. I just can't believe it was your first time."

"Well it was."

"Are you going to do it for me again?"

"If you want me to…but not now."

"I know. Listen. Next time I want you to swallow it."

"No. It tastes nasty."

"A man's cum isn't nasty. It's good for your hair, skin, and nails."

"Well my hair, skin, and nails aren't in need of any help."

"Okay, well…will you think about it?"

"I will."

"You my baby?" I couldn't stop blushing and shyly answered, "Yes."

## Chapter XXII

The next morning I woke up in excruciating pain. My vagina was swollen, and it was red and on fire. I ran to the bathroom because I had to pee, and I wanted to find out what was wrong. When I sat on the toilet I was afraid to go. I could see how red it was because I brought a mirror into the bathroom to get a closer look. Andre and I didn't have sex so I was confused. I knew about condoms, or at least enough to know I needed to use them to avoid getting pregnant or catching an STD, so I was boggled as to why my vagina was in so much pain. Just then a drop of urine came out, and the fire turned into a volcanic eruption. I couldn't pee! I took a cup and filled it with cold water. The problem was I poured out all of the water before I could pee. Only drips of pee would come out. When the urine would touch my vagina, the fire arose. This was ridiculous, and I needed help. I got into a tub of cold water, and although the water was comforting to my vagina, the rest of my body suffered. I urinated in the cold water to relieve my vagina from some of the pain. This was of great help, but as soon as I got out of the tub the pain returned.

I went into my room and lay in my bed, all the while crying and holding myself. I had to be at Temple in thirty minutes, but there was no way I could make it so I continued to lay there. Sandra knocked on the door and peered her head in. "What's the hold up?"

"Nothing. I'm not going today."

"Why?"

"Because I don't feel well."

"Since when did that stop you?" She burst into my room and pulled back the covers. I was naked, holding my stuff. As she continued to question me, I began to tear up. I was embarrassed and I didn't want Sandra to know what I'd done. But she lost her patience and started screaming at me. Instead of opening my mouth and further disgracing myself, I showed her. "You had sex! What the fuck are you thinking?"

"I didn't, Sandra I swear."

"Who in the hell you do think you're talkin' to? Just get dressed Sunshine. Now!"

Sandra took me to her doctor and I cried all the way there. She didn't say a word to me, but I could feel she was disgusted. The feeling ran through my entire body. Lil Jermaine was sitting next to me in the back seat (because I didn't have the guts to ride shotgun), and he was confused as to why I was crying. He kept asking for hugs, but I didn't want to touch him because I thought I would contaminate him. At the doctor's office all I could think about was what I was going to say. I wasn't going to tell Sandra or the doctor about Andre. I didn't know what was going on or why my vagina hurt. I just wanted to be seen. The wait was long and I had to pee again, but this time there was no tub and the little cups of cold water did not ease my pain. So I just gunned it. I let it out as fast as I could, and the cost was hefty. I was burning inside and outside of my vagina.

Finally, after waiting an hour and a half because I was a walk-in, the doctor called for me. I thought I had to go by myself, but Sandra came with me. When we entered the exam room the doctor asked, "So what's going on?" Sandra looked at me, and I looked at her, but I didn't know what to say. "Can you use the small clamps on her? This is her first exam." Sandra made that statement then left the room. "Sunshine you can get undressed from the waist down and put this gown on. I'll be back in a second." That's all she gave me too, a second. I barely had the gown on before she came back in the room. I got up on the exam table and she showed me how to position my legs in the stirrups so I could have a pelvic exam. She pulled out these plastic clamps that looked similar to the tongs used at a barbeque, and they worked like a jack that's used to change tires. There was no way they would fit in my body, so I spoke up. "Excuse me, but I didn't have sex and please don't put them inside of me."

"Sunshine relax. I'm going to do an examination with my hands first, and then I will show you how these work."

"Okay."

"So where is the pain?"

"All in my vagina, but it hurts even more when I have to use the bathroom."

"Okay, so it burns when you urinate?"

"Yes."

"Is there any discharge?"

"Huh?"

"Yellowish, cottage cheese looking?"

"Oh no. I haven't seen any discharge, this just happened after yesterday."

"So what happened yesterday?"

"Please don't tell Sandra."

"I prefer if you tell me what's going on with you so I can help you... Listen Sunshine, you're not the first girl to come in here with an STD, and I need to treat you and your partner for this."

"For what? I never had sex! I know what STD means and I didn't have sex."

"Did you give him oral sex or did he rub his penis on your vagina?" My cover was blown. Dr. Patel had pulled my card, and I truly didn't feel like holding back anymore. If she had the key to stop the burning so I could pee, I had to open up, but Andre had to remain a secret. "Dr. Patel, I went over to my friend's house, and I let him suck on my breasts. He did rub his penis against my vagina, but he never put it inside of me. He kissed on my vagina, then he asked me to suck...you know what..."

"What?"

"His penis."

"And?"

"And I did."

"Do you know you can catch STDs from having anal, oral, and vaginal sex, and even from allowing an infected male to rub his penis up against your vagina?"

"No, I thought as long as I didn't have sex with him I'd be okay."

"Okay, I'm going to examine you. Lay back. First you're going to feel my fingers, and they'll be a little cold from the K-Y Jelly. Does that hurt when I press here?"

"It burns everywhere. I can't tell what hurts. It all hurts!"

"Okay, okay, now I'm going to insert the speculum. Bring your bottom all the way down to the end of the table."

"I feel like I'm about to fall."

"No, you're okay. Keep coming down. Okay, you're alright. Now relax. Let your legs dangle free in the stirrups. Don't tense your muscles up because it makes it difficult. Okay, it's in. One more swab, and I'll be done. I see some discharge but no apparent signs of penetration. Okay, you can sit up now. Wipe off with these paper towels, get dressed, and I'll be right back with your results."

Violated! It was embarrassing having a female look and feel around like she did. The long Q-tips she used to swab for discharge were the only comforting aspect of the entire event. They were cooling to my insides, and the depth they reached to rub this itch I had was amazing. But it was still an unpleasant event. I had my butt hanging in mid-air, with my legs up in stirrups, while she was checking for an STD. What had I gotten myself into? Sandra would probably put me out. I hadn't even have sex with Andre but still I was now diseased.

Within a few minutes Dr. Patel returned. "Yes, Sunshine, you have an STD. It's called Gonorrhea, and it's sometimes referred to as being burnt or burning. This disease is very contagious, and in your case you could have gotten it from him rubbing his penis up against your vagina or from oral sex."

"Can you tell my sister that I didn't have sex?"

"I will, but first we need to discuss treatment. I need you to take these pills, all four at once. They will clear up this infection, and you need to abstain from sexual activity, rubbing or touching of any kind for at least seven days. We clear?"

"Yes. Crystal. Can you please tell Sandra I didn't have sex?"

"Give me a minute. Now what type of birth control would you like?"

"I don't want any."

"I'm going to give you condoms. Even though you didn't have intercourse, if you decide to in the future, it's better to be prepared. Do you know how to use them?"

"No."

"Okay. What you want to do is pinch the tip of the condom, but not hard enough to puncture it. Then roll it down onto your partner's erect penis. Make sure it rolls all the way down, and that's all."

"I won't be having sex."

"I'm not saying that, but I want to educate you on all of your options because you saw firsthand what the consequences are. Now I will talk with your sister, but by law I'm required to tell her I'm treating you for Gonorrhea because you're underage. And I will let her know it doesn't appear you were sexually active vaginally."

Sandra looked relieved when she finished speaking with my doctor, but she quickly reverted to being revolted and disappointed once we got home. All she wanted to know was who I let rub up against me. The doctor was kind enough to leave out the oral sex edition. Sandra had never been this upset. She was yelling for hours, which ended with me being placed on punishment. I was restricted from all activities except for going to the program, and I was given a set amount of time to get there and to get back. She even threatened to tell Mrs. Archie what happened, and that sent me into tears. My vagina was already burning away, and I didn't need any more embarrassment. I was sent to my room until she could think of more ways to punish me. I knew chores would be added, and phone privileges were taken away before we left the doctor's office.

When I woke up the next morning, the swelling had gone down and the burning had subsided. I no longer needed pitchers of cold water to accompany me to the bathroom. Sandra gave me the entire spiel from the day before as I left the house for Temple. When I got there, all I wanted to do was curse Andre out, and as soon as I got a break I went over to talk to him. He was smiling at me, but the flames were leaping off my face. He quickly parked his smile into neutral. As soon as I approached him, he asked if we could talk outside. We walked away from any spectators, and I drilled into him. He had no response. Instead of looking smart and intelligent, he looked like an ass. Why was he acting as if his dick wasn't on fire? As hot as I was, there was no way his body hadn't felt the flames. I yelled at him for a good twenty minutes before I realized Mrs. Archie had walked past both of us. I knew I had to get back to class because getting caught talking to him was a sure sign of a problem.

Before I could react to my emotions with Andre, Mrs. Archie had called for me to stop by Anderson Hall before I went home. She was all over me with questions about Andre. Why was I talking to him? Was he trying to talk to me? What was I thinking, arguing with a college student? I didn't have the best planned out response, so I just stated I was mad at him because he erased my project from my floppy disk, and that I had to turn it in today. I knew Mrs. Archie was a smart cookie, but luckily she fell for my bull. She told me to talk to my professor about recovering the lost data or to ask for an extension, and to be more careful the next time. Before I walked off she also threw in, "Don't yell at Andre because he was trying to help you." If she only knew he had helped my pussy-cat reach the gates of hell, she might have beaten both of us up.

Andre called the house twice while I was on punishment. The first time he called, Sandra let him off easy by letting him know I was on punishment and not to call back. After three weeks passed, I guess he felt lucky because he called again. Profanity was the name of the game, and Sandra laid him out, but his repeated calling catapulted the entire situation back up again. Now she wanted to know if he was the guy, if I had ever stayed with Lil Bitts that day, how many times I had thought about sex, and why didn't I tell her if I had those thoughts. With her, silence isn't golden because I was given two more weeks, added to the year of punishment I already had, for not responding. Instead of being frustrated with Sandra, I started thinking about Andre. I wanted to be with him, but how could I trust him? I really didn't get a chance to express myself the way I needed to because we were at Temple with crowds passing by. We both wanted to talk to each other but with eyes on us and me on restriction, there was no way.

One day I was in the lab when Andre quickly handed me a letter:

*Sunshine don't hate me. I didn't know I had a problem. I'm often at the courts playing basketball and sometimes I don't wash my hands before I go to the bathroom, so I must have gotten it from there. But I went to the doctor, and I'm all better now. I wish we could talk and be friends because I want more from you, but you're acting like you're done with me. I never had anyone make me feel like that, with only using their mouth. You have real talents and I want us to enjoy each other again. Call me when you get a chance.*

*By the way, how come you didn't tell me you're fourteen? I could be in jail right now. Maybe I should be the one mad at you?*

*Andre*

After reading his letter I started to think about my meeting with Dr. Patel, and I never heard her say it was airborne, or that you could get it from touching a basketball. She did say you could get it from rubbing body parts against each other or having sex with an infected person. I wondered if you could get it from not washing your hands and then touching your penis or vagina. Either way I didn't want to try anything with him again. He was unclean, and I was too scared to venture back to the realms of hell. The fact that he knew my age didn't matter to me, and it didn't seem to bother him because he still wanted to see me. I made up my mind to ignore him and my feelings for him, and to strongly remember sitting in a cold tub of water just to pee.

   I concentrated on my classes and dealt with my punishment. It went from a summer of freedom and fun, to a summer of school, chores, and no phone. Because I had nothing else to focus on, I studied intensely for Spanish and learned how to insert charts and graphics for my CSI reports. When the program drew to a close, my hard work had paid off. Mrs. Archie called the house in regards to my grades, but she wouldn't tell me. She wanted to speak with Sandra first. My phone privileges were reinstated when Mrs. Archie told her I received a B for Spanish 101 and an A for Computer Science Information. As a treat, Big Jermaine said he was going to take me shopping. Lately he had been distant, and I was unsure why, but on our way to the mall when he started talking about having protected sex and what was an appropriate age for sex, I knew Sandra had leaked the news. Thankfully she kept the news in the home and not in the hands of my mother or Mrs. Archie. My mother would have finally had a reason to make me move in with her, and Mrs. Archie probably would have thrown in the towel.

## Chapter XXIII

Temple provided me with a weekly stipend over the summer, but when the program ended so did the compensation. I came to the conclusion that money was a beautiful thing, and I wanted more of it, but I no longer wanted to depend on Sandra and Big Jermaine for cash either. So when my freshman year began at Dobbins I started searching for a job after my first day of classes.

Directly across the street from my school was the avenue of 22$^{nd}$ Street and it had plenty of stores. I applied to as many of the stores as I could by asking for an application or an on-the-spot interview.

I instantly realized I would have a problem getting paid with a paper check because I had no working papers and I didn't like the idea of paying taxes. So I looked for jobs that would pay under the table. There was a store called "Talking T-Shirts", and their pay style was right up my alley. The owner was a really sweet guy and offered me a job working three days a week from 4:00-6:00 pm and on Saturdays, noon-5:00 pm. I ran the idea past Sandra, and she was okay with it as long as my grades weren't compromised. I was sure my job wouldn't interfere with my school work because all of my classes were easy, and I didn't have a single challenging course on my roster.

My job was in complete harmony with my school schedule. My last class (you won't believe this) was Spanish. It was like taking a breath with healthy lungs – too easy. School let out at 3:20 p.m. so I had some time to hang on the wall before I went to work. Dobbins was famous for its wall. There was a shopping center across the street from our school, and they built a knee high wall that surrounded the parking lot. Everyone sat on the wall and got their talk on, even people who didn't attend our school. Although the wall had some clique sections, we all seemed to share it. It was also a meeting ground. Guys and girls who went to other schools would drive up and park their cars in the parking lot, then come up on the wall to see who they could meet. The wall was our unofficial hang out.

I started my job on the third day of school, which was a Wednesday, and the owner went over my duties. I had to be polite to the customers, dust the stockings, and stock the shelves when the knee-highs, socks, or hats got low. My pay would be sixty-five dollars a week. This was good for me and the first day went without incident, better yet without customers. The next day we had one customer who wanted a t-shirt with his name on it. I wanted to do it, but the owner said he was the only one that could iron the letters on the t-shirts. On Friday, I had one customer who came in for a pair of knee-highs. That was at 6:00 pm on the dot.

When Saturday arrived, I was pumped up to go to work because a lot of people shop on the weekends. Plus Sandra kept asking me how it was going, and I figured I would definitely get some customers today and be able to give her some positive feedback. Big Jermaine dropped me off. He came in to check out the store, but I think he was sent there to verify if I had a job and not a boyfriend. He bought a pair of socks and left. From noon till 3:00, my only customer was Big Jermaine. I started nodding off at the register. Most of the time the owner stayed in the back of the store watching TV and laughing so he didn't notice my nodding. Still I didn't want him to catch me. To rejuvenate myself I went for my twenty-minute lunch. I got a turkey breast sandwich, soda, and a bag of salt & vinegar chips. I thought my lunch would keep me awake, but it only made me sleepier. When it was time for me to get off my eyes were so low, you would have thought I was high. When the owner paid me I knew I had to quit, but I was too scared to tell him. I figured he'd ask why, and boredom didn't sound like a great response so I decided on my next scheduled day I would do a "no-call, no-show". When I got home I told Sandra and Big Jermaine what I had decided. They laughed because Big Jermaine knew I wouldn't last. He figured the store didn't get enough business and he had a bet running with Sandra for fifty bucks (which she didn't pay) that I was a goner.

After school on Tuesday, I started a new search. There was a beauty salon called "Doing Big Things" with a barber shop upstairs that had a help wanted sign in the barber shop window. I walked up the staircase and could hear voices before I made it up the steps. For me this was a great sign because that meant they had customers. When I got upstairs, all eyes were on me. I was so nervous because all fifteen of the people got real quiet and stared at me. "Hello, and how is everyone?" I nervously began. "My name is Sunshine, and I'm looking for a job. Is the manager in?" They all said yes then burst out laughing. One spoke up amidst the noise. "I'm the owner. I'm Shareef. What do you wanna do?"

"I was hoping to shampoo for the barbers."

"Okay, so you wanna be a shampoo girl?"

"I don't like that terminology, but it'll do."

"You uppity?"

"No, I just don't like that title."

"Lift your arms up."

"Why?"

"You want the job, don't you?"

"Yes."

"Lift 'em."

"Okay."

"Alright y'all, come check it out." Four guys came over and smelled my underarms. I was in shock. I knew this wasn't proper hiring practice, but at least they had customers.

"You good! When can you start?"

"Why did you do that?"

"What, smell your pits?"

"Yes."

"Because the last shampoo girl we had was funky, but you alright with us. How old are you?"

"Sixteen."

"Just old enough."

"For what?"

"Just joking. But yo, you can't be workin' here actin' all snooty."

"I'm not. I have a sense of humor."

"Good, you can start tomorrow."

"How much do I get paid?"

"Oh okay, I'll talk to you in tha back." Shareef walked me to the back of the shop. They had turned the back portion of the shop into an office, but it looked more like a mini gym. They had weight benches with all different sizes of weights, ropes, and other gym equipment, but no desk. Shareef sat on the weight bench and laid down the rules. I had to come to work as soon as I got out of school, and I worked every day, except Sundays and Mondays until 9:00 pm, and Saturdays he wanted me to work from noon till 10:00 pm, later if they still had customers. Shareef was the owner, but there were four other barbers – Mike, Ralph, Dave, and Tyree – who worked with him as well. I was responsible for washing all of their clients' hair, and my base pay would be seventy-five dollars a week, plus any tips I made.

I was excited about working in the barbershop, but Big Jermaine had doubts. He knew one of the barbers, Tyree, and made sure he kept him up to date on what I was doing. Sandra surprisingly didn't give me any slack about working there. She was all about my grades, and I assured her there wouldn't be any problems. I had finally broken down and told her about Andre, how I let him rub his penis up against me (I vowed to take the oral sex details to my grave) but that he didn't penetrate me. She was pissed, but it restored some of the trust back into our relationship. Now I could go to work without feeling like she didn't trust where I was.

My first day on the job, Shareef already had a nickname for me that he said was more suitable for my character. Shorty Shamp. I liked the name, even though I wasn't short, because it was ghetto, but still cute. The job was fun because the barbershop did big business, and there were no shortages on clients. The shop cut all the guys from the neighborhood: children, policemen, priests, local celebrities, even two professional NBA basketball players.

I worked hard at my job. I learned all of my clients' names and how each one liked their hair washed. Some wanted the extra hard scrub, others the sensitive scalp wash. There was the scratch-up-the-dandruff-before-you-wash wash, and the put-your-gloves-on-before-you-even-look-at- my-scalp wash. I hated those kinds. There was this one guy in particular that truly made my skin crawl. I never learned his real name, but they called him Juice. I wished he would go bald so he'd never get his hair cut by us again. He had razor bumps that began on the back of his neck and went all the way up to the middle of his head. It was disgusting and hard to look at. I put on my gloves as soon as he walked up the stairs. When I washed his hair, I just poured the shampoo on his head and used a disposable comb to rub over his hair. I threw away the gloves and the comb, and then I would bleach the wash bowel. Shareef cut his hair, and it was the only time I wasn't impressed. He used his old outdated clippers – a pair for Juice's head only. But besides Juice, I had wonderful clients, and they tipped well. As long as my nipples showed through my shirt and my jeans were fitted, they kept tipping. When I washed their hair, I would catch them looking up at my breasts. Believe it or not, that small view brought great tips. It didn't bother me that they looked as long as they didn't touch. I was bringing home three to four hundred dollars a week. The more I did for my clients, the more they tipped. Some of them were tipping as much as they were paying for their haircuts. In addition to washing their hair, I would get them breakfast or lunch, listen to their sob stories about women, or massage their shoulders, but I wouldn't let it go further than that.

My biggest tippers were the big time drug dealers. They didn't care if they spent five hundred a day on lottery tickets, and some of them did. For them to tip me twenty or forty dollars was no big deal. One of them had a thing for me, Kalil. He was so sexy with his brown skin, his faded wavy hair, his medium build, thick hands, juicy lips (I love lips), and his tall, athletic body. He bought me breakfast every Saturday morning and tipped me fifty dollars each time I washed his hair. He got his haircut weekly and never short-changed my tip. When I had time to rub Kalil's shoulders after washing his hair, he would include a twenty with my regular tip. Seventy dollars for three to five minutes of hair washing and a five-minute shoulder massage? I couldn't beat that.

My finances were on the up and up, and whenever I got a free minute I was shopping. Still a fan of the thrift shop, I made sure they got a good chunk of my cash. I was the queen of making a dollar shirt look like a seriously sought-out, one of a kind. I racked up on so many clothes that my room looked more like a large walk-in closet. I also had an infatuation with boots. I liked shoes, but I loved boots! I spent four hundred dollars on a pair of pink gator boots from Dudes, off of South Street. They were perfect and just one pair of my seventy-two shoe and boot collection. Not that all my shoes cost four hundred dollars – which is cheap to some people, but the ones I most adored I didn't mind spending my money on. I bought girly shoes from stores like Bakers, Easy Pickens, Strawbridge's, and other not so expensive retailers. I would buy five or more at a time, but with my boots, they were a one buy deal. My lover and my enemy was Nordstrom. Once I spotted a pair of boots I loved, my savings would automatically decrease. There was nothing I wanted that I couldn't afford or work to get, except a car. Not that I couldn't afford it if I worked my butt off and saved, but I wasn't old enough to drive.

As a kind (questionable) gesture, Shareef told Kalil about my infatuation with boots. One Saturday he handed me a bag. I wanted to rip the bag open, but all the guys were watching and I didn't want to look like a nut, so I played it cool. "What's this?" I asked him, holding the bag out in front of me.

"It's for you."

"Thanks, but you didn't have to."

"I know. I wanted to give someone special a special gift. Open it."

"Right now?"

"Yeah, right now!" So I opened it. It was a pair of seven hundred dollar shoe-boots from Nordstrom. I had drooled over these boots, even put them on my wish list. But I didn't expect to get them because my limit was set at four hundred and fifty dollars, and they weren't going on sale anytime soon. My kitty was moist. Weird, I know, but boots turned me on. In my eyes, I wasn't materialistic, but shoes were my weakness. I took the bag and went inside the office to try them on. Inside of the box there was a note with his phone number on it and five hundred dollars. The message read:

"It's all about me and you!" Plenty of my clients had tried to talk to me, but I ignored them. They had propositioned me with money, jewelry, cars, but none of them had ever done it in a public light. I wanted the shoe-boots more than the money but not at the price he was asking. I wasn't as naive as he may have thought, and I was not about to lie down for some boots and a few dollars. I made enough of my own money, and I wasn't going there. I sat in the office for a while before Shareef yelled for me to come out and show off my boots. I was uncomfortable but I knew I had to show my appreciation. After all, if I had to give anything back, I sure didn't want it to be the boots. It was Saturday and crowded, but I modeled the lovely shoe-boots, blushing the entire time. Everyone was staring, some of the guys were laughing. It was all in fun and I laughed at myself, and then I went outside for a break. Kalil walked out behind me and asked me if I liked the boots. Then he said, "Shareef gonna let you get off early today, okay? I'll be back at six." There was nothing more for me to say. I had a date at six.

Kalil showed up at 5:30, and Shareef told me it was okay to go. Why he was being so nice, I didn't know. Maybe he figured somebody would get some coochie from me, even if he couldn't. I got my shoe-boots and my pocketbook, and I left. Kalil was flashy. You could tell by his clothes, his jewelry, and his cars. He decided to pick me up in a shiny black BMW. I wasn't a car person, but I knew luxury when I saw it. When I walked up to the car, he opened the door for me and closed it behind me. Once he sat down he turned over to me and said, "I want you, and I'm not gonna play games with you. I'm gonna take care of you, and you're gonna be mines. Do you have a problem wit that?"

"I don't even know if I like you."

"Oh you like me."

"But I don't know you."

"You'll get to know me, and you'll fall in love with me."

"Money can't buy me."

"You can have the money and the boots. That ain't about shit. Baby girl, ain't no strings attached. If you don't want me, keep that stuff. I gave it to you. It's yours. You should

135

know I'm not a petty dude. So what's up? Are we goin' out, or do you wanna go back to tha shop?" I was silent for a moment and then decided to go along for the ride.

Our first date was a trip to the mall. "Get whatever you want," he kept saying, but I didn't want anything. Everything I saw I wasn't interested in, and I didn't want to come off as money hungry. Had I been broke and in need of an outfit, this never would have happened to me. He was being way too nice to me. I was very skeptical. "You think I want some pussy, don't you? I don't want some pussy. I want yours, but I want you too. I take care of people I want." "So how many people are you taking care of?"

"None, not like the way I'll take care of you."

"Whatever."

"I don't have to lie to you."

"I never said you did. I'm just unsure of why you decided to be so nice to me."

"You couldn't tell I had a thing for you?"

"There's having a thing, and there's buying me those expensive boots and giving me that money."

"Why can't you just trust me? What, you been hurt before."

"Yeah, but what does that have to do with anything?"

"A lot. Don't let that man's ignorance become my fault. Just trust me." Once I let my guard down, I started to have a really good time. Since I didn't see any clothing I liked, he bought me panties and bras. My sets were forty dollars apiece, and he bought me ten pair. He didn't make me spend any of the money he gave me. He wanted me to use that money to open a bank account instead. Kalil wanted to take me, but I was scared the bank would ask my age or for my birth certificate, and I didn't want him to know how old I was. I told him I would go with Sandra, and he was okay with that as long as I showed him the bank receipt. Later that evening we went to a restaurant and had a very romantic dinner. It was a cozy, candlelit restaurant in New Jersey. He held my hands, rubbed my thighs, kissed my hands, and even fed me.

After we ate, I realized it was 11:30 and I needed to call Sandra. I didn't want to get into any more trouble so I went to the back of the restaurant to use their payphone. Big Jermaine answered and asked, "Where you at?" I told him I had finished my last customer and would be home within half an hour. I wasn't sure how I was going to pull it off because I couldn't let Kalil know where we lived, and it was going to take forty minutes to get back to Philly plus another twenty for me to get home. I called Lil Bitts because I figured she would be up. The plan was for her to have a cab ride waiting for me at her house that would give me a ride home. When Kalil dropped me off at her house, he said he'd be back in the morning to take me car shopping. He didn't give me a chance to respond, he just pulled off. First of all it was Sunday, and I didn't know car dealerships opened on Sundays. Second of all, I couldn't drive. And third of all, I didn't live there. I didn't have time to wonder about those issues because I needed to get home. Lil Bitts was on point with the cab ride. Within two minutes of me arriving, the cab pulled up. She was being all nosey, asking me tons of questions, but I wasn't in the mood for talking. I needed an excuse for Sandra so I told the cab driver to give me a minute. I called Sandra and told her I caught a cab to Lil Bitts house first because she was at the shop waiting for me, and now I was on my way home. She told me to hang up, and then she called right back. She said she wanted to make sure I was actually at Lil Bitts' house and told me to spend the night there. She didn't want me to catch a cab home that late, and if it was okay with her mom, who could care less because she was on her way out the door, I could stay there.

I didn't want to stay with Lil Bitts because it was crowded in her house. Wait, let me stop lying. I just wanted to be with him. Since Sandra was okay with me staying the night out, I told the cab driver never mind and gave Kalil a call. Within ten minutes he came back, and we were on our way to his house. He lived downtown in an amazing two- bedroom condo. The view from his apartment was incredible, and his furniture was up to the minute. The leather sofa was so soft; it caressed your body when you sat on it. He had white carpet through the entire condo, and I took my shoes off at the site of its fluffiness. We went into the bedroom. He undressed and got in the bed while I sat on a chair and watched TV until my eyes started to clunk out. I was about to sit on his bed with my jeans on, but he gave me this look. Then he tossed me a t-shirt and told me to put it on. I went in the bathroom to get undressed and he came in right behind me. He undressed me and carried me into his shower. It was a walk-in shower with an overhead dispenser, and the tub sat on the other side of the bathroom. The water was so hot steam was filling the bathroom and my body. He washed me, licking and sucking all my tender spots along the way. He cleaned every part of my body and left no crevice concealed.

After the shower he took me to his bedroom and started to dry me off. The more he dried me off, the wetter I became. He took me over to the leather chair and sat down. He tried to ease me down on top of his dick, but I pulled up. He was bigger than Andre, and I didn't want him to break me open. But this time I wanted to at least try it. He could see the resistance in my eyes so he started kissing me to reassure me. Then he slid me slowly down onto his penis. I let out the softest, sexiest moan when his tip entered, but midway in I was singing a different tune. He started talking to me. "This pussy is so damn wet and tight. Just like I love it!"

"You love it…I…I…" I was losing control of my senses. With each trip down his rollercoaster my body was experiencing feelings I'd never had before. When I got to the tip of his penis and was headed back down, he took my hips and moved them in a circular motion; and as I swirled down my legs begin to tremble. At first he helped me by telling me when to go faster, slower, and deeper, but then he told me to show him what I was working with. This was my first time. I was working with a virgin kitty, but I didn't want to dissatisfy him so I let my body lead the way. When I got to the tip of his penis, I showed him a trick I had learned. When I was younger I used to take a bath toy of mine and fill it with water. Then I'd squirt the water into my kitty and release it slowly and then faster. I had control over my muscles, so when I came to the tip of his penis I made my muscle suckle him, and then released plenty of juices when I was going back down on the ride. He loved it! He started chanting my name and telling me I better not cheat on him because I was his girl now. Then he bust in me, but he didn't stop. He tossed me on the bed and started fucking me from behind. He was pounding my pussy and slapping my ass but with the perfect amount of pressure. My legs were all over the place and he was all over me. He had me bent over the bed, on the floor, on the kitchen table, on the chair, and he fucked me while he walked around with me. He was strong, and his dick was tasty and meaty. I didn't think he'd ever stop, but when I sat back on top of my rollercoaster and let my juices flow, he came again and was out for the count.

His bed was comfortable and huge (king size), and I wanted to drift off in its tenderness. My kitty was swollen, but luckily not infected, and my legs were trembling for nearly twenty minutes after the ride was over. I needed to rest and I was falling asleep, but Kalil wanted to talk. He wanted to know if I dealt with anyone at the barbershop, what type of car I wanted, how I felt about living with him, and when could I move in. But before we went any further I told him my age. I was fifteen and had just turned fifteen, but everyone at the shop thought I had just turned seventeen. Then I told him I couldn't let anyone know where I lived and that I didn't know how to drive. He wanted to know who knew my real age. And when I told him nobody, he instructed me to keep it that way. His response was basically
- I was with him now and not to worry about anything. As far as where I lived was concerned, he didn't care because soon he said I'd be staying with him.

My life became all about Kalil. When I wasn't at school or work, I was with him. He wanted me to quit my job, but I told him I liked working there. I know I didn't need the money because he gave me a weekly allowance of five hundred dollars, but working gave me a sense of independence. Sandra became concerned because she knew I was making too much money to simply be working at the barbershop. Every week I had new earrings, bracelets, designer pocketbooks, boots, shoes, and more clothing. Big

Jermaine didn't even bother asking if I wanted to go shopping anymore because I was running out of places to put all my stuff. I took a Saturday off from work so Sandra could take me to the bank to open an account. My first deposit was in the amount of forty-five hundred dollars, which created a stir with Sandra. When we left the bank she asked me how I got the money. I told her the truth - I had a boyfriend who looked out for me. She knew he was older and immediately assumed he worked in the shop. We got into a heated argument, and she demanded I break up with him and start acting my age.

At home, I started packing up my clothes. Then I called Kalil and told him what happened. He told me to catch a cab and not to worry about my things, but I wasn't going to leave everything I owned. Sandra came in my room and asked where I was going. "You're only fifteen, where you gonna go?"

"I have a place to stay. And it's not with your mother."

"Who, Mrs. Archie?"

"Nope."

"You gonna live with your boyfriend? Sunshine you better get ya fuckin' head out of the clouds and stop playing yaself. You don't move in with someone you barely know."

"Didn't you?"

"Yeah but that was different though."

"No it wasn't."

"Sunshine please don't do this."

"I love you Sandra but I'm leaving."

"No, you're not."

"What are you going to do?"

"Oh yeah, you really startin' ta smell yourself."

"I'm leaving!" As I was heading towards the door, I stopped to pick up one of my bags, and Sandra punched me. She hit me hard enough to stop me in my tracks, but instead of reacting I took the bag and sat on the porch. She looked at me and said, "Have it ya way!"

When I pulled up to Kalil's house he was happy to see me, but I had tears in my eyes. How could I leave Sandra after all she had done for me? And why did she have to say I was smelling myself? I wasn't trying to act or be grown; I just wanted to do me. When I got out of the cab I burst out in tears. Kalil hugged me and said, "Don't worry 'bout the rest of your stuff because I'll buy you more." Did he really think I was crying over some clothes and shoes? It was so much bigger than that. Clothes were the least of my worries. I started worrying about getting back and forth to school, but before I said anything, he told me he'd take me to school and pick me up from work. I still didn't feel right. I wanted to call Sandra, but what was I going to say to her? I had lost my virginity, and I was in love with Kalil. I didn't want anyone trying to stop me from seeing him. So I had to let her be. Once I sat down and tried to get my mind around living without Sandra, Kalil and I talked about the rules of the house. There definitely were some similarities since Big Jermaine and Kalil worked in the same line of work. No one could know where we stayed, I couldn't spend the night out, and I needed to let him know my whereabouts at all time. After he laid the rules down, he laid me down.

## Chapter XXIV

With the start of summer, I was desperately seeking a way out. Kalil had me on lock down and I was in dire need of air. He bought me a pager and paged me constantly. If I didn't call him back within a minute, we would argue when he picked me up and when I got home. I couldn't even find refuge in my car. My car and my insurance were registered under the name Tasha Reed. I also had a driver's license (showing that I was twenty-three) in that name, because Kalil knew someone who worked at Penn Dot's driver's license center. Even though I wasn't old enough to drive, he taught me how. My first lesson was on Broad Street, which in my mind was a suicide mission. He didn't want me to ride around vacant lots or parks because he said it didn't teach you how to drive. Once he was satisfied with my comfort level on Broad Street, he took me onto the Expressway. I did okay, but as soon as the first exit came up, I jumped off. My car was a silver, two-door Buick Rivera, but it was more for show than use. If I wanted to go anywhere Kalil always wanted to drive me. Even if I took my car to work he'd be there to pick me up, so I often left my car parked at the barbershop. It took about a month for me to go through a full tank of gas.

Kalil's jealousy was another demon I was getting tired of dealing with. He thought I was sleeping with everyone in the barbershop, co-workers and clients. If he came in the shop and I was talking to anyone, he wanted to see me outside. Every time we'd go outside to discuss the situation, it turned into me getting yelled at for twenty minutes or more. It was getting to the point where I think Shareef wanted to fire me. And if it wasn't for the fact Kalil was supplying him with work, I'm sure he would have gotten rid of me.

I was isolated. He banned me from seeing Lil Bitts because he didn't like her, and I was too ashamed to call Sandra and tell her what was really going on. When I did talk to her I gave her the sunny-side-up version of my thunderstorm, even though I thought she could sense it was stormy in my relationship because she always asked me if I was really okay. I had also voluntarily secluded Mrs. Archie because I quit Temple's Upward Bound Program, and that really broke her heart. She knew a tidbit about me moving out, and anytime I called Sandra she begged me to give Mrs. Archie a call. That would have taken some serious courage, but I couldn't face her. Though I let go of the program, I didn't let go of my education. For the entire school year my grades were all A's and B's, but my chances of getting a scholarship through Upward Bound were over.

All I had now was Kalil and my money. It was always Kalil and me, me and Kalil, and I was just tired! I tried to talk to him about easing up, but that led to arguments and me being accused of cheating. As a way to keep me closer, he took me to the Bahamas for a week. While we were there, he was the man I had first met – kind, caring, easy going, and romantic. We had candle-lit dinners on the beach; we went kayaking, waterskiing, shopping, skinny dipping, snorkeling, and had more sex that week than we did in our entire relationship (hypothetically, of course). The atmosphere put both of us in a passionate, sexual mood, and we bit into it. On our first night in the Islands, once we got into our room, it was on. He took a pair of scissors and cut my halter dress off. And when his lips touched my breasts there was an explosion in my panties. He went down on me, and then his tongue decided to travel to a land he had never visited before – my anus (ass, butt, whatever you call it). Different but erotic, I welcomed this new form of pleasure, but I was not going to return the favor. Once we finished in the room, we headed to the beach and started fucking there. It was late night, but to tell the truth I know people saw us. When I looked up at our hotel I could see a couple watching us from their balcony, but I didn't want to stop. I think it turned me on more.

There wasn't a Jacuzzi, bathroom, beach chair, pool, or ocean we didn't fuck in. We had sex more than we ate, it was that good. The mood was defined to be sexual. When we weren't having sex, I was sucking. I sucked his dick in the back of a taxi, under the table at a bar, in the bathroom of a restaurant, on the beach, by the pool, and in it. I needed this!

I wanted things to work out, and if he could just loosen up we would be alright.

When it was time for us to catch our flight I started crying. Returning to the States meant I had to go back to the same jealous, lock down routine. At the sight of my tears, Kalil promised me things would be different and assured me he trusted me. He said he had been stressed with all the worrying he does, and he would ease up. Before, I was sure he trusted me because I knew where all his money and drugs were. He left me in the house with three hundred thousand dollars, had me separating it and placing it in stacks of a thousand. But money wasn't the issue. He didn't trust me with men. However, the thought of sleeping with anyone but him sickened me. He knew my body and knew everything I wanted done to it. He knew how to stop my spoiled ways by laying down that aggressive fuck, that had me calling him Big Daddy and running around answering, "Yes sir," for weeks. He also knew how to make love to my body and when it was time to let me take control. He taught me so many things about my body, and showed me how I could bring him to his knees just by placing his balls inside of my soft, juicy, warm mouth. Also Kalil had been there for me when I decided to leave Sandra. He supplied everything I needed, emotionally and physically. Why in the world would he think I wanted to trade in an all-inclusive lifestyle for some guy who lived paycheck to paycheck? I just wanted things to improve.

When we got home things were going well, and on Saturday we made plans to spend the night at the Embassy Suites on the Parkway. We wanted to relax and do a little shopping downtown before Sunday, because we were headed to New Jersey for some rock climbing. I loved going rock climbing. Kalil thought it was a white thing, but he sure was great at climbing. I told Shareef I would work a half-day because I was going out. By now he was used to my routine and as usual he didn't give me any problems. I was waiting for Kalil to come pick me up and whatever time he showed up, I would leave. The shop got really busy, and I lost track of time. It was a typical Saturday, with the music blasting and all the usual barbershop talk, so it was easy to get lost in the riffraff. I had fifteen missed pages from Kalil by the time I realized I'd left my pager and pocketbook in my car. I tried to call him back but he didn't answer. I kept working until someone came in the shop and told me he was outside. When I went down to tell him what happened, he ignored what I was saying. "Get your shit and get in the car."

"This is what I'm talking about Kalil. Why do we have to go through this?"

"Shut the fuck up and go get ya shit!"

Saturdays in the summer were extremely busy and people were hanging around outside. I didn't want anyone else to hear me getting cursed out, so I went and got my stuff. When I got in the car he didn't look at me or say a word. I assumed we would go home, but we did go to the Embassy Suites. When the valet came to open my door, Kalil yelled at him, "Let that Bitch get it herself!" The tears started, but I didn't let them drop. We had gone from perfect back to this nonsense.

When we got in our room it was a nightmare. He choked me and shook me. He kept asking what I was doing and why I didn't call him back. His grip on my throat was so tight I couldn't get the words up my windpipe. He thrust me on the mattress and ripped off my clothing, all the while I was begging him to stop. He smelled my pussy and stuck his fingers in me to make sure no one's cum was up there. My body had gone limp. He was choking me so hard my eyes started to roll in the back of my head. I was losing consciousness and could no longer fight the urge to black out. Then he started fucking me. But not like anything before. He was truly hurting me and my body was too weak to fend him off. I could no longer cry or move. When he was finished torturing my pussy and vigorously biting my neck, breast, and face, he told me to get out. I was breathing heavy and was in disbelief. I tried to stand up and get my composure, but I needed help. I was so out of it. Then I started to gather my clothes and my pocketbook so I could go, but he yelled, "You think I'm playin' wit you! You ain't takin' nothin' outta here."

"That's my money that bought those clothes."
"You wanna fuck around on me, after all I did for you."
"But I wasn't..."
"But my ass. Get tha fuck out!"

I tried to build up a little energy to leave, but my knees kept buckling. My body was shaking. I didn't want to leave the room naked. I fell back on the bed and he started walking towards me. I picked up a glass that was by the nightstand and threw it at him, but it missed. The next thing I remember seeing was a huge black hole, big enough to blow out my entire eye socket. He was pointing his gun at my head. "Bitch, you wanna play wit me. Didn't I tell you to get the fuck out?!" I left everything in the room and walked out naked. He slammed the door and I walked towards the elevator. Three rooms down stood a room service attendant. I wanted to scream for him to help me, but I didn't want Kalil to hear me. He stared at me as I mouthed the words, "Please help me." He didn't move, but I continued asking him for help while he stood there looking. At the very least, he could have gotten his manager.

I pushed the elevator button and waited for it to open. By this time I didn't care if anyone else saw me. I was going downstairs in the lobby to get a cab and a towel; everyone would just have to see me naked. I tried to tell myself – they're just ass and tits – but don't think for a second the idea of being seen nude didn't scare me to death. The elevator opened and it was empty. I knew someone would soon see my naked body, but the emptiness gave me a little more time to prepare myself. The doors began to close when suddenly one of the hallway trashcans came slamming into the elevator. The doors opened back up, and Kalil was standing in front of me with a devilish grin on his face. I moved to the back of the elevator. He told me to get off. Just at the sight of his face, and all I could think about was him shooting me in the head. I shook my head no because it was too painful to speak. He was blocking the elevator from closing and started yelling at me to hurry up and get off. He yanked my hair and pulled me into the room. Then he threw me on the chair and started laughing. I closed my eyes and

started praying to God. I was about to get murdered b e c a u s e
I didn't hear my pager going off. How could he treat me like
this? Kalil had scared me before but he had never behaved
like this. I didn't know if I was going to see tomorrow. I was
still going in and out of consciousness. At one point, I looked
up to see him jumping on the bed, saying, "I'm a real nigga."
When he finished bouncing up and down, he gathered all of
my belongings and left the room. I started to get out of the
chair when he came back in and told me, "If you leave or
call anyone, Imma kill you."

My first instinct was to call the cops, but I figured when
they'd arrive he'd see them first and run upstairs and blow
my brains out. I wanted to call Sandra but what was she
going to do or say? Someone was banging on the door. I made
it to the peephole without passing out and saw the same
room service attendant who hadn't helped me. He had a steak,
mashed potatoes, string beans, and some sort of liquor. I
walked back to the chair, but he wouldn't stop knocking.
Instead he started knocking harder. I went to the door and
told him I didn't order anything, but he insisted I take the
food, something about it being my boyfriend's orders. I pulled
the cart into the room and then he asked if I was okay or if I
needed him to call anyone. I slammed the door and went
back to sit down. The food had to be for me because it was
what I always ordered when we went out, unless it was a
seafood place. I drank the liquor because I needed to calm
my nerves, but I placed the food on the table. My windpipes
were swollen, and if I had been hungry the food wouldn't
have fit down them. I stayed in the chair. The next time I
opened my eyes, it was morning.

## Chapter XXV

By summer's end, I had two black & purple eyes from two different occasions. Kalil was hostile and there was no room for error on my part. He didn't listen or believe anything I said, and crying was "a waste of water works", as he called it. I had to do precisely what he said in order to make him happy. Otherwise there would be trouble. The first time I dealt with the black eye was when I didn't answer my pager because the battery had died. No answering of my pager equaled a hearty punch in the eye. I got the other black eye because I went to the mall without telling him. I only went to get a pair of sunglasses because my left eye was healing but still had a ring around it. I didn't know I would need the shades to cover both eyes. Not only did my eyes enter a sunglasses prison, but my freedom had also been snatched away. He had changed the locks on me, and now he could lock me in from the outside. To complicate matters, only he had a key to that lock so if he wanted me to stay in, I had to stay in. The lock usually went on for the weekends, when I wanted to be out the most. My home was now "Kalil's State Penitentiary," and I wasn't sure how long my sentence would be. I thought about killing myself on a daily basis and cried myself to sleep often. But I had to conceal my pain because if I showed him any signs of discontent, I'd get choked, slapped, and told how ungrateful I was. I still had to have sex with him, but when I did my body was so lifeless. My kitty would still juice up, but emotionally I was gone. I used to enjoy sucking him off, at my leisure, but now it was mandatory. I was terrified of him and didn't know what to do, but I didn't want to involve anyone else. He was crazy, and if he was willing to kill me I was sure he wouldn't have a problem shooting anyone else.

When school resumed, it was a repetitive routine of there and back. I didn't have a job anymore because as soon as we left the hotel he called Shareef and quit for me. I tried to find enjoyment in my shop, which was fashion design. My classmates were cool and they knew I had a car, so sometimes they tried to bum a ride with me to the fabric store. But I couldn't allow it because everything I did had to be run past Kalil first. And most things I asked were disapproved. Without cause, Kalil often grilled me after school with questions. He wanted to know if I had met anyone and if I was messing around. If my reply didn't reassure him that he was the only one in my life and I would never step out on him, we would get into it. Once I caught an attitude because I was tired of him asking me the same damn questions time and time again, and he slapped me clear across the room. That was the last conspicuous attitude I caught with him.

Sandra became my therapist but I limited the information I divulged. I didn't tell her about the black eyes, the slapping, or the dreaded chokings. When I vented, she was a great listener and without hesitation she often said, "Our door is always open." She and Big Jermaine had bought a new house, and they were moving soon. I was glad because they really weren't hidden in Oxford Circle. So far they had racked up six properties, and four of them were occupied with tenants. Big Jermaine really took care of my sister, and I missed being a part of their family.

Sandra kept me abreast on her family, and on my mom and the kids. My mom now had eight children (seven girls and one boy). She named the twins Shonda and Shameka. They were toddlers now, going through their terrible two stages. I had never seen the twins, but Sandra promised to have them at her house, along with Lil Jermaine, whenever I came to visit. I really missed my nephew. Sandra said he looked just like his dad, and that he tried to imitate his every gesture. My brother Shawn was busy running around chasing girls, and my sisters had adapted to Pastor Jordon and were doing fine. My mother did marry the Pastor. I knew that was a positive example for my sisters and brother because two parents are often better than one. With everything going on in my life, I had eased up on the sworn hatred for my mother and Pastor Jordon because I just wanted to spend time with my family.

Kalil hated me doing anything without him, and I knew it would take some convincing before he'd allow me to visit my family. At first he said when I had a free weekend I could go, and I was so excited because I knew I had nothing to do. But Kalil always managed to hinder me from getting there. Every weekend when I asked him to go, he kept saying we were going out. Not that we went anywhere special, but as long as he said we had something to do, I couldn't go. Unexpectedly, one Friday before I left for school, he said I could go. My lungs started to open up because I would be free of him. I didn't care if it was only for a few hours. It was more freedom than I had had in long time.

My visit with my family went so well that I didn't want to leave. Sandra asked me to move back in with her, but my situation was out of control. Kalil was snorting, and his temper was not to be trusted. When I found an empty coke bag, I asked him about it, and he beat me up and threatened to make me snort some if I asked him any more questions. And there was the time he got upset with me for overcooking his eggs. He pulled out a rusty looking twenty-two and sat it on the kitchen table. I was going to go back in the bedroom but he said, "Have a seat". He emptied the barrel and loaded one bullet back in the chamber before spinning it. He said that ladies should go first and he held the gun at my temple, and then pulled the trigger. But he didn't take his turn. Instead he said I should get two turns for fucking up his eggs. I think I wanted to die, because instead of running I sat there as he spun it again and pulled the trigger. He shouted, "It must be ya lucky day!" and walked away from the table as if nothing had happened. Sandra's invitation might have sounded good, but I knew if I left him I wouldn't be so lucky next time.

The twins and my nephew had me in tears because it felt amazing to be around my family. The twins were having problems pronouncing my name and kept calling me, "Tuntine". It was so cute. Kalil was the furthest thing from my mind, until my pager started buzzing. That's when I realized I had to go. I was two hours late, and he was standing in the doorway awaiting my arrival. His annoyed eyes were a sure sign that we were going to have a problem.

No words were tossed, just a choking and some slapping as soon as I entered the door. When I picked myself up off the floor, I went to get a few of my things because I was gone. I was tired of wearing sunglasses and walking on pins and needles each day. Sandra said I could come back and now I needed to. I was so used to getting hit, slapped, and choked that my body was becoming immune to the abuse. When he hit me I didn't cry as much, and the pain was endurable. Kalil also knew I had grown a resistance to some of his hits, and he tried to hit me harder and harder each time to get a reaction out of me. When I got to the door the lock was on. It was the weekend and he was angry with me, so of course he put the lock on. I tried to kick the door down, but it wasn't coming off.

Monday came and I was still locked in the house. I didn't care that he hadn't come home, but now I was missing school. Kalil never interfered with me going to school, and I was pissed because I had missed my sewing assignment. My academic classes were manageable and boring, but fashion design was the only joy I got out of going to school each day. I quickly learned how to make bags, shirts, bathing suits, even dresses. I had a sewing machine in the house, and when I wasn't in pain from getting beat up by Kalil, I sewed. I made the twins bathing suits and Lil Jermaine a jumper without a pattern, and my teacher said I really had a knack for sewing and design.

Now I had to sit and wait for him to come home so I could go to school. I sat on the couch, dressed and waiting for the door to open, but school had let out and I was still locked in the house. I paged him until his pager was full, but he still didn't return my calls. I called Sandra and told her that I missed school and was locked in. She wanted to come over and break the door down, but I had never told her where I lived so she couldn't. Sandra tried to squeeze the address out of me, but at this point I was more afraid of Kalil than of Sandra, so no juice came out.

Wednesday morning came and went, and Kalil still hadn't called or come home. I had missed three consecutive days of school and hadn't been outside in four days. Kalil was taking this too far. My stomach was growling, and our food supply was running low because we didn't go food shopping on Sunday. I couldn't even order delivery because they didn't have a key to get in. Again I called Sandra, but this time I told the truth about the abuse and my fear of Kalil. Sandra was crying and pleading with me for the address. "You better tell me where the hell you at!"

"No, I can't."

"What the fuck, you gonna let him kill you…Sunshine you smarter than this. Where are you?"

"I'm scared."

"Tell me now. I ain't fuckin' playin' with you. Imma call the cops and have them trace this call if you don't tell me. You know we don't even play with the police so start talking!" I couldn't stay in the house for another day. I was scared to give up the address, but I had to get out of that apartment.

After I hung up with Sandra, I packed most of my things and put them by the door. The phone rang and I was petrified. The phone hadn't rung the entire time I was locked in. It must have been Kalil calling to see if I had learned my lesson. I didn't want Sandra coming if Kalil was on his way, so as soon as I talked to him I would tell her not to come. "Hello, Sunshine?"

"Yes. Who's calling?"

"This is Beverly, Kalil's mom."

"Hi. He's not here right now. I'll tell him to call you when he gets home."

"Don't bother. Listen, are you sitting down?"

"Actually, I am."

"Kalil was found this morning in his car…he's been murdered. They shot my baby in the back of his head…and…well…Oh, my baby…He was always so careful. I don't know who did this to my baby…Sunshine are you there? Hello…Hello…"

I dropped the phone and fell face-down into the carpet. I could hear a knock at the door and a distant cry coming through the phone. "Sunshine are you in there? Back away from the door Jermaine is gonna kick it down!" Nothing was registering. How could he be dead? Who did this? What was

153

I going to do? Where was I going to go? Who was going to take care of me? I went from loving Kalil to hating and fearing him, but I didn't want him dead. I did love him?

## Chapter XXVI

The following week I had to pick out Kalil's outfit and meet his mother at S.T. Willey's funeral home. Beverly lived in New Jersey so that gave me about an hour to get his clothes together. A day after the cops found him, she called me to discuss his funeral arrangements. His mother and I had previous brief encounters, during which she was always pleasant, so planning the arrangements with her didn't seem impracticable. Since she had access to his safe and his bank accounts, and was listed as co-owner on all of his real estate, she was going to send her son home in style. From the flowers, to the coffin, to the limo, to his outfit, she was spending top dollar.

When I got to the funeral home, she hadn't yet arrived so I went in to view his body by myself. It was my first time seeing him since I found out he was murdered. His head was swollen, and he didn't look the same. When I touched his face it was cold and stiff. The makeup they used on him made him look like a mannequin, but they did a great job, considering the circumstances. At first we were sure he'd have a closed casket, but the funeral director worked a miracle. While I was standing over his body, I hadn't noticed but my legs started to give way. The funeral director ushered me into the family room.

By the time Beverly arrived, the shock was wearing off, and my emotions gave way to tears. She did her best to comfort me, and I gathered myself so we could make the arrangements. The funeral director was clearly numb to my tears, but he did his best to appear sympathetic before going over our options. While he described the services they offered and the fees, his mother said she only wanted the best. If they would have offered a golden casket, she would have taken it. Ultimately, it didn't matter to me. Whether they burnt him to a crisp or put him in a pine box, he was dead. The corpse I had viewed was not the same man I had laid with or fought with. His spirit was gone. I detached myself from the body, but I struggled with the scars and the memories I couldn't bury. Beverly paid for the best and it was her money, so I didn't care. I just wanted to get back to the apartment and try to sort out some things, if that was at all possible.

When I got home I asked Sandra to come over and keep me company. I had been struggling to write a poem for the obituary, and I didn't want to write it but Beverly asked me to. Truthfully, it didn't seem like a request, more like a demand. She wanted the woman her son was crazy about to write him a final love letter. When she said he was crazy about me, she got the crazy part right. His mom never made mention to any beatings or choking's, so maybe she didn't know. Regardless, it was hard for me to write a love letter when I was questioning my love for him.

Another pressing issue was my living arrangements. I would be okay for at least three more months because Kalil paid up things (the rent, utilities, insurance, etc.) in threes. But after that, I was gone. There was no way I was shelling out eighteen hundred a month in rent. Even though Kalil didn't leave me high and dry, paying that much for something I didn't or wouldn't own didn't seem logical to me. There was thirty-five thousand left in the house, which was mine, and I had twenty-two thousand and some change in my bank account. Thankfully he never allowed me to touch the money in my bank account, and he always gave me money to save. Maybe he knew this day was coming.

When Sandra arrived I had a poem prepared:

*Never fall in love with a lie*
*He'll beat you until you cry*
*And maybe one day you or he may die*

She balled the paper up and then hugged me until I felt a sense of love inside of me. "Sunshine if you can't write something positive, call Beverly and let her know you can't do it. She'll understand. Have you thought about where you're gonna live or how you're gonna support yourself?"

"I haven't put too much thought into it but it has been on my mind. I want to get an affordable apartment because I do like living on my own."

"I take it you have a few dollars?"

"Yeah, I'm alright."

"Okay, well I think you need to be around family right now."

"I will, but I do need to be by myself too, so I can think about my life and how I got here."

"This is gonna take some time and I don't wanna say the obvious, but you know you can always come back home."

"I know."

"Do you?"

"Yeah, I know. And I know I haven't said this in a while, but Sandra I love you and I appreciate you."

"Well be grateful by not letting go of me again. You know I'm your ride or die sister and I'm here to tha death. You see how I got Jermaine to come break that door down? And I would've done it myself if I didn't have bad ankles."

"Since when?"

"Since I said so." Our conversation made me feel better, and my mood was elevating. Before Sandra got ready to go, she handed me my notepad, gave me a kiss and then left me to write.

The day of the funeral the limo came to pick me up, and Beverly and I headed to the church. The consoling and reassuring Beverly I had seen the other day in the funeral parlor had now metamorphosed into a complete wreck. She had bags under her eyes that resembled potato sacks, and she cried and shook the entire ride to the church. At first she had presented a strong front, but the reality was her only son was about to be laid to rest at the young age of twenty-six. I don't think any mother would be able to hide such devastation. I wasn't the greatest comforter, but I did the best I could, feeling uncomfortable all the while. I hugged and held her as she cried on my shoulder, saying how much she loved him and how we shouldn't stop communicating because Kalil was gone.

The church was crowded. Kalil knew a lot of people, but I never imagined it would be this many. It was a struggle getting in with all the spectators. On my way into the sanctuary a few people stopped me to give me hugs and offer their condolences. Everyone from the barbershop was there, and Shareef handed me an envelope with the words "Shorty Shamp, we love ya" written on it. Once I finally made my way in, I had a chance to settle my eyes on my surroundings. Never before had I viewed a funeral as a fashion show or spectacle, but from the expressions and outfits people had on, they weren't all there because they loved him. I knew some of the females came to meet other weight dealers, and some showed up to make sure he was dead. Kalil's temper was responsible for issuing plenty of pistol whippings and beat downs, and a few of his victims were there. There's no way they showed up because they had instantaneously found God and made their peace with him. I couldn't even be sure if his killer wasn't among us. The women Kalil slept around on me with were present, and they were cutting their eyes and whispering to their girlfriends about me. They were all older than me, and the look of jealousy was so intense it had turned the darkest brown eyes into the deepest envy green. If they only knew what went along with being his so-called main-join, they may have turned their eyes back a color.

Once in my seat I signaled for Sandra and Big Jermaine to come sit with me on the family's side. I didn't want to feel alone. Although Beverly and I sat together, she wasn't my family. The services began, and my nerves were getting the best of me. I knew my name would be called soon because Beverly didn't want a long service. Everything was to move quickly, just like her son. I couldn't stop my legs from shaking, and Sandra did her best to calm me. When my name was called I walked up to the podium and looked down at his face. I had an instant flashback and felt his hands around my neck. My words wouldn't describe how I really felt about him because I didn't know what to feel, but I didn't want to offend Beverly so I read the script:

*We loved in a way most will never understand*
*Me as your woman and you as my dedicated, understanding,*
*loving Man*
*There was never a problem that you couldn't solve*
*You were my rock, my provider, and my knight in disguise*
*Someone from heaven called out your name*

*And with that call I know your death will never be in vain*
*Your father wanted you near to him*
*So he took you to be by his side*
*So when you see me shed tears*
*It's for the love I have inside*
*But sometimes I cry because my love for you seems as if it*
*goes unattended*
*But our father touches my heart and our love I will always*
*remember*
*So see you later*
*I say to my Man*
*I know our love will never part*
*Because although they took your body from me, they will*
*never be able to take your heart.*

*Love You,*
*Sunshine*

When I was done I couldn't wait to sit down. My heart was aching and my emotions were all over the place. On one side I was angry for all the hurt he put upon me, but on the other side I remembered how he touched me and once showed me love. He was there for me when I needed him, but he had changed. I looked at his body and tried to come to terms with reality. He was gone, and the beatings were over. Maybe if someone hadn't killed him, I would have been lying in the casket.

To my surprise I made it through the rest of the service and the burial without passing out. My body was weak and wanted to give out. After the burial we rode over to a banquet hall that Beverly had rented out. They were playing home movies of Kalil when he was younger, and she had pictures of him placed all around the center. There was a beautiful spread of food, free drinks, and a DJ who played songs that reminded me of him. Beverly wanted this to be a celebration of his life, and she didn't want anyone moping around. I took the cordial approach and walked around speaking to a few of his friends and family members. Everyone wanted to know how I was holding up, but I couldn't respond truthfully, so "I'm fine" or "Okay" had to be the next best answer. I had been asked if I was alright and how was I doing so many times, that I stopped answering those questions. Not because I wanted to be rude but because I wasn't alright or doing okay. And I didn't think if their lover had their brains blown out, that they would be okay either.

After his mom and I made an announcement, in regards to our appreciation and thanks for everyone's support, I decided to get something to eat. The baked chicken and the baked macaroni and cheese were calling my name. It suddenly dawned on me that I couldn't remember the last time I had something to eat. I had been operating off of pure shock. But no sooner than I had eaten the food and started to enjoy the feeling of a full stomach had it decided to come right back up.

## Chapter XXVII

Ten straight mornings of vomiting, nausea, and dizzy spells required a check-up. For the moment Lil Bitts was staying with me, and she suggested I get a pregnancy test. The thought had never crossed my mind, but I took her advice and bought a test. The test was simple to read – two lines meant baby and one line meant no baby. I didn't know which way the test would read, but when I went in the bathroom I knew I'd have an answer to one of my questions in three minutes. When I looked at the test I had to count more than one line, so I was definitely pregnant. Now I had one answer, but what was I going to do about it?

Sandra took me to my doctor to confirm the truth. There was no escaping it, I was pregnant and about to have Kalil's baby. My doctor, who knew I was only sixteen and was aware of my mental state because she had me on anti-depression medication, was sure to inform me of all my options. Sandra wanted me to get an abortion because she thought I was too young, and I would ruin my chances of graduating from high school. My doctor was pro-life and thought I should seriously consider giving the baby to a family that would provide for him or her physically, financially, and emotionally. I wanted to have my baby, and I wanted to raise it. I could handle being a single mother, and with help from my family and Beverly, I didn't see a problem. I wasn't worried about the finances because between Beverly and me, it was do-able. I tried to reason with Sandra by saying, "The baby is growing inside of me, and I have an attachment to it." But she quickly replied, "How can you have an attachment when you didn't even know you were pregnant yesterday?"

With no regards to my wishes or wants, Sandra called the abortion clinic and scheduled my appointment. When she hung up the phone, she told Lil Bitts to keep her mouth shut, and for me to cut all communication with Beverly until the pregnancy was terminated. Sandra knew she would have tried to convince me to keep the baby, because at the funeral she told Sandra it was a shame she didn't have      any grandbabies. Sandra didn't want any conflict so I was forced to agree.

Based on the date of my last menstrual cycle, which I couldn't believe was two months ago, I had to go in as soon as possible so they could see if I had passed my first trimester. My first visit to Planned Parenthood was scheduled early in the morning for an information session. They had three a day, and the first one I was told would be the least crowded, and it was. A few girls showed up, and two brought their boyfriends. The caseworker greeted us, and then she explained it was mandatory to watch the tape- because by law, if we failed to view it, they couldn't give us the abortion. The video looked outdated, as if it was recorded in the doctor's basement by his wife. The footage was shaky, and the audio kept going in and out. *"Welcome to Planned Parenthood. My name is Dr. Tripp, and I will be talking to you about your abortion procedure..."* Dr. Tripp explained to us the procedure, what to do the night before and after the procedure, and about the side effects of having an abortion. The worst side effect was death, and when he said that, I was looking for somebody to run out the clinic so I could go with her, but they all sat still. After the video tape everyone was reminded to sign the attendance sheet, and anyone getting sedated was asked to stay for an additional two minutes. The three of us were reminded not to eat or drink anything after midnight and to bring the first morning urine sample with us when we returned.

The next day when I arrived at the abortion clinic, everything was different. My first visit was informative and I was fine, but now the clinic was intimidating and scary. I thought I would be the only person there besides Sandra, but it turned out that everyone was getting an abortion because this was a big business. The seats were practically filled, and there was definitely a wait. When I signed in, the clerk had me fill out several pages of paper work. Two forms asked about family history – if you had or have sexually transmitted diseases, previous pregnancies or abortions, and the other forms explained the abortion procedures. Because I was a minor, Sandra had to fill out the forms for me, and because she wasn't my mother, we had to wait to see if they would perform the procedure without my mother's consent. When they called us in to speak with the counselor, Sandra had her game face on and her lies together. She told the woman my mom had been on crack since I was born and we had no clue as to her whereabouts. Midway through her story, I started crying because I didn't want to get an abortion, but that backfired because the caseworker thought I was crying about my absent, crack-addicted mother. Without asking me any questions, the abortion was granted. Sandra signed the final forms and we were sent back to the waiting room.

The ultrasound procedure was heartbreaking. I pulled my shirt up, my sweat pants down, and then lay down on the examination table while the technician squirted cold gel onto my lower abdomen. She rolled the device over my stomach and a picture of my baby appeared on screen. After four or five clicks on her machine she had the baby coordinates and told me, "You can wipe off now. You're twelve and a half weeks." I asked for a picture of the baby, and she looked at me as if I had asked to take the baby remains home. It was already messed up that I didn't have a say about getting the abortion so at least I could have a picture for my memories. After she asked me if I was sure, she gave me the photo. You couldn't see much, but I knew it was my baby. I was further than most of the girls there but the most concealed. My stomach did not show any signs of gas or bloating, let alone pregnancy. Without this ultrasound I wouldn't have believed I was this far myself. My next step was to get blood drawn, and height, weight, temperature, and blood pressure taken. With my mini-checkup over, my picture, and all my papers signed, the next time I'd be called would be to get the abortion.

After two hours of waiting, they were finally ready for me. Sandra and I followed the nurse to a security door that led to the back of the clinic where they performed the abortions. The nurse said Sandra wasn't allowed to go in the back with me, and my nerves started percolating. Sandra hugged me and sat back down. Down the corridor there was a recovery room you waited in until it was your turn, and after the procedure you rested there until the nurse deemed you were okay to go home. It was set up with eight reclining chairs, four on each side of the room, and with a small nurse's station. I saw some women who looked drugged and relaxed, while others were holding their stomachs begging for pain medicine. Before I could run out the door the nurse walked up and handed me a basket to put my clothes in. Maybe she could tell I was nervous because she said, "Don't worry sweetie. You're getting a twilight procedure, and you shouldn't feel anything. Go in the bathroom and get undressed, and put this gown on with the opening in the back. And make sure you put your pad in your panties and place them on top of the basket. When you're done, have a seat in the blue chair by the door, and they'll come get you when they're ready." When I was in the bathroom I could hear the screams of a girl coming from the room where they did the procedures. Sandra and the nurse had told me I wasn't going to feel anything, but with those screams I wasn't so sure.

With my plastic gown on and my basket by my side, I went to take my seat in the blue chair. I don't know if I was cold because I was naked or if my nerves had me shook up, but I was freezing. The more I looked around, the more I wanted to get out of there. The anesthesiologist called my name and took me into the room. The room was no bigger than the examination room at my doctor's office. The only differences were the two suction devices on the floor next to the examination table – the ends of the devices were covered. That was fine with me because I didn't want to see what was in them. I sat on the examination table and put my legs up in the stirrups as I was told. I had to come all the way down to the end of the table until my bottom hung off a bit. At this point it was no different than getting a pap smear. I wasn't a big fan of needles so I tried to get as comfortable as I could because the anesthesiologist was about to stick me. "You scared?"
"Yes!"

"I'm not going to hurt you. Child, I've been doing this since before you were born. How old are you?"

"Too young ma'am."

"You're not the youngest I've seen. I want you to do yourself a favor and be careful out there. You have to take care of your body because this is not a form of birth control. Okay?"

"Yes ma'am."

"We're all done now, just give it a minute. Okay, you can start counting back from ten now."

"You mean one hundred?"

"No, ten."

"Okay. Ten...Nine...Eight...Sev..."

When I woke up I was sitting in the recovery room, and I was dumbfounded. I asked the nurse when I would get my procedure, and she said, "You already had it, Hun. You're done. Do you want any crackers?"

"No. How did I get here?"

"Didn't you come with your sister?"

"No, in this room!"

"Oh, they brought you in here by wheelchair when they were finished."

"Are you sure?"

"Yes, I saw them with my own eyes. Sometimes the medication makes people fall asleep and some forget the whole experience."

"Oh."

"Your blood pressure and temperature are fine. And in a few minutes I want you to go to the bathroom and tell me how's your bleeding, okay?"

"Okay." My stomach felt a little cramped but nothing more than my menstrual cramps. When I went in the bathroom to check myself, there were two spots on my pad and not a dot more. The nurse said it was normal and that my monthly should come on shortly. I thought I would be groggy and disorientated, but I was doing fine. The caseworker led me to her office and asked me what type of birth control I wanted, but since I was unsure she gave me condoms and told me to follow up with my primary doctor. Then she gave me a post-abortion instructional sheet that suggested no heavy lifting or strenuous activities, and no sex until after your post-abortion exam, which was in two weeks.

There were only four people left in the lobby, one being Sandra. She was asleep so I nudged her, and we headed for the car. The first question she asked was how I was doing, the second was if I was hungry, and the third was why I was crying. My body wasn't in pain and I had no desire to eat, but my heart was aching. I had been through a rough trip with Kalil, and after having had an abortion, I just felt atrocious. Well, guilty I should say, because I had killed my baby, and because I didn't let Beverly know what was going on. Nothing Sandra said made me feel any better – this was one of those events that could only heal with time. I was so out of my mind that instead of going home I stayed with Sandra. The remorse I felt put thoughts into my head that would have reunited me with my child's father.

## Chapter XXVIII

Staying with Sandra was currently a necessity but definitely not a permanent fix because I missed being on my own. I needed a new place where I could create some enjoyable memories, but of course only with Sandra's help. After all, I was underage and lacked credit and a source of verifiable income. At first Sandra had suggested I stay in one of her houses and pay her a small fee because she knew I wouldn't take the place without giving her something. However, I wanted to have that sense of independence that I was lacking, so I respectfully declined her offer.

It took me a few weeks, but eventually I found a reasonably priced one-bedroom apartment on 15th Street near Allegheny Avenue. The monthly rent was four hundred dollars, and to move in the landlord wanted twelve hundred dollars to cover the first month, last month, and one-month security. At first I was going to take Sandra along because I was nervous that he wouldn't rent to me, but I brought something much better. When I got there, instead of waiting for him to ask me any questions about where I worked or the traditional rental inquiries, I showed him the twelve hundred dollars along with six additional rental payments. He didn't ask me any questions. Instead he handed me the keys and told me I could move in immediately.

Coming from my luxurious, carpeted, lavish condo with high ceilings, a skyline view, and a doorman, this was a definite downsize. It was like going from the CEO of a company to becoming the janitor, but at least it was mine. I hired some guys to clean and paint the place from top to bottom, and once everything dried I moved my furniture in. It wasn't the condo, but if you closed your eyes real hard, I mean real, like super hard...well, let me stop kidding myself. It wasn't the condo, but it did the job.

When school let out Lil Bitts decided to bunk with me. She wanted to get away from her mom, and I could respect that so I let her stay. I took the room and she slept on the sofa bed unless she had company, and then I would let her use the room as long as she washed my sheets. Our initial agreement was for both of us to get jobs so we could split the bills, but I ended up paying the majority because she only made sixty dollars a week at her summer job. I was working as a wash girl for another barbershop, and she was employed as a receptionist with Phila-Job. They were an organization that allowed teens to work for their approved companies or individuals. The implied benefit was invaluable work experience for the teen, while the business owner was rewarded with cheap laborers. Unfortunately neither one of our jobs worked out. After my first day I knew I didn't want to return to the barbershop scene, and Lil Bitts quit once she realized her paycheck didn't reflect the amount of hours she actually put in. She worked harder than most of the adults but only received a teaspoon of their pay.

With no job or restrictions I had all the freedom in the world. Still it took some time to get used to. For a while I stayed in the house and waited for Sandra to take me places, even though I had my own car. But after realizing I didn't have to answer to anyone, I soon loosened up. Lil Bitts and I started going everywhere – the mall, the thrift shop, the movies, out to dinner, paint-balling, the club's let-out, and joy riding whenever we ran out of ideas. In next to no time I realized I was spending most of my time in my car. The only time I went home was to change my clothes and to sleep.

At first Lil Bitts and I were like Thelma and Louise, but she quickly converted to a homebody once she hooked up with a guy from our block. Jamal was nineteen and to speak frankly he was ugly as all hell. Whenever he came over I tried not to stare at him because his lips and nose were bigger than his face. It was like he had a green pepper for a nose and a baked potato for lips. Apparently that's why she liked him because he used his whole face to eat her out and because he was hung. But she knew he was ugly too. That was why she only called him over at night so they could "you-know-what". One night I came home in the middle of their session and heard the headboard jingling, and the all too familiar sounds that accompany the doggie style position. My body started to reminisce and instantly I was wetter than a kiddy pool. I hadn't had sex in over four months, and my body was yearning for the touch of a man. I didn't want to feel like a pervert, so I went outside and sat on the steps. That didn't work because my mind was on men and my panties were drenched, but I hadn't met anyone new and to be honest I was skeptical about dating. The last time I could remember somebody trying to "holla" at me was during the days following Kalil's funeral. Ironically, many of Kalil's friends, or so-called friends, had put their bids in, but I wasn't biting.

My loneliness prompted me to start checking out our neighborhood to see if it had anything to offer. It was filled with non-job seekers, high school drop-outs, corner boys, and the all too familiar drug entrepreneurs. I wanted a man, but I refused to be desperate and set my standards at zero, so when the broke-ies tried to whistle or call to me like they were looking for their lost pets, I kept it moving. I felt that if you were broke you best find a different stroke. Not because I thought I was better, but I just wanted better.

The best thing the neighborhood had going for me was the same thing that I was trying to leave behind. The block captain's name, the drug dealer who was currently at the top of the food chain, was Reds. He was bright light-skinned, with red orange hair, and he was a former boxer so his body was toned in all the right places. His beard, hair, nails, and his attire were always well-kept and only added to his sexiness. I caught him eyeing me a few times, but I did my best to keep my eyes focused on other things because I didn't want to travel that route again. I knew how he earned his money, and the thought of him hitting me or trying to control me kept me from falling victim to his seductiveness; at least for a while. Initially I was diligent in being non-responsive to his stares or witty come-on lines, but Reds was persistent. He sent the local crackhead, Emo, to knock on my door and say, "Your presence is being requested at the corner." I couldn't stop laughing. I was in disbelief because this fool had the nerve to send a crackhead to knock on my door as if he was inviting me to a ball. Emo was dirty, but I had to give him respect because from our brief conversation you could tell he had some smarts with him. Still it was too funny. Once I got a hold of my composure, I kindly said, "Tell him I'm not coming," and I started going back in the house. But Emo grabbed my arm. "Miss Lady I need you to walk to the corner and see what he wants."

"I know what he wants, and I'm not interested."

"Why you gonna mess up my hit!"

"So he promised you a rock if I come down the street?"

"Yes, and if you come now he might give me two."

"Oh."

"You know he likes you, and if you don't want him, just tell him, but wait until I get my payment, okay? At least one of us wins."

I reached in my pocket and handed Emo what I pulled out, then said, "Huh, now leave me alone." His face lit up like he had just won the lottery because I gave him ten dollars, and he said, "Anytime you need me to do anything just holla."

Two minutes later, Emo was back banging at my door. Reds had taken his ten dollars and told him, "If she don't come down here you ain't gettin' ya money back." He then told the corner boys, "and y'all better not serve him eitha." Emo, a grown man, dirty and all, was about to shed tears over his rocks. He was pleading for me to come down and asked me if I wanted him to wash my car, braid my hair, wash my sneakers, take out my trash, paint my house, wash my clothes, clean the steps and the sidewalk, beat anyone up, steal anything, flatten some tires, or bust somebody's windows out, just to convince me to go down the street. I didn't need anything from him at the moment, but I decided to go so I told Emo to give me a minute. Then he said, "I'm gonna sit right here and make sure nothing happen to you, but can you hurry up?" Emo was in love with those rocks. He showed me the power of drugs and recertified my belief that they were a substance I had no use for.

Before I left I had to take a quick look in the mirror to make sure I was right because I had been lying down before he came, and my hair was a little out of place. I had on a short pleated skirt, a tight white tank top, and some cleats (they were in style then, trust me). When I came outside Emo was all smiles and asked, "Do you need me to hold your hand?" He got the look and walked his behind with me down the street. When I got to the corner, Reds had walked to the Deli, which was a block away, and Emo was so scared I would leave he clutched my arm and insisted we meet him at the Deli.

"Okay, Mo, ya job's done." He shook Emo's hand and turned his focus on me. "What's up shorty?"

"Nothing, what's up with you?"

"I'm good."

Emo quickly interrupted. "Um, excuse me, can I get mines?"

I had to laugh because Emo was amusing.

"Here Emo, and get ya ass outta here. Good lookin' out though." He turned back to me and smiled like he wanted something. "So what's up?"

"I don't know. Maybe you can tell me what was so important that I had to come down here and meet you?"

"Listen, Imma keep it real with you. I wanna get to know you. Take you out, wine you, dine you, and do some others things, if ya interested."

"So basically you want to fuck."

"Why would you say that?" I stared at him and waited for him to give me a real answer.

"I do, but not right now. Maybe tomorrow."

"Stop it."

"No, you stop it. I saw you lookin' at me... You know I'm sexy."

"You need to stop. Now, you alright, but that's about it."

"Listen, you alright too with ya peanut head."

"What!"

"Alright, I'll stop. So when we hookin' up?"

"Tonight if you're not working."

"Come on now, you know I got workers out here. I'm the boss!"

"Whatever. Just stop past when you're done collecting."

We went out to eat and to see a movie and I really enjoyed myself. Reds was fun to be around. He kept cracking jokes and made me smile most of the evening. Yet he also showed a mature side as he opened the door for me and held my hand on the way into the movies. Afterwards we went to Kelly Drive to take a walk down the drive and look at the scenery. It was a quiet night and not too many people were out. Usually the drive was jam-packed with cars and people talking, walking, cuddling, and doing the couple thing. When we got to the benches, we sat down and talked a bit. I blushed the entire time as he complimented every inch of my body. Then he started playing with my hair and caressing my face, which quickly resulted in him getting down on his knees. Next he gently pulled me to the end of the bench and put his face under my skirt. Without hesitation Reds moved my panties to the side and launched operation "eat her out". I wasn't shocked or scared. I was happy and thankful that someone had touched a part of my body that was yearning to be touched.

He was good, and if it wasn't for me opening my eyes just to make sure I wasn't dreaming I wouldn't have had to stop him. "Somebody's coming," I whispered.

"I know."

"No, someone's really coming."

"So."

"Well I don't want them to see us."

"Well don't look at 'em, and they'll disappear."

"No seriously, stop it!"

"Alright Punk." He was a pro, and if it wasn't for the couple coming up in the horizon, I would have never stopped him. I wanted him to finish so when we got in the car I lifted my skirt up and he started again. Every time I reached my hands for his dick he pushed me away. I wanted to feel it to see if it was worth opening up my tight kitty, but he wouldn't let me get a hold of it. I couldn't take any more foreplay and my knees had become weak from the tongue lashing.

After having multiple orgasms in his car, we went back to his house where I took my clothes off and got into his bed, but he told me I wasn't getting any and to chill. When I questioned why, he said I wouldn't be able to handle it. Laughing out loud was the only option I found to counter his foolish suggestion, but he would have the last laugh because no dick went inside of me that night. He put on a movie, but my mind was in another place. I wanted him and he knew it, but he wasn't giving in. I let the movie watch me as I tried to rub my ass up against him, but his will power was far superior to mine because he didn't budge or bulge.

Since my needs weren't going to be met I fell asleep but was promptly awakened by the sound of creeping footsteps. The sound of the light switch being turned on caused me to sit up at attention. There was a short, petite, brown-skinned woman staring at us with the look of hate and rage in her eyes. "What tha fuck is goin' on! Reds, who is this bitch?"
"Come on wit all this bullshit. You know we ain't together!"
"Oh now we not together?"
I looked over at Reds and asked, "What's going on," but was swiftly interrupted by this girl.
"Bitch you need to get dressed and get tha fuck up outta here, that's what's goin' on!"
"Renee this ain't ya house so go tha fuck head with the orders."
"You gonna fuck this bitch in our house, in our bed!"
It was obvious that they had previous and probably current ties, and now unfortunately I was in the middle of their mess. I didn't think there was anything I could say to clear up this situation, but I told her, "I didn't sleep with him." Then I looked at Reds and said, "Take me home."
But she wasn't having that. "He ain't taking you nowhere."
"Reds, take me home!"
"Bitch didn't I tell you he ain't taking you no fuckin' where…"

She came up on me with her right fist heading towards my face, and I had no choice but to beat the living shit out of her. Being a domestic abuse victim, my strength had definitely grown and those baby taps she was throwing didn't faze me. I didn't want to fight her. I was going to leave as soon as he gave me a ride, but instead, Renee - who I'd never met or seen before- got her ass whooped in her own house. After Reds broke us apart (she was on the floor getting a mud hole stomped in her head), I used their phone and called me a cab. Then I went into the living room to get dressed and all of a sudden I noticed photos of her and their baby all throughout the house. There were also hair curlers and hairspray in the bathroom that I saw but didn't acknowledge earlier. If I had, maybe I could have avoided this entire problem.

I waited on the porch because Reds had to keep her in the house. She kept acting as if she really wanted to come outside and fight me or hit me with the hammer she had in her hand. I wasn't worried about it because she only got one chance to swing. If that hammer didn't knock me out, I would have made sure she never got up off the ground. But since she couldn't get loose, she started yelling through the screen door, "I'm gonna get you bitch. I hope you get AIDS." I started thinking, maybe that's why he didn't want to have sex with me, but I had condoms in my purse. Either way, we didn't have sex so I was cool.

On the ride home the cab driver wanted to know what I was doing out so late. He was an older guy, in his late fifties or early sixties, with a very old school demeanor. I told him the full story and he couldn't stop laughing. He kept saying, "All of this on your first date." With all the laughs he received I thought he was going to give me a discount, but he wanted his full forty-two dollars. Coming from the far northeast down to Allegheny Avenue was costly, and he wasn't about to lose out on a penny of his money, even if he had a good laugh or two. Lil Bitts was up when I got home and I couldn't wait to tell her what happened. She wanted to go back up there and tear Renee up but she already got mangled so what would be the point? My pager started going off while we were talking, and of course it was Reds. He started calling my phone, but I ignored him. Why did he want to talk now when he should have put his girl in her place and driven me home? I had nothing to do with their situation and no previous knowledge of her. And furthermore he endangered my life. Honestly, if I was a hard sleeper she could have stabbed me to death, or worse, shot me and let him live.

The next day I came outside and guess who was sitting on my steps apologizing? Reds had excuse after excuse, and he didn't want me to be mad, but I was trying to figure out if he understood exactly why I needed to be angry. I wasn't mad that I beat up his baby mom. To tell the truth it helped me get some stress off my back, but he could have told me about her. He swore up and down that they were broken up but she was still in love with him. Was her being in love with him supposed to excuse the fact that he forgot to tell me about her? His rationalization was clearly idiotic. The bottom line was he should have told me about her, or taken me somewhere where nobody had spare keys. I wasn't feeling him so I told him to take that walk. He walked to the corner only to send Emo back to my door, as if Emo could convince me to forgive him. Don't get me wrong. I liked Emo. He was a very knowledgeable man, crackhead and all, but Reds was cut off. I didn't want any more drama. Besides, I was just getting over a bad situation.

Emo and I sat on the steps discussing men, bad relationships, how he got on drugs, when he was going to get off drugs, what I was going to do with my life, and if I was going to accept Reds' call or go down the street and talk to him. We both had questions and plenty of answers, but any solutions in regards to Reds weren't yet determined so I kept quiet on that subject.

Later that night Reds came over with a dozen red roses and a box of heart candy. Lil Bitts slammed the door in his face and told me some nut was at the door. Don't ask me why, but I let him in and we went into my room to talk. However he didn't give me a chance to speak because he ripped off my panties and started sucking my pussy. At first I tried to stop him, but soon I felt like I'd won a grand prize. This time no one was going to interrupt us and I wanted to get fucked. And believe me when I tell you he gave me just what I needed – rock hard, lengthy, meaty, dick meat. He knew how to maneuver my body, and his stroke game had to be ranked in the top two. He was a beast at his craft and worked me out in every position. When he looked me in the eyes and commanded, "Put them legs up, get 'um up," it was all a turn on. "Bend ova, arch ya back, and throw it back...Didn't I tell you to throw it back...What, you can't take it?" He was in control, and I loved it. At one point he put so much dick in me that I started out in alto but moved

175

straight up to soprano. And when I acted as if it was too much for me to handle (and some moments it was), he grabbed me by my hips and gave it to me harder, then made me ask, "Daddy, can I please have more?"

When our first session ended, it only took him a minute or two for us to get back into another one. Then Lil Bitts had the nerve to come knock on the door with a request for us to keep it down. In my head I was thinking she better go sit on the steps like I did, but then he said, "Get out!" and I laughed as we went back at it. When I heard the echo from the front door slamming, I got even louder and wilder. He flipped me over, and I grabbed him by his neck and started to ride him. I locked eyes with him and popped my pussy to the beat of his pulse, and he loved it. He placed his hands on my hips as I rotated them like a belly dancer, up and down, faster and faster, slow wind, round the globe, and I ended with the irresistible rattle-shake.

"Oh shit, Oh shit, I'm 'bout to cum… Where you want it at!"

"No, don't stop, please don't stop!"

"I…I…Oh, here it come!" I looked at his face while he squinted, shrieked, and made some of the ugliest expressions, knowing he had just cum all up inside of me. The first time he came he pulled out, but now he was blaming this one on me, saying since he told me he was coming, I should have popped off. I wasn't on birth control, and by the look on my face he could tell I was worried. He told me to go to the bathroom and sit on the toilet.

"Sunshine you wanna put some effort into it."

"What? You told me to sit on the toilet and let it come out."

"Push your muscles like you have to shit."

"No!"

"Yeah, it's gonna come down."

"I know, but some of it already came out."

"Not enough though, push. Matter fact, put ya feet on the toilet seat like ya squattin' to pee, then push." At first this was too funny. I wasn't having a baby. But with a few pushes from my abdominal and vaginal area, the cum did flow down into the toilet. Soon after I started thinking about

Renee and the HIV comment, and nothing seemed funny. Was there any truth to her statement, and would a squat and a push really prevent pregnancy?

## Chapter XXIX

Reds was full of shit because Renee was his girlfriend, but he sure didn't need one. His definition of commitment was promiscuity. All he wanted to do was run around sticking his pipe in new holes, while often going back to the old holes he was fond of. Being in the drug game benefited him monetarily and he was under the impression that it also allowed him to sleep around; and at the moment no one was proving him wrong. I certainly didn't need his money, but I demanded it and took it each time he gave it. That wasn't the reason why I kept sleeping with him. He left a great first impression between my legs, and it seemed to get better each time after that. When his pipe called to me, I would call him over or walk down to see him. Often Renee or some other chick would be posted up with him on the corner, so I'd walk to the Deli, just to be sure he saw me. When Renee was around she gave me dirty looks, but she wasn't dumb enough to open her mouth. Not that I wanted to be seen fighting over her man, but if she pushed me, I would.

It didn't take too long for me to stop stalking him and I settled for the "when he was available, we'd fuck". When I had enough of his nonsense – because being available meant I was truly on his time-table – I gave him the cold shoulder. Then he'd send Emo for me, and sometimes I'd give in, but I was slowly moving on.

For a minute Lil Bitts had been trying to introduce me to a few guys, and since I was trying to forget that dick, I made myself available. We started double dating. Sometimes it was worth it; other times it was the biggest mistake I'd ever made. We dated two brothers, Walt and Will, who were these tall, sexy, twenty-two-year-old twins. They were fraternal and easily recognizable – Walt was light-skinned, almost see-through, and Will had a caramel complexion. Lil Bitts started out with Walt but soon decided she wanted Will. She wanted us to switch partners, but the dilemma for both of us was that we already had sex with them. Although they were twins, they didn't share the same dick size. Lil Bitts wanted my twin because he was packing, not

Mandingo status, but he was alright. And she said Walt had a pencil that had been sharpened too many times, and she could no longer fake it just because he was cute. I didn't have feelings for Will so I didn't care if they went at it, but I wasn't about to sleep with pencil dick either.

I asked Will to come over to the apartment and told him not to bring Walt because Lil Bitts wasn't home. We sat on the couch, and I got on my knees and began putting my face in his crotch and gently blowing on his dick. He was rubbing my hair and palming my head as if he wanted me to start sucking him off immediately. "Sit down, and don't get up," I said to him.

"Where you goin'?"

"I'll be right back."

"Okay, hurry up." I got up to cut the lights off, and that's when Lil Bitts crept in the room. It was pretty dark in the living room, and because she was light on her feet he didn't hear her sneak in. She slipped right in and started to give him head. Now I know at some point he realized Lil Bitts wasn't me, especially when he felt her breasts. She was an A cup, if that, and half my size, but I guess it's true when they say men only use one head at a time, especially when they're getting head. Quietly laughing I sat in my room. I could hear the sounds of sex so the operation was a success. By now he knew we had switched and obviously didn't care. They were at it for about forty minutes to an hour before he came knocking on my door. "Yo, why you do that? I thought it was you!"

"No you didn't. You couldn't tell the difference? You see these breasts? You see how tall I am, how curvy? You see my hair? Now cut the shit! You wanted it, no matter where it came from."

"So, you mad at me?"

"Nope, but I'm busy. I'll call you later." After Will left, Lil Bitts came in the room asking my permission to continue seeing him. He had a mighty stroke and she fell victim to it. I could care less because at this point in my life my sentiment towards men was whatever, and whenever I felt like dealing with their B.S. I would be bothered.

I thought I would try to get some sleep, but the neighborhood was poppin'. Everyone was outside and one side of the block was filled with cars that Emo was about to wash. Lil Bitts and I sat on the steps, and I saw Reds at the corner with a couple girls. One was all up in his face so the others were probably her girlfriends. He looked up at me, but I ignored him. Then he yelled up the block, "What's up, Red Bone?" I rolled my eyes and continued talking to Lil Bitts. He must have thought he was big pimping, but I was about to show him that two can play that game. He wasn't the only player on the block.

Some guy rolled down the block, and when he pulled up in front of us he turned his radio on blast and stared us down. We were in a playful mood so Lil Bitts and I got up and started dancing. I slapped her on her butt, and she bent over and started poppin' her booty like a stripper. It was too funny. I yelled to the guy, "What, you just gonna watch? You better come get some of this." I don't know if Reds started walking up the street when he saw me dancing with Lil Bitts or when he saw the guy get out of the car, but he gripped me up and told me to go in the house. I laughed in his face, then pushed him out of my way and tried to keep dancing with the guy. But that punk got scared and pulled off. "Okay, you can go in tha house now. I wanna talk to you anyway."

"You can talk to her right here." Lil Bitts spoke up, but I waved her back.

"Lil Bitts, I got this."

"Lil Bitts betta mind her damn business."

"Don't talk to her like that Reds, and no thank you, I don't feel like talking."

Lil Bitts must have been feeling feisty so she said, "Um...I guess it's time for you to go."

"You got jokes? Didn't I tell you to mine ya business?" Reds was getting heated.

"I can't hear. Too much wax build up, ya know?" Reds walked away, cursing me out and calling me all types of nuts while trying to hold on to his pimp credibility. I was going to let it go until he called me a bitch. I wasn't about to take

181

that, so I said, "How you got a main join but you tryna give out directions to your side girl? Ya dick too little for that!" Everybody laughed, especially Lil Bitts. Red's face went from pimp to limp. But he did the best he could to clean up his reputation by saying, "If it's so little why you keep chasing it and stalking me?"

Okay, the little dick comment was a flat out lie, but he deserved a little salt on his game. Besides now he knew how I felt.

Lil Bitts and I continued sitting on the steps, flirting with whatever cutie that drove down the block. It was 2:30 a.m. before I knew it, and I was sleepy so I went in. As soon as I laid my head down on my pillow I heard shots. At first I thought somebody was playing with firecrackers, but when Lil Bitts came running in the house screaming and trying to duck at the same time, I knew it was much deeper than that. We both lay on the floor in my room. I was trying to ask her what happened, but she didn't know. As soon as she heard the gun go off she ran in the house, but she was positive the shots came from the corner. I started to think about Reds and went to the door to see if he was okay. Everybody outside was screaming for somebody to call the cops. I didn't know if the shooter was still outside, but I made my way to the corner to see what was going on. The closer I got to the corner I could see him and her lying on the ground. I ran up to Reds and started punching one of the neighborhood crackheads in the face. He was stealing his money out of his pockets and trying to get a ring off his finger. I kept calling Reds' name because he was shaking like someone who had seizures, but he wasn't responding. I held his head so he wouldn't keep hitting it on the ground, and started looking to see where he was shot. He screamed when I touched his chest and dimly said, "Get me some help." Emo came running up. I told him to call the cops. When I looked over at the girl, she wasn't moving. Blood was everywhere, and I couldn't tell where they were shot.

The ambulance ride was unreal. Even if you watch cops or have heard about people getting shot, it's nothing like seeing it up close. It is an unimaginable horror flick. I kept talking to Reds, telling him I was there, and begging him not to fall asleep because he kept saying he was tired. The paramedic had cut his clothes off and started to pump here, poke here, and tried to get him to answer his questions. He was going in and out, and at one point it didn't seem like he was going to come back around. We were taken to Temple Hospital, which was only two minutes away, but once we entered the hospital I wasn't allowed in the operating room. So I sat in the waiting room, trying to be patient, but I couldn't contain myself. I continued asking the nurse how much longer, and the response was still, "I don't know. The doctor will be out to talk to you." I had blood all over me and the shock wasn't wearing off. And when the cops came in asking me questions, the only appropriate response was a distant stare. I didn't know what to tell them. I was still waiting for somebody to tell me something. I hadn't seen anything, and even if I did know something my mouth was shut.

The cops told the nurse I must be in shock because I couldn't talk, and when they left she came over to exam me. But as soon as she came I asked again, "How much longer?" With the mutter of those words the doctor came out and asked who was there for the double trauma. I walked over to him, and he took me into a private room. "I'm so sorry, but she didn't make it."

"Who?"

"The female who came in with the male." I didn't know who she was, and I couldn't give him any information so he could identify her.

"I'm only here for Reds. I don't have any family contact numbers for him, but how is he?"

"Well, right now they're still working on him, and that's all I can say for now. If you need someone to come to the hospital, feel free to call them."

Lil Bitts drove my car up to the hospital and brought Emo with her. She had been crying, and when she saw all the blood on me she started crying again. I tried to comfort her, but she needed to let it out so I started questioning Emo instead. "What happened?"

Emo was silent.

"Come on, Emo, this is me. What happened?"

"Red Bone, I don't know who did it."

"Neither do I, but what happened?"

"Reds was out there wit Trina and her girlfriends chillin'. They started kissin' and all that lovey-dovey shit, so her girlfriends went home. I was down at the Deli and saw a car driving up on the corner real slow. Next thing I know somebody was like, 'I told cha I was gonna get ya.' Then they just started shootin'. He was supposed to get all them shots, but he used that poor girl like a shield..."

"Seriously?"

"What's up wit her?"

"She's dead weight."

"What?"

"Yeah, the doctor just told me a second ago. They wanted me to identify her or help them get in contact with her family, but I don't know her."

"I know where she lives, but..."

"But what? Emo just show me. I'll tell her peoples."

"What about Reds?"

"He's still in surgery, and that's all they're saying."

On our way out Renee came in the hospital like a bat out of hell, loud and throwing things around. She was begging the nurses to let her see him, but she got the same response I did. As soon as she laid eyes on me she went off. She ran up on me as if she had learned how to fight or forgotten our last run-in, and I planted a jab dead center on her forehead. That stopped her right in her tracks, and she had to regain perspective on what she was trying to do. The security guard ran up to find out what was going on, and she got hype. He quickly grabbed her and took her to the side until she calmed down. I understood she was scared and not sure of what happened, but why did she feel the need to lash out on me? I left because Emo had to show me where the girl lived. We were going to come right back, but I didn't want to be there with Renee. Realistically, Reds was her man so she could handle it.

I knew most of the people around our way, but this girl slipped through the cracks. She lived in my neighborhood so it took no time to get to her house, but I wish it had taken longer because I wasn't ready. I was uneasy, and when we got to her house Lil Bitts and Emo said they were too scared to get out of the car. If I had offered Emo a rock he probably would have gotten out of the car, but I wasn't thinking clearly. I didn't even think to change my blood-stained clothing. It was now or never, because the more I waited I thought about turning the car back on and pulling off. So I said a quick prayer and knocked on the door. I began talking as soon as someone answered it. "Ma'am…Um…"

"Oh my God. What is it? Oh my God…No, no, no…Where is she? Was she in a car accident?"

"There's been an accident, and the hospital is trying to reach her family."

"What type of accident?"

"Ma'am I'm sorry, but that's all I know. Please get to Temple as soon as you can." I hurried to my car, desperately trying to keep my feet to the ground because they were in sprint mode. I knew that she wasn't going to get to the hospital and find her injured, living child, but only a soulless corpse. At this point I was crying because I wouldn't want to be in her place. Her daughter didn't deserve this. She didn't even know Reds like that, but now she was dead. Emo and Lil Bitts stared at me as I wept like a baby because there was nothing that could be said.

We all went back to the block and sat on the steps. The cops had put the yellow tape up, and the detectives were working on their homicide investigation. Emo wanted to be nosey so he went down the street to get an up-close-and-personal view, but I think he was looking for any loose rocks that may have fallen. When Emo got too close the detectives sent him home, wherever that was. Without notice, the sun had risen, and I still had blood all over me. It was in my nails, in my shoes, on my face, and my dress was drenched with it, so Lil Bitts ran me a bath. I was too afraid to be alone so I asked her to sit in the bathroom with me while I bathed. And she didn't mind because she didn't want to be

185

alone either. We didn't do much talking although there was plenty for us to talk about. I took two baths, one to get the blood off of me (a good soaking), and one to clean my body. When I was done Lil Bitts asked me if she could sleep with me, and I was glad because she had saved me the trouble of asking her. It took her no time to pass out, while I kept trying to convince my mind to shut down. The thought of me being used as a human shield wouldn't disappear. Then I started to feel guilty because if I had let him in earlier maybe this wouldn't have happened. Eventually my body and mind started to wear down and I felt myself falling to sleep. I called 'time" just before I dosed off. "The time is now seven thirty-eight and seven seconds."

## Chapter XXX

Reds was paralyzed. He had been shot in his lower spine, his left side, and once in his leg. The other five bullets made their home inside of Trina. She had been shot in her neck and four times in her chest. Word on the street was she died at the scene, and the only reason the paramedics had performed resuscitation was to forfeit any possible lawsuits. Two days after the incident, her family held a candlelight vigil on the corner. I went down to pay my respects, but the mood of the crowd was more of anger than remembrance so I left. Everyone was blaming Reds, and many of the men in her family wanted revenge. One of her cousins had the nerve to knock on my door and ask me about Reds, but if he was looking for answers I had none. My response was simple, "I didn't see nothing, don't know nothing, and I barely know him. I was just trying to help two people who got hurt."

Two weeks after the shooting Reds called me and asked me to come visit him. My initial thought was to go see him and make sure he was okay, but I didn't want to see him like that. Even more I didn't want anyone to think I dealt with him and then I'd end up getting shot. However my concern got the best of me so I went to see him. He looked different, thinner, but he was still sexy. I know that's a horrible way to think, but he was. He had lost weight but he still had his charm and his sense of humor. I sat on his bed and rubbed on his legs, but he quickly pointed out that he couldn't feel anything from the waist down. Feeling insensitive, I started to tear up but he said, "Yo Red Bone, hold onto them. You supposed to be up here to lift up my spirits, not bring them down." Then he rubbed on my head and asked me to suck his dick, but we both started cracking up because if I did he wouldn't feel it.

We talked for a while, mostly joking around and keeping the conversation upbeat, but I didn't want to play charades. I wanted to get deeper. "I know you want me to be lively and all, but I want to know how you really feeling, like what's really going on with you..."

"Man when I first came to I was surrounded by my big ass family. My mom started cryin' and Renee started prayin'. It was a good feelin' to see them though. I don't know why but the first thing I did was feel for my legs. Then I asked the doctor to help me up because my legs felt heavy like they fell asleep or somethin', but I couldn't feel any numbness. Yo, everybody got quiet, and my moms looked at me and said, 'You paralyzed.' Imma grown ass man, but...Sunshine, I cried like a fucking newborn. This some shit I just can't get used to. Real Rap. I can't stand having people wait on me hand and foot, and not being able to get up and go when I please...I asked about therapy an' talked wit my doctor about my chances of recovery."

"So what did he say?"

"They brought that wheelchair in here last week... Those are my chances. That's my new hot ride, my life-time partner." I stayed with Reds for three hours before five of his family members came into the room, and their timing couldn't have been more off. I wanted to ask about Trina and if he used her as a shield, but when I left I buried those questions because whether he did or not she was dead. And in my mind I was thankful it wasn't me.

Of course when I got home Lil Bitts wanted the scoop, but Reds had disclosed his feelings to me in confidence so I respected that and kept them private. Emo came up the block with his nosey self-wanting the gossip too, but he sensed my hesitation and told me he'd settle for a "he's alright". Then he asked for a dollar. I had given Emo enough dollars to buy a super rock, but he was my buddy so I gave it to him anyway.

Lil Bitts and I sat on the steps and watched as the news van pulled up on the corner. Trina's mother was holding a news conference to speak out against the shooting and to get help with catching her daughter's killer or killers. Her whole family came up on the scene once the news crew pulled out their cameras. Lil Bitts wanted to walk down the block and see what the fuss was about. But I didn't like the way some of the family members had been looking at me, so I opted to stay put. She went down for about five minutes before she came back telling me my name had been used. I went off but felt like a fool once Lil Bitts said they were speaking positively about me. Her mother had praised me for locating her and delivering the heart-wrenching news. That was shocking because the looks I kept getting from many of the family members didn't have positive connotations behind them. I just wanted to be out of the mess so I stayed clear of the news (who came up the street asking me to do an interview) and her family whenever I could, seeing as we all shared the same zip code.

I was back at trying to find ways to take my mind off of everything. School was right around the corner, but I had no real concerns about it because I had money, clothes, and my car was still running well. So I had to search for an alternative mind stimulant. Sandra was pressuring me to move, but I liked where I lived. It wasn't the nicest place I'd been, but it certainly wasn't the worst. The neighborhood had a welcoming appeal, and to keep it honest I wanted to be in the mix of the mess. Being locked in a condo made me shy away from any quiet atmospheres. The best and quickest distraction I could conjure up was to meet some new guys. I wasn't in a relationship and definitely had no commitments to anyone, so I took a dive back into the market. I met a few people at the mall and at the local clubs. I even revisited the barbershop to do a little hanging out, but nothing too serious. I was a hot commodity there but I wasn't giving up any coochie. Therefore I kept my visits basic - talk, flirt, and roll.

## Chapter XXXI

When school started back I was a dedicated woman, and not a moment too soon. I had unintentionally gone on a sex binge as if I was at a wine tasting event, taking a sip from this glass, a sip from that glass, and oh yeah, that one too. The splurge resulted in me sleeping with ten new g u y s before the summer ended, not including my new man. Two of which I couldn't remember their names, only the places we had sex – one at the park on the bench at 1 a.m., the other in a club in the men's bathroom. The others were quickies in cars, their mom's basement, or in their apartments. Eight of the ten wanted me to be their girlfriend, one of them at the very least wanted me to have sex with him again, and the other one's penis was so small I asked him, "Could you do me a favor? How about you tie a rope to a big rock, then tie the other end around your neck and go jump off a bridge into the deepest ocean in the world." It might sound mean, but I had to say it (on the phone, of course) because there couldn't be a woman in the world he could have satisfied. But now Robbie was in and everyone else was out. This time I didn't lie about my age, my address, or my phone number, and I vowed to be as honest as possible – except when he asked me how many men I had slept with. The given answer was two. This question, if you ask me, is personal and nobody's business. I had been asked before and the answer was always two. Though I felt awkward for telling this little white lie, I didn't felt guilty enough to reveal the truth.

Robbie came with one specific feature that I would no longer allow to be a bonus. It was mandatory at this point – his own place. It was a nice change. We stayed at each other's place whenever we felt like it, but we didn't share the open door policy. When he gave me his key I was sure he wanted mine in return, but thankfully he took a hint from my hesitation and said I didn't have to return the favor. I was impressed with his maturity and his somewhat immediate level of trust in me, but I struggled with distrust in myself. And that's why I kept my key. Don't get me wrong I felt committed. But I had recently fucked someone (ten someones) without a second thought and had no desire to see them again; whether the sex was good or not. Indeed there was something about Robbie that set him apart from the others, and yes, he took good care of me emotionally and physically, but I could never be completely sold on the emotional part. My trust never rested within a man, and even if they had shed blood to prove their dedication and love for me, my feelings could never be completely reciprocated. It was as if I was mortally wounded and no one, including myself, knew how to heal the inner me so I did the best I could with what I had to give.

I spent more days and most of my nights at Robbie's, so Lil Bitts was living it up because she had the place to herself. Sometimes I called her and jokingly asked if she'd turned our place into a revolving door of dicks, but she'd always laugh and promised me she had her two and wasn't bringing any more home. Robbie was now paying my rent and all my utilities so I didn't bother asking Lil Bitts for her measly monthly contribution of fifty dollars. As long as she provided her own food, which she did, we stayed cool. I was generous but the idea of me feeding her, in addition to providing room and board, didn't sit well; especially when she had two dicks in our apartment.

It had been three months into our relationship and Robbie wanted to take me to Mexico. It seemed like a good plan, and if we went in the middle of the week for a three or four night escape, missing two or three days of school didn't bother me. The trip was booked. He came over two days before we were to leave and gave me some money. After school I went to the mall and picked up some bikinis, sandals, and some shades. With Lil Bitts' help, I quickly packed and for two nights I went to bed extremely early because I couldn't wait to leave.

At 7:30 a.m. Wednesday morning, I was packed and waiting at my place for Robbie to pick me up. Did I say I was waiting? The wait went on and on, and the phone calls I made went unanswered. I paced my apartment (inside and out) and kept calling his phone leaving messages. By noon I had a feeling we weren't going, but I hadn't heard a word so

I kept waiting. When Lil Bitts came in from school and saw me sitting in the living room, she started grilling me with questions. "What happened?"

"I don't know."

"Yo why you still sittin' here?"

"When I find out you'll be the first to know."

"Stop playing, he didn't call you?"

"No call, no show."

"Oh so he playin AWOL...he ain't shit."

"Why you say that?"

"Cause you're still sitting here. So what did he say?"

"Girl didn't I say he never called? I keep calling, leaving messages, and he hasn't called me back yet."

"So what you gonna do?"

"What can I do?"

"I guess you have to wait." So I played the waiting game, the pacing game, and the leave messages but no one will call you back game, for the rest of the night.

The day of the trip he got locked up, but I didn't find out until Thursday. After he had been processed and given phone privileges he gave me a call. He was making a delivery before our trip but had gotten pulled over by the cops. They found a few pounds of weed in his car. After I heard that there wasn't much I could hear him say because I started crying. Not for what had happened to him, but because what was wrong with the men I selected, and why had he lied to me? Robbie told me he worked for a construction company, as the supervisor, and that he put in long hours and got great overtime pay. That was his explanation for how he could afford to take such good care of me and himself. Now the truth was out, and I felt like I should be too. He called and called and begged for visits but I wasn't comfortable with visiting him in jail, although I was trying to consider it. I wasn't up on the visiting procedure so I asked Emo. He explained to me that a woman guard would have to search me, which entailed removal of shoes, checking your bra, and finally she would take her hand and outline the top of your panties to be sure you weren't smuggling anything in. I didn't feel comfortable with the search and besides what could I really say to him? He was in jail and had no clue as to when he would come home. Our relationship was fresh, and although I appreciated him and was ready to be committed, I hadn't signed on for this division. I wanted a man and not the bars that separated us, and I knew my deep-rooted fear of jails would only interfere with our chances. Ever since my dad's incarceration, simply driving past a prison would bring semi-forgotten memories and tears to the surface.

Ignoring Robbie's pestering phone calls for me to visit didn't stop the letters from pouring in. I often felt in the wrong for not visiting so to lesson my guilt I made sure to write weekly. He sent me letters that included handmade cards, and for a minute I thought he was drawing them until Emo let me know they had a resident jail artist that would do cards for perks (extra phone time, naked pictures, food, etc). In the beginning I wrote telling him how much I loved him and wanted us to be together. To which he demanded to know why I hadn't visited if I loved him so much. I finally broke down and told him about my fear of prisons but left my dad and the molestation out of the narrative. He seemed satisfied with my response and requested that I write as much as I could to keep our love strong, but he wanted me to try to muster up the courage to visit. I wrote as much as I could but got angry when many of my questions went unanswered. He never responded to my questions regarding the terms of his prison sentence, and if I pressed him about the issue he would give a vague response by saying "soon". It was apparent that the truth was something he pledged to hold on to. I knew our relationship would soon get fuzzy because of all the lies, and then quickly fizzle out.

To take my mind off of Robbie being away, I joined the cheering squad at school. This also gave me an excuse to cut down on writing him letters. The try-outs were easy, and it appeared that the coach was more interested in how we looked than how well we performed. Our coach was a black woman in her forties, a very stylish dresser who wore six- inch stiletto heels, whether rain or shine, tailored suits, and the sharpest hairdo with not one hair out of place.   She ranked us on our appearance, on our ability to smile, flip, split, and on the sixty-second cheer we had to choreograph. One girl who tried out left all of us in tears. Even the coach laughed at her before she even opened her mouth. She stood about six feet tall and had a huge head with glasses that were bigger than her face. To top it off, she wore a size thirteen shoe and had her socks pulled all the way up to her knees. In all honesty, if she made the team she would be great as a lifter for building pyramids, but at the end of the day only six girls were added to the team and she wasn't one of them. I felt bad for her but what could I do, I was a newbie.

We practiced four days a week, but the combination of the varsity girls and the new squad wasn't a perfect match. There was too much jealousy, and the varsity squad behaved as if we were rivals instead of teammates. They readily pulled rank and had us doing push-ups if we made one mistake. They never got tired of making us run their errands. I ignored the mess and was rarely exposed to it because the captain enjoyed the rides home I gave her and she knew they would immediately stop if she or the varsity squad stepped out of line with me, so I was able to enjoy being on the team. We cheered for the football team in the fall and winter months and for the basketball team during spring and summer. The football team smelled musky and none of the guys were cute. Even though most of the players were my age or older, their mannerisms were too immature for what I could tolerate. I witnessed this firsthand when a senior varsity player asked to take me out. When I asked what time he was going to pick me up, he said I could catch the bus and meet him there. Although he knew I had a car he didn't ask me to pick him up, which was fine with me because I didn't want to get into the habit. I drove while he took the bus. Once we sat down he acted as if he couldn't read the simple Applebee's menu. I suggested he get a steak- well done, with a side of mashed potatoes, and the seasonal vegetable. The conversation between us was non-existent because all he wanted to talk about was football and his ex-girlfriend, who happened to be the current captain of the cheerleading squad. To add to my aggravation when he cut his steak, he screeched the plate because his mother never taught him how to use utensils. Then he spent a good hour trying to place the lemon slice in his water at the bottom of his glass by only using his straw. Not only did he and that worthless date get on my nerves, but it caused a bit of tension between the captain and me. But once I explained to her my disgust for him, she didn't hesitate to throw it in his face, and that removed any issues she and I had.

Our football games had some scattered spectators, and the only time attendance was up was when the opposing school's team was popular. We ended the season two and twelve and I was happy to see it and those musky players go. On the other hand, basketball season was nothing like football. The games were always packed, and I wanted to date all the senior varsity players but I knew that would be tacky. Also with basketball being an indoor sport, it was an excellent climate change for cheerleading. We hated cheering outside in the rain and snow, and we were often so stiff because we had to wear so many layers of clothes just to keep warm. Now that we were indoors we had a chance to show off our stuff. Most of us flipped the top of our skirts down, to shorten them an inch or two. Those desperate for attention flipped theirs twice. Then the varsity squad demanded we wear bikini cut panties instead of our cheerleading briefs so when we did our jumps, splits, or flips, a good portion of our booty was visible. That was a brilliant little stunt because when we went out on the floor, all our classmates and visitors clapped like they'd never seen our routines before.

While cheering at one of our home basketball games, I met Herc, a sharp, up-to-the-minute dresser that stood out in the crowd. He and a few of his friends followed the high school games and regularly bet on them. Not the five and ten dollar bets but more of the fifteen hundred dollar bets on this team or that team. That could only mean one thing – drug money. I knew I had sworn off drug dealers, but I was curious to find out how he had received the nickname Hercules. After the game I made sure to accidentally bump into him, which sparked a conversation, transfer of phone numbers, and an invitation to get something to eat later that night.

When he picked me up it was obvious that he was flashy just by his choice of jewelry, clothes, and his car. Thankfully his personality was humble and down to earth. While riding to the restaurant I abruptly asked him why he sold drugs and his reply was, "I have no knowledge or desire to work for someone...but moving that product...now that's something I know how to do. My pop always said stick to what works for you."

After dinner I suspected the house we were in was not his home because he didn't have much in there. Besides most guys who sold weight and had a big stake in the game (their lives) wouldn't allow strangers to know where they laid their heads. He pulled his mattress into the living room so we could talk and relax. We did more relaxing than talking, and we started kissing, but then he quickly moved to sucking my breasts while he stroked his fingers through my hair. He was a horrible kisser, better yet I labeled him a pecker, but he knew how to activate arousal through a latching mechanism he did on my nipples. Within minutes my clothes had been removed and I was on top of him ready to mount up. Then he pulled me close and said, "Look at me."

"I am."

"You want it..."

"Huh?"

"You heard me."

"Yes, I want it."

"Then take it!" I quickly and anxiously propped up my butt, arched my back, and started riding him. "Oh my...Oh my god. I know why they call you Hercules. Oh god, I know." He had a smirk on his face, but I could only imagine what my face looked like, considering I had a monstrous pipe inside of me. My natural lubricant was gushing and squirting distances while my pelvis vibrated. I was five seconds from screaming, "I love you daddy!"

I heard a noise as if someone was scratching on the door, but I kept riding him because it was so pleasurable. Suddenly I could no longer ignore the distraction because someone was punching me in the back of my head. If you've ever been hit off guard it takes you a little minute to recuperate, but I didn't have a minute because this bitch wasn't stopping. "I'm gonna kill you bitch! What the fuck is this?!"

"Get off of me... Just get the hell off of me!" Hercules had pulled the girl off of me, and when I got my head in order I was ready.

"Let that bitch go!"

"Who you callin' a bitch?"

"Let her tha fuck go! He ain't holding you for real, you can get loose!" I started in on her but punched him dead in the face because he wouldn't let her go. She was kicking and scratching me, but it didn't affect me because I wanted her loose. No matter how hard I hit him he wouldn't let her go. I put my clothes on while she talked her shit, and I waited for the moment he let her go.

My mind had me tripping. I had to be in the twilight zone because this wasn't happening to me again. I mean I was sure that lightning doesn't strike the same spot twice, and if it did it had to be a one in a billion chance. Yet here I was getting caught up in the same situation. He took her outside and put the latch on the door, and then he came back in and tried to explain to me what was going on. He said it was over between them, but she couldn't get that through her head. Without delay I said, "Listen I heard it before and I ain't buying it."

He responded with, "I said it before, but this time it's true." She began banging on the door and yelling for him to let her in or for me to come out. Then she threw a rock through the window and shattered it. I opened the door and beat her until the cops came. This time Herc didn't try to break us up. I think he wanted me to whoop her ass because she broke his window.

"Nobody move. I mean it...nobody fucking move!" Cops are dramatic and bad actors. We were fighting not shooting, and I wasn't going to stop because they said so. They grabbed me from behind and slammed me on the ground. She was already down and out of it so they pulled her to h e r feet and asked if she was okay. But I wasn't about to calm down or be quiet. "Don't play the victim now, bitch. You thought you were gonna whoop my ass right?"

"Shut up," one of the cops shouted at me.

"No!"

"Don't make me…"

"Make you what?" He got right up in my face, acting all tough.

"You better get the hell out my face after I just got attacked by that bitch. Call my lawyer!" I started cracking up laughing after I asked for a lawyer because not only did it sound like a line off of TV, but I knew I didn't have a lawyer on file. The cops were looking at me like I was crazy. One officer pulled Herc to the side and asked him what happened. The other officer was listening to the girl's side of the story as she sat in the cop car crying. I was being treated like a killer, ignored and sitting in handcuffs. After they got clarification, they removed the handcuffs and apologized. "Stupid ass cops. Now who's going to pay for the damage y'all did to my wrists? …Cat caught some tongues? They should've sent someone here with a brain."

"Now that's enough young lady."

"No! It'll be enough when you haul her off to the district because I want her arrested for assault." Hercules didn't want me to press any charges and he wasn't worried about the window, so after he begged me to let it alone, I agreed. Then the cops let her go home with a warning.

From that day on I was attached to his hip. The day after the incident with the cops, I moved into his place, and I think the aggression from that experience fueled our month long sex expo. I know you're thinking you can't have sex every day. What about those days you have a visitor? Well, he ran red lights, and even though I was hesitant, he had a way of making me do whatever he wanted me to.

Lil Bitts was enjoying staying on her own as well as living rent-free. He wanted me to drop the place because he didn't see the sense of him paying my rent when I never stayed there. At first I was nervous about giving up the apartment because I didn't want him to kick me out, but I

199

had some money and a backup plan if necessary. So after some serious consideration I told Lil Bitts I was out and she had a month to find a place, or she could take over the lease if the landlord approved. Realistically I knew she couldn't handle the rent because neither she nor her boyfriend worked, and they didn't have any money for the security deposits. So when the month ended she moved back in with her mother while I was off to bigger and better things.

## Chapter XXXII

"Where's da fuckin' money?"

"I don't know!"

"So you think this is a fuckin' game?"

"I swear to God I don't know!"

"No what you don't know is that we ain't fuckin' playin'! Bitch, I'm tired of askin'. This ya last fuckin' chance. Where da fuck does he keep da money and dat work?"

"I don't know!"

He started to pistol-whip me and I could taste the blood building up in my mouth. My arms were tied behind my back, and my legs were duct-taped to the front legs of my bedroom chair. I had just gotten off the phone with Hercules, and I was lying in bed when three masked men burst in the door, guns drawn and pointed at my head. He had gone out of town for a week (on drug business) and wouldn't be back for two days. All I could see were their dark, fearless eyes and tons of black because they were dressed in it from head to toe. There was five thousand dollars on the night stand, but when I mentioned it they weren't impressed or concerned with that. It appeared they were looking for something in particular. I pleaded with them to let me go because I didn't know where anything was, but they ignored me and continued to search the house. They wanted more, and someone must have told them there was more to find because I could hear them tearing the house up.

They came back in the room and told me if I wouldn't tell them the hiding spot they'd all take their turn with me. The thought of three men forcefully having sex with me sent me into a panic. I started screaming and begging for them to leave me out of it. I told them to take the five thousand and leave, but they looked at me with devilish smirks and began to remove the duct tape and the rope. They threw me on the bed and tied my arms to the headrest. One of them put my nightgown over my head while the other two held my legs down. Then one by one they rotated positions, each having unprotected sex with me. After the first guy I didn't have enough energy to fight back or scream because my body was worn down. So I laid there with my eyes closed while they fucked me like a dog. One had the nerve to pull my nightgown down so he could cum in my face, and if he had been a little closer, I would have risked my life because I would have bitten his dick off.

In a situation like this each moment is an eternity and you lose track of real time. Disgusted is not a word you want to use because it does nothing to express the emotions you are feeling. Words truly serve no purpose. I was burning inside and out, itchy, and unable to wipe the nut off that was running into my eyes and mouth. They started discussing who was going to kill the witness and I tried to make my peace. Then they told me to count to ten. I might have complied, but considering cum would have dripped in my mouth if I opened it, I figured I'd rather die than swallow. The same guy who removed the nightgown from my face (I'll never forget his eyes) replaced it. Then I heard his gun cock. I saw my dad's and my mom's faces flash before me, and I asked God to make it as painless as possible.

Instead of pulling the trigger I was left there, tied to the bed, and unable to get loose for two days. I urinated on myself two maybe three times, even though I tried my hardest to hold it. By now I was sure they were gone, and it was only a matter of time before help arrived. There were times that I thought I was dead, but I stopped hallucinating when I realized a dead body wouldn't feel so dehydrated and weak. When Herc came in the house, he called to me. I didn't scream for help, talk, or cry. I just lay there. I felt the wind from him rushing to me to untie my arms, and when he did my body collapsed onto that filthy mattress. He talked, but my mind was closed. I couldn't respond to any voices. I saw people come in and out, but I couldn't talk. When I got to the hospital they wanted to do a rape kit, but they needed consent from a guardian because I wasn't eighteen. Herc called Sandra and she gave verbal consent, and then she assured the doctor she'd be at the hospital to sign whatever forms they needed. During the exam, the detectives came in the room and started asking me questions, but I still couldn't find my words. I just stared into their faces but I couldn't answer. Herc tried to hold my hand, but I never latched on. He was crying and tried to console me by rubbing my face. Although I couldn't speak, he understood I didn't want to be touched when I callously pushed his hands away. I started to feel pain and without seeing my face I knew it was swollen. I could still taste the blood in my mouth. Several tears began to drop from my eyes when he convincingly whispered in my ear, "I'm gonna get them." That was what I wanted. Not only did I want them to suffer, but I wanted them dead – execution style. I wanted to ask him if he knew who did it but my words were still scrambled.

I had all types of IVs in my arm because I was dehydrated, and they needed to get some fluids into my system. To make matters worse they had to draw blood to test for a number of things, including STDs. When Sandra arrived I was beginning to leave my comatose state, and I wanted to talk to Herc, but Sandra came in snapping on him. "You almost got my fucking sister killed pussy! I should kill you! What the fuck were you thinking? She's a fucking baby... Oh my God, look at her face... Why did they do this to you Sunshine?" The hospital's security had to come and escort Sandra into the waiting room until she calmed down. I desperately had questions to ask Herc, but I needed Sandra to see I was alive and trying to be okay, so I told him to leave. He firmly said no, but I insisted and he finally agreed to leave us for an hour. Immediately after he walked out, the nurse came in suggesting I see a psychiatrist. But I wasn't in the mood to talk to any strangers so I requested they send my sister in. When Sandra returned to my room she cried so much that I started crying. I begged her to stop because I wasn't trying to destroy myself. I felt suicidal and filthy, and the more I cried the more I thought about cutting my wrists or blowing my brains out. She did her best to hold her tears back, and I attempted to tell her what happened but my inability to get my sentences out assured both of us I wasn't ready. What I was ready for was a bath, but the hospital only had showers. I wanted to bathe away some of my pain, even though I knew that wasn't logical, but at least a bath would have been a starting point. Sandra helped me shower, but when she told me she had to leave the bathroom to get a towel I started panicking. I was sure from that moment I couldn't be alone because I wasn't able to deal with the silence. I needed her with me every step of the way.

I was curious to see what damage was done to my face so I asked her to get me a mirror.

"Why?"

"I want to see how my face looks, and the rest of my body for that matter."

"It's not pretty Sunshine. The gun messed ya face up, but the good thing is it's all swelling, and as soon as that goes down, with the bruising, you'll be back to your beautiful self again."

"Please get the mirror Sandra! I know it's fucked up but I want to see for myself!" I shouldn't have asked for t h e mirror because at least the images of my face wouldn't have haunted me. I looked puffy, black and purple with red highlights. My left eye was shut and my lips and face had blown up like a blowfish. I had two black eyes even though I didn't remember getting hit in my eyes. But I know if you get hit hard enough in the face your eyes are vulnerable to bruising. I looked down on the floor. I had urinated dead center where I was standing. I didn't have a weak bladder, and I was embarrassed and began to cry and scream. My behavior became too much for Sandra so she had to get the nurse to calm me down. Two nurses came and cleaned me up and then laid me down. Then one gave me some medication to relax me. The medicine was fast acting because within five minutes I went from hyperventilating to drifting off. It was so powerful that it knocked me out so hard I didn't dream or think about the incident.

I stayed in the hospital for three days, during which Sandra never left my side, except when Hercules came to sit with me. The hour a day visits with him were refreshing but brief because by the end of the hour Sandra would return from running errands, and she wanted him to leave. Each day he brought fresh flowers, and on the first day I could sense his lips moving to ask about the incident. But I made it clear I wasn't ready to have that conversation. It was such a horrendous ordeal, not only physically but emotionally. I had to wear a catheter because if I thought about it too much I'd lose control of my bladder. I had to get help for this because at my age with school, and just living, I didn't want to be known as Pissy-Ann, so Sandra set up my psychiatrist appointments before I left the hospital.

Sandra and I decided the best place for me to live was with her because I didn't feel safe with him anymore. No matter how many times he promised to protect me I wasn't going back to any of his houses. The house we were staying in was supposed to be top secret and only a selected handful of individuals knew where it was. This could only that mean it was an inside job and knowing that, I was sure the drama and danger were just beginning.

My first day home from the hospital was a hard teaspoon of tea to swallow. I persistently checked the doors and stalked the windows to see if anyone was coming for me. I was in a constant state of panic and couldn't sit still without the help of medication. My brother and my mother came to visit me, and I got the same reaction from everyone who saw my tortured, battered, swollen face – tears, pity, and then anger. There wasn't much they could say to me, and Sandra explained that crying only added to my torment so they tried to cry as little as possible. My mother's reaction was to pray for me. For once I wasn't angry with her because I appreciated her concern and right now I needed her. Shawn kept asking questions but I had no answers for him. The silent treatment wasn't normal for our relationship but this incident had changed everything. The incident was real. It happened, and I was worried about my safety, Hercules' safety, my constant nightmares, my bladder, not to mention my face returning to normal, and my biggest concern – my STD results. The initial tests taken came back negative, but those results didn't ease my worries. I had to get weekly testing for a month, and for the HIV test I had to get retested in three months, then six months after that. So if I wasn't being as open as I could with my family, they would just have to understand that the incident currently had full control over me.

When they left Sandra wanted to talk about my living arrangements and my school plans. "Sunshine you know you can stay here as long as you want and I don't want you to think about going back with Herc. Your life is more important to me than you having a boyfriend."

"I know, but one day I'm going to have to get back out there on my own, but right now I'm scared to death."

"Aww, don't cry girl, you don't have to rush nothin'. Listen, once you start seeing your therapist, she's gonna help you get through all your problems, and your face will be healed in no time. I bought that aloe plant, and that really works. Remember when I burnt my leg on the iron?"

"Huh…"

"Why you laughing?"

"Yeah, I remember."

"Don't laugh. That shit hurt."

"I'm sorry, but how did you burn your leg when the iron was on the ironing board and you weren't even ironing?"

"I don't know."

"I think you suffer from the clumsy curse."

"Curse or no curse, just thinking about it hurts."

"Listen, if Jermaine don't come home tonight, can I stay in your room?"

"Sure, I can use the company because he won't be back for a while."

"Did you tell him?"

"No because I know he's gonna get at Herc to try and find them. Right now I'm trying to keep the situation as calm and as safe as I can."

"You know I love you. You've always had my back and been like a mother to me."

"That's what a big sis is for. I love you too."

Sandra got me excused from school, and then she set me up with a home-school tutor. I did the assignments she requested, and she came twice a week to go over my lessons. The work was too easy, and she was often bored because I'd have everything completed quickly and accurately. Now only if I could commence sleeping in the same manner. Falling asleep and staying asleep had become a traumatic mess. The worst outcome was a bladder that wouldn't get right. I wet the bed for two weeks straight (yes, my first night home I peed on Sandra) before getting the courage to get out of the bed and go to the bathroom. I had to resort back to putting plastic bags under my sheets so I wouldn't ruin my mattress. All it took was one nightmare and I'd instantly wet myself.

Each day a new step had to be taken, but these were definitely baby steps. After the incident I was drugged up all of the time. This worried my doctor because I was taking more pills than prescribed. When I ran out of them so quickly she cut down my doses and gave me fewer pills. I also had to overcome my color fears. Anytime I saw someone wearing all black I panicked and my bladder gave way.

Herc tried his best to stay in contact with me and offered numerous times to take me out, but anything involving him wasn't happening. I needed some time to myself. The cops never caught the guys who hurt me, and neither did he, so how could I be sure they weren't waiting to come back and finish the job?

Out of everything and everyone I had to deal with, when I met the psychiatrist she pushed me to my limits. "How do you feel?"

"Excuse me, but how do you think I feel?"

"What do you dream about? ...Do you dream?"

"No dreams."

"Do you think this was your fault?"

"No I don't. I know it's not my fault!"

"What scared you the most?"

"I really don't feel like talking."

"If you hold it in you might continue to wet the bed."

"Who told you that? That's not true! I don't do that anymore!"

"Okay. Well, Sunshine, this room is for honesty and healing and you can't truly heal if we don't talk."

"Okay, fine, then I won't heal!" I was pissed off because Sandra didn't have to tell her about the bed-wetting. Why would she tell my psychiatrist?

When Sandra picked me up from my session I got in the car and shouted, "Why would you tell her I wet myself?" She laughed at me and told me that my doctor had told her. I was under the impression that the information known by my general doctor wasn't to be shared with my psychiatrist, but now I understood that being under the impression isn't the same as being informed. I had to get over the embarrassment and get myself back into therapy because I had to get control over my bladder.

The sessions were intense, and tears poured as the preliminary questions about the incident were asked. At first she wasn't able to get me to open up so she tried several approaches. She quickly learned that asking questions would leave her coming up empty. On the other hand if she allowed me to get to know things about her, like her past trauma, I was able to see her as a person that was concerned about me. Once we built a relationship I opened my flood gates and talked to her about my past, my father, my mother, and Kalil. Finally I began to purge the incident. The sessions involving the incident had no time limits. I was her last patient, and she allowed me to speak for as long as I needed to or until my tears had drowned my voice.

With my fears a bit in check I was now able to talk to people I had cut off after the incident – Lil Bitts, who was worried because the streets had tangled the truth and she thought I was missing a leg, and finally Herc. I finally had the strength to sit down with him and discuss the incident in detail. I arranged for us to meet in the back of a quiet restaurant, for privacy, and because I knew Sandra didn't want him at the house and neither did I. I drove my car to meet him, and it felt strange because now I was used to being driven around by Sandra. At that moment I realized I had to take a piece of my freedom back. He was at the restaurant first, and when he saw me he got up and hugged me. I pulled back because it was too passionate and I wasn't ready for that type of embrace.

"Hey Baa, it's so good to see you. I finally get some one-on-one time with you."

"Yeah."

"Your face looks real good. In a week or two you won't be able to tell...I mean it'll be back to normal."

"No, it won't ever be back to normal, but I know what you mean."

"Come sit on my side."

"Naw. I'm alright over here."

"I understand."

"Listen, I know you want the details because they'll help you figure out who did this, so I'll do the best I can."

"Sunshine I didn't ask you here for dat. I wanna spend time with you...I mean I want to make sure you're alright."

"Well I want you to know."

I told him everything I could remember. At times I was talking so fast I thought my tongue would choke me, however once I got it all out, I felt relieved. He cried when I gave details of the sexual assault, and I can't imagine how it feels to hear that your woman was raped by three men. But I sure know how it feels to *be* raped by three men. The waitress had to come over once because Herc began sobbing and slammed the table a few times during my playback so I assured her that if she brought us two cups of tea and some water we would be on our best behavior.

After everything was out, it took him some time to digest it all. Then he asked me if I wanted to go home. I thought after I told him my story I would be in a rush to get back home, but I felt comfortable being in the restaurant with him so I stayed. Now it was my turn to ask him a question because we hadn't truly spoken with each other, so I started with a simple, "How are you?" He let me know his stash house was robbed, that they had taken his work along with a substantial amount of money. That was surprising to me because I thought he had sense not to keep his money and work in the same place. As a result he wasn't doing well financially, and he, well, we both were paranoid. Luckily I had an escape now I was staying with Sandra, but h e couldn't trust anyone. He had to cut everyone off because he knew it was a set-up, but he didn't know who to point the finger at. Furthermore, I knew he was strapped because he kept his hands close to his pants, and with any distraction or noise he'd place his hands in ready-for-action mode.

Not long after we discussed his misfortunes, our conversation took a turn onto a road I didn't want to drive on. As foreign as it sounded to my ears and as uncomfortable as he must have felt saying it, he asked to borrow fifteen thousand dollars until he got on his feet. The only reason he knew I had it to lend was that he saw my bank statement when we were staying together. At that moment I recalled him being impressed with my savings but equally curious as to how I got the money.

My initial thought was to laugh and let him know it was my trust fund. Then we'd both smile and hopefully that would end that conversation. But neither one of us was laughing or smiling. It had seemed too coincidental that only yesterday I checked my account balance, which had dwindled down to eighteen thousand dollars and some odd cents and now he wanted fifteen! Why did he have to ask me? Was that the definition of a ride-or-die chick? To get raped and almost killed, and then to give up my monetary assets? I had that money for my life, my expenses, and thankfully the hospital had a rape victim fund because between their fees and my therapist sessions, I'd be empty already. If I gave him the money, he promised to pay me back along with a bonus of six thousand dollars. I tried to find the logic in lending him the money, but no logic could guarantee he'd pay me back. If my savings weren't so low I wouldn't have second-, third-, and fourth-guessed my decision, but ultimately I decided to help him out. He was good to me, and when he was up, I was up. Knowing that I was okay with giving him the money because if I debated any further the answer would be no.

To withdraw my money, I needed Sandra because after all, I was officially a minor. My account was set up with her as the guardian, and although I could deposit money and withdraw funds by using my ATM card, she was the only one who could withdraw large sums of money. Since I had no intentions of letting her know what I was doing, because the answer would be "hell no" and she'd probably have me admitted to the psych ward, I had to come up with a plan. I stole her ID from her pocketbook and went to the bank dressed in full Muslim garments, including the niqab (face cover). All the bank teller could see were my eyes, and I knew she or the manager would never ask me to remove the religious garments. I made my request; the teller asked for my ID; and then she told me to wait a moment while she got her manager.

"Hi Sandra how can I help you today?"

"Well I need to close this account today."

"Sure, I can help you with that, but can I ask why?"

"I just need to close it."

"Oh no problem. I was only asking because we have other options for your money, such as money market accounts or bonds that you may be interested in."

"I appreciate that information, but we're moving out of state and I need to close it."

"Well you know we have branches all over."

"Yes, I'm aware of that, but I'll be closing this account. You see my little sister was raped, and since they haven't been successful in capturing her perpetrator, that money will help us relocate out of state."

"Oh my, I'm so sorry to hear…Give me one second, and I'll get you squared away ASAP."

"Thank you."

"Now how would you like that, cashier's check or cash?"

"No check. I'd like to have it in cash. Big bills, if possible?"

"No problem. I've got you covered."

She handed me the money in one of those big yellow envelopes, and I quickly stuffed it into my pocketbook. Then she walked me to the door and said, "Take care of your sister, and I hope they catch that loser." Just like that I had removed all of my savings. My next step was to meet Herc at the same restaurant where he had asked me for the money, because he was about to go on a road trip in order to make his money back. When I walked in the restaurant he was smiling. I quickly handed him the envelope. I could feel that he wanted to say something that would put my worries at ease.

"Hey baby, how you doin'?"

"I'm okay. It's all there. Be careful with that."

"You know I will. Thanks again for this."

"Uh-huh."

"Baa why you look nervous...you know I'm gonna give ya money back, right?"

"It's not that I don't believe you, it's just so much going on right now."

"I understand, but it's gonna get so much betta, trust me."

"Okay."

"This some real ride-or-die shit and you know I'm gonna have ya back always...you love me?" I didn't want t o answer because what did love have to do with me getting my money back? But I unconvincingly said, "Yeah." Not surprisingly, he wasn't satisfied with my response and did his best to convince me that not only was he going to give me my money back but that he loved me. "What you mean, 'yeah.' It's a yes or no."

"You know I love you."

"Then don't worry 'bout notin'. We gonna be back on top, just trust me."

"K."

"I'll see you when I get back."

"Alright." Herc hugged me and walked me to my car. I was nervous. I wanted to snatch the envelope back from him, but it was too late. I had given him the money. Now all I could do was wait.

## Chapter XXXIII

Bad luck was following me because Hercules got arrested for having two raw bricks in his car. Not that I was an expert on drug quantity or lingo, and I certainly didn't know the difference between a cooked or uncut brick, but I did know he was facing serious jail time. The lockup had the neighborhood buzzing. It also involved three other well- known hustlers, and while the details were still hazy, it was clear to see that prison would become their new homes.

Instead of crying or falling into a severe depression because I knew I wasn't going to get my money, I decided to take a drive to evaluate my situation. I had driven so far that I had gotten lost, and when I looked around I knew I was out of the city because the roads were barren and what houses I did see sat quite a distance apart from their neighbors. At this point in my life I wasn't afraid of being raped or killed – I often thought it would be a blessing if it happened – so I decided to bunk in my car. I pulled my blanket out of my trunk, got into the backseat and began to write in my journal. My therapist suggested I write in it daily, giving thanks for all the good things in my life. However the plan always backfired because I wrote and recognized more wrongs than rights. Another exercise I actually found enjoyable was the duck factor. Each time I had a negative thought or I was about to say something to be hurtful, I had to quack like a duck. When I was by myself I quacked a lot, and I even flapped my arms like a duck. Silly, I know, but it helped me. That technique even opened my communication with my doctor as she and I would quack it up in her office.

That night I quacked for as long as I could before bursting out in tears. I started remembering Kalil, the rape, the abortion, and now the arrest. I was broke and felt cheap, but I was too embarrassed to call Sandra and confess the truth. Besides, I had gotten myself into this situation and now I needed to come up with a plan to fix my mess. I don't remember falling asleep, but when I woke up there were still uncertainties looming around me. I didn't know where I was or how to get home, if I could come up with the courage to tell Sandra what I had done, where I was going to live, and if I did go on my own how I'd pay my bills. I was left with three thousand dollars and I knew that could disappear like a cup of kool-aid in a project refrigerator. The only thing I knew for sure was being a burden wasn't on my agenda. Sandra had opened her home up to me, again, and I was eternally grateful but, being fiercely independently, I had this overwhelming need to stand on my own.

Thanks to the help of an Amish woman I returned home with no problems. Word had gotten back to Sandra, and when I walked in the door she wanted to know how I felt about him being locked up. It was easily sensed that she didn't care he was in jail because she blamed him for the rape, and whether she admitted it or not she was happy we were separated. Her concern seemed more sarcastic than genuine so I went in my room to think of a way to get some money back into my pockets. Since I was uninsured and low on funds I immediately cut the therapist sessions. Although I needed therapy, I needed money more, and I didn't want Sandra paying for them. Trips to the Thrift and the mall had to be cut or ceased (unless the sale was too good to be ignored). Plus not shopping would also save money on gas. Finally that left eating out, which was one of my ways of dealing with my depression. Now I'd have to paper bag it unless someone else was treating.

With my budget in place I tried to go back to school, but it was difficult because everyone knew what had happened to me. Once the news of Herc's arrest became public information, it only increased the stares and gossip. At times I felt overwhelmed and I'd lash out at teachers. Thankfully they knew what I was dealing with and didn't suspend me. The principal who was trying to be my hero, or maybe he was just doing his job, assigned me to daily mandatory counseling with the school's guidance counselor. Sometimes when things are free it's just as they say: "You get what you pay for." The sessions were a waste of time, and I completely shut down because I had nothing to go off of. She was one of those people who'd ask you if you were okay when she already knew there was no way possible you'd be okay. Then to make matters worse she'd stare at me like she could read my eyes. I would have been better off going to see a psychic or talking to Emo because this counselor had no clue on how to help people. It had taken everything I had to get close to my therapist so I could speak openly with her. I couldn't do it again, especially with someone I knew wasn't qualified.

Feeling the need to relocate I had a long talk with Jermaine and discussed moving to another city, with his help of course. He was supportive and under the impression that I had some money saved. I knew he wouldn't have a problem putting some funds to the money he thought I already had, but I wasn't about to live another lie so I told him what happened to my money. His immediate silence was action enough of his disapproval, but thankfully he didn't try to give me a father-daughter talk. Our relationship had grown to one where he understood that I was living my life. He would try to steer me in the right direction but would never stop me from making my own decisions. Fortunately for me, he had a few places in various locations so he asked me how I felt about staying in New York. At first, all I could envision were dollar signs but when he offered me a monthly allowance and told me the spot was paid for, New York began to look like the place for me.

"Sun this spot would be good for you, yah-mean. It ain't Manhattan, but it ain't the hood eitha."

"Okay."

"You'll be safe, and I might have to stop through here and there but ain't no illegals takin' place."

"That's perfect. I just need a change of scenery."

"So you talked to Sandra yet?"

"No, and I don't want her to know just yet. Not until I get on my feet and stay on them for a minute."

"Listen you my peoples, and I'm not gonna see ya out there fucked up. Gimmie a week to put things in motion and we out."

The week's end was in sight, and I didn't know how to tell Sandra or how I was going to get out of school. I knew manipulating the guidance counselor was a must because she was the only one who could give me the approval to go out on leave. During our next session I cried to her and said how people were openly discussing me being raped and blaming me for what happened. She was immediately outraged and wanted the names of the students, but I told her I feared they would kill me so I'd never name names. I explained to her how suicidal I felt and let her know that was the reason I didn't talk much during our meetings. She sympathetically apologized for my suffering and asked what she could do. I immediately smiled internally because I knew exactly what I needed her to do. I asked to be placed on home school, minus the tutor. Based on my grades and the previous report from my tutor, stating that I was an independent learner and that her involvement was minimal and sometimes unnecessary, she put in an immediate request to the principal. If the request was approved, and based on the counselor's tone it would be, all I had to do was return the mailed assignments to her within a week.

With that out of the way I had to deal with telling Sandra, which was going to be awkward, uneasy and unscripted. What could I say to her that would put her mind and heart at ease? Honestly, nothing, because she wanted me with her, or in arm's reach so she could come running if I needed her. Knowing I couldn't, in her mind, come up with a good enough reason for moving, Jermaine and I left on Saturday while she was grocery shopping. I knew she would be curious to know where I was because I took most of my belongings, so I left a note that read, "I'll call you as soon as I get out of Philly. Love you. Don't worry about me, but I had to go."

As promised, I picked up the phone and called her as soon as my feet touched the floor in my new home. "I love you Sandra."

"I love you too, but where are you?"

"I moved?"

"I can tell that by lookin' at ya room, and by the way thanks for the note."

"I know I should have said something, but I was scared of how you'd react."

"Well where are you staying?"

"I'm in Jersey, and I know you wanna see where I'm at, but I need a moment to stand on my own cavaliers."

"So you felt as though you couldn't tell me though?"

"Yes I did, and I know I hurt you."

"Hurt? Try confused. I love you lil' sis, but you...you know what? I'm not gonna keep you from living your life. If you need me, you know where I'm at. I love you. Call me later."

"I love you too."

NY was scary, exciting, and new! My house was small, but the décor was sexy, flirty, and elegant. Jermaine had excellent taste, and his money was reaching an all-time high. He owned over twenty properties, including singles, duplexes, triplexes, and two large commercially-zoned buildings. He was a smart businessman. He tried to get Sandra involved, but no matter how hard he pushed her to step up or just learn the business, she was too satisfied with being a stay-at-home mom. I often wondered why she'd never moved into one of his singles or out of state, and the only explanation that made sense was she stayed to watch over me. Now there was no excuse for her. I was too far away for her to come running to my rescue. From here on out I would have to figure things out on my own.

My monthly allowance was a thousand dollars. I felt that was more than generous because my expenses were minimal – food and any activities I did. Eventually I was going to invest more of my time into finding a job but for now I was trying to learn my new surroundings. Everything in New York was busy and at first hard to understand. Not only did the cars drive fast, the people talked fast and they walked so fast they might as well have been running. Fortunately Jermaine showed me around the city but mostly the tourist parts because he didn't want me going to any of the boroughs he visited. Then as an introduction to New York's world of fashion he took me shopping and I almost lost my mind when I saw the price tag on a pocketbook I had been eyeing. To purchase a three thousand, five hundred and thirty-eight dollar pocketbook, that at the moment was more money than I had to my name, was a foolish move so I kept looking. I wasn't cheap and had bought myself some expensive gifts, but I wasn't in a position to do such things like that right now. Jermaine acted as if he was in these stores on a daily basis, and he probably was because Sandra's wardrobe was full of designer names. Still she rarely got dressed and most of her clothes still had the price tags on them, which made me question her appreciation. However, when he purchased my pocketbook along with a matching scarf, it was clear I treasured my gifts because I immediately wore both and smiled until my jaw locked up.

After a week of showing me the ropes and getting me some very nice pocketbooks, shoes and jeans, Jermaine left me to myself. I thought Philly was a big deal, but NY quickly showed me how much of a small-towner I was. At first I traveled lightly because I was scared to ask strangers for directions, but eventually I got up the guts to find my way. My biggest step was riding on the subway, which was nothing like Philly. At times the subway was as crowded as a sold-out concert, and the people on the subway could be as crazy as a war vet suffering from schizophrenia. On the bright side, the subway offered an array of talents. Singers and rappers performed in hopes of getting a few dollars or getting discovered because you never know who you are sitting or standing next to in NY. In addition to the performers, the abundance of products offered – from a pair of socks to a fake ID and social security card - were easily obtained from the endless hustlers who made riding the subway better than taking a trip to the department store. After riding for a bit I loved the subways, because I knew driving in NY was an accident waiting to happen. You had to be crazy aggressive, like the cab drivers, or you'd be the one causing accidents. And with the overflow of traffic and the limited parking spaces, it was quicker to get from point A to B by subway.

I soon found two places I couldn't resist – Central Park and Sylvia's Soul Food Restaurant in Harlem. At a minimum, I ate there two times a day because the food was fresh and amazingly delicious. What I couldn't finish went home for leftovers. Surprisingly for NY, Sylvia's prices were more than reasonable. And as for Central Park, I just loved it! Although it was humongous I felt safe, and every time I saw a bird it reminded me of my duck therapy and I'd immediately be at peace. I enjoyed watching people holding hands, jogging, playing with their children or dogs, and I often daydreamed of a life with Hercules. I thought of a life without pain, without sadness, a life where my past would stay there and not interfere with my future. Nonetheless I'd always remember that in my current reality I didn't have the power to make these things factual, but that didn't lessen my desires.

With more than a month of living in NY, I had completely neglected my school responsibilities. I hadn't been back to Philly to pick up my school work, nor did I want too. I loved NY, and I thought about asking Sandra to mail my homework out to me, but I still hadn't decided whether I should let her know where I was staying. When Jermaine called me to make sure things were on the up and up, he let me know she often asked about me. Sandra knew Jermaine and I communicated and she was okay with not knowing where I was, as long as I was doing fine. It made me feel good that she cared about me, but was willing to let me grow up a bit.

Jermaine was coming to visit me soon and he promised to take me out and show me much more of the city. There was so much to do in NY, I didn't think I would ever be able to see it all. When he showed up he took me to Times Square so we could catch a play, but the good ones were sold out. We walked around checking out billboards, people, and scenery, until we decided to take a ride on a New York City tour bus. It seemed like an easier way to see more of the city, and I wanted to get off my feet anyway. After we paid for our tickets and were about to board, a very feminine looking man approached us and asked how we were. Jermaine instantly became protective and answered, "Fine," but as we tried to board, the man interrupted us again. "Well she's beautiful, isn't she? Have you ever modeled?" I laughed because I was flattered and because I had never even thought of modeling. I wasn't a stick figure, and I didn't want to lose weight, which I had heard was the norm in NY. However, before I could say thank you, but no thanks, Jermaine said, "No, she hasn't, and why?"

The feminine man replied, "Well I'm a talent scout, and I see she has potential."

Jermaine looked unconvinced but kept the conversation going, "Potential for what?"

The man quickly laughed and said, "To be a successful model. Well I'm going to leave you guys my card, and if you're interested call me, but don't hesitate. I wouldn't want a beauty like her to go undiscovered." I was excited but Jermaine was seriously questioning the authenticity of this man, probably because he was a homophobe. The man had on a touch of red lipstick and black eyeliner. For a man, he was pretty. After the tour ride we went back to the house and Jermaine let me know he had to go but he'd see me soon. He tried to get out of the house without giving me the card, but I quickly reminded him. He was reluctant, and I had to beg him to give it to me while he kept saying I shouldn't trust faggots. However I eventually got the business card.

Faggot and all, the card was legit, and when I got to the modeling office my body was immediately filled with intimidation. Tall, beautiful, thin women filled the office. I started to feel out of place, but I told myself I belonged there because I had potential. After waiting twenty minutes or so – which seemed like an eternity because the mere images of those gorgeous women had me somewhat convinced I was an ugly duckling - my talent scout appeared, dressed in red patent leather from head to toe. "Baby, you made it! How was your trip?"

"Good, I'm not too far from…"

"Never mind that, let's talk business. I get twenty percent of each job you book, and there will be no side deals. Absolutely no side deals! You work for the agency. I work for the agency, so better yet just assume you work for me. Okay, let's make it happen."

"Okay."

"Now do me a favor and go in our swimsuit room and try on a kini. Okay?"

"Yes." I don't know what scared me more, his pink lipstick or trying on a bikini. Before I got there, I wasn't ashamed of my body, but after looking at paper figures, I didn't think my curves would go great with the agency.

When I came out of the dressing room, he walked me into a small studio without saying a word. He just looked me over. Once the photographer snapped a few Polaroid's of me, my new agent said a few words. "Sweets, you probably won't do any runway here because you have too much umph, and even with those long legs you're just too damn short, but trust me you'll work! We have many clients that want a fresh look and print work pays just as well, and sometimes better than our runway gigs. Listen, I want you to have a good look in the mirror! You have a good body, but it could be better. I want you to lose about fifteen pounds or more so I can market you to our higher end clients. Right now I have some catalogue work for you. Everything okay with you...Well, don't answer, just make sure you cut out the chips, dips, and everything else you don't need."

I started working immediately. They marketed me in the thirteen to twenty age group, and most of my immediate work was in the pre-teen division. I knew I had a fresh face, but not newborn. I was running all around NY taking photos, changing clothes, and getting my hair and make-up done. It was amazing and breathtaking when I'd open up a catalogue and see me with my backpack, or look in a magazine and see me in a toothpaste ad. I was finally making some of my own money, even more than I expected. If I booked a full catalogue ad, I made twenty five hundred for a day of glamour and posing. The hair, toothpaste, or shoe ads paid a base fee of five hundred dollars. Once my agent booked me for a lingerie shoot, and the male model felt me up. Even though other female models said this was a common practice, it was uncomfortable, especially when nothing was being done about it and most of the people at the shoot were men. The memories of the rape were always close to the surface, and I wanted to walk off but I finished the shoot. Afterwards I told my agent I didn't want to do any more gigs involving lingerie or male models, and he scolded me and said, "You have to move on to bigger things. Sun you have to follow the money! Now grow the hell up!" For the moment, though, he didn't book me for those shoots. Instead he started looking into some television ads in the teen category. I was happy because I wanted to milk the teen work as long as I could.

## Chapter XXXIV

I only had twenty minutes to get from my house to work, but everything was spinning, and the more I stood, the greater need I had to vomit. I'd been watching my weight and barely eating, but lately I was putting on pounds, and it was affecting my booking ability. Although Pinky was a great agent, he had no tolerance for my weight gain, and he held no punches when it came to telling me how he felt. I was afraid of losing my contract if I didn't get the weight off, and he threatened to drop me because I wasn't keeping up with my end of the bargain. Once he called me an ungrateful bitch because a client who had used me before said I'd put on too much weight and went with someone else. I understood his frustration and like many other agents Pinky had a potty mouth, but honestly at times I wanted to slap his ass straight. Not that it was possible, but I was eager to try. Besides I was doing everything in my power to stay thin. At the office I worked out in the gym, and when I was home I did crunches and sit-ups to make sure my mid- section was tight.

I struggled to get up off the couch. As soon as I was standing, I made a dart for the bathroom but everything came up before I could get there. To begin with, I didn't have much in my stomach and that made it much sorer, and to add to my stomach woes I caught a case of instant diarrhea. There was no way I was going to make it in to see the catalogue client, which had been the break I was waiting for since my print work had dwindled due to my weight gain. Partially undressed, I laid on the bathroom floor as if I had been out all night drinking and getting high. I tried to get up, but each time I lifted my head off the floor I had to throw up and use the bathroom, a true double bubble.

I placed a call to Jermaine because I knew he was in the city. He came past and took me to the hospital. Every time we hit a bump or if I lifted my head up too high, I vomited in his jeep, and before I could finish being triaged I had to throw up again. The nurse immediately wheeled me to an ER room and said the doctor would be right in.

"Hi, how are you?"

"Not good."

"I see. Well I'm Dr. Finnegan, and I'll be helping you feel better. Well let's see here Sunshine, when was the last time you ate?"

"Two days ago."

"Why?"

"I was so busy I forgot to eat."

"Well you can't go days without eating, whether you're busy or not. When's the last time you had some water?"

"Yesterday."

"You sure?"

"No."

"It appears to me you're severely dehydrated, but we're going to run some tests to be sure. Nurse start a line on her and get a blood and urine sample." As soon as they walked out of the room, Jermaine looked at me like I'd been starving myself, but that wasn't true. I wanted to explain myself but I was too weak. I wanted to get up and give the urine sample because the sooner I got that over with, the faster I could lie back down; but my legs weren't supporting me so I had to use a bedpan. The nurse offered me something to eat, but I was too weak to eat, stand, or pee on my own, so she drew her sample, cut off the lights, and left me alone.

I fell asleep, but the doctor came in and hastily woke me up. He wanted another urine sample. By now I was feeling much better and hydrated so I quickly made my way to the bathroom and left the sample at the nurse's station. I wanted to go back to sleep because Jermaine had gone to get something to eat from the hospital cafeteria, but as soon as I cut the lights off and laid down, the doctor came back into the room. "Sunshine do you know you're pregnant?" Maybe the doctor wasn't really standing in front of me, maybe I was dreaming, but then that would have been the dream I hoped for, not my reality. This doctor just said I was pregnant. I was beyond a state of confusion. "How? I just had my period."

"Well the urine and blood tests are conclusive, and in some cases women have a regular menstrual cycle the entire course of their pregnancy."

"But where is it? I gained a little bit of weight but nothing major, and I haven't had sex in months."

"Well I'm going to do an internal exam and an ultrasound to make sure all is well with the baby. I'll have a better estimate for you then."

Tears were better than words for now, but I had to quickly clear them because Jermaine walked back into the room. He wanted to know what was wrong. What could I say? I didn't believe I was pregnant. I was still in denial regardless of the blood and urine tests. Where was the belly, the movement, or any other warning signs? Jermaine held me while I cried, and when Dr. Finnegan came back he asked, "Are you the baby's father?" My secret was out. When the ultrasound technician let me know I was seven months pregnant, my denial was gone as well. Jermaine looked confused, and I was confused, but I had found out why I was so ill. Now it was time for me to go home.

On my answering machine Pinky had cursed me out in five different languages for missing the booking and let me know my services were no longer needed, but I didn't give a damn. I was still trying to figure out how I could be pregnant for so long and not know it. Bigger than that, who was I pregnant by? My mind quickly returned to the rape because that was about six to seven months ago. I was tested not only for STDs but also for pregnancy, and nothing came up on my doctor's radar. However at my next scheduled appointment, I wasn't tested for a possible pregnancy because my period was on. To add to my frustration I wasn't able to pinpoint the last time I had sex with Herc, but I knew it was around the same time period that the assault occurred. I had plenty of sex with him before the assault, but afterwards I shut down shop. "Who is my baby's father?" I forgetfully screamed at the top of my lungs before recalling Jermaine was downstairs. Thankfully he was asleep because I didn't feel like telling him that just maybe I was pregnant by one of the rapists. And I had to take another look at myself because how could I be so far gone and not notice a change in my body. When I looked in the mirror I still didn't see a woman who was seven months pregnant. It was obvious to me I had put on a few pounds, but nothing that would indicate a pregnancy. Just imagining me pregnant by those ruthless dudes made me want to take a gun and blow it out of me. I began acting erratic, thinking of ways to get rid of the baby. My bed was pretty high off the ground so I fell off my bed, straight onto my belly. That didn't do anything but give me a stomachache. I tried falling midway down the steps in hopes of having a miscarriage, but that just hurt my head, back, and foot instead.

Frustrated with my ineffective attempts to self-abort, which only resulted in me feeling unnecessary pain, I called a place in NY that offered third-trimester abortions. I was embarrassed because getting an abortion wasn't a cause for a celebration, and having to get one so far along in your pregnancy was viewed as a greater sin. Not only to others, but to me as well. I was scared and wrestling with feelings of guilt. I wanted to talk to one of the girls at the agency. To them, abortions were like eating a bag of skittles or walking down the street, no big deal, but I never heard of anyone getting one in their third trimester. Realistically, the baby could survive outside at this point, and I was too afraid of being judged so I didn't call. I thought about calling Sandra, but that thought quickly faded when I realized I hadn't kept in touch or picked up my assignments as I promised. Now that I was in trouble I would ring her phone? I decided the best thing for me would be to get the procedure, especially if I wanted to get back in good with Pinky. He would never accept me back into the agency with a belly or any stretch marks.

My appointment was exactly one week from the day I found out I was pregnant, and every day I had to wait I felt as if the end would never come. The center was nothing like a first trimester abortion center. There was no big crowd in the waiting area. It was more like a very private surgical center. I was greeted by a friendly representative and had a quick price confirmation with her. Thankfully the thirteen hundred dollar price tag wasn't an issue for me. The staff tried its very best to comfort me and explain the procedures of a third trimester abortion, but I blocked out most of what they said because I didn't want to know. All I wanted was for this thing to be taken out of me and discarded.

The process was a two-part method of dilation and extraction, which would result in me coming back in twenty-four hours once my cervix dilated. It was as if I was actually giving birth to a baby. As a precaution, I was required to stay overnight. After I watched the informative third trimester video, I was ready for part one of my procedure – the dilation. They prepped me in a room that looked more like a birthing suite compared to the small room I remembered when I had my previous abortion. Once in the room, I had to wait for the doctor to come and insert two one-inch long dilators into my vagina. The nurse said he would be right in, but the last time I checked it had been over fifteen minutes and now I was having second thoughts. The last thing I needed was time to listen to my conscience, and it didn't help that I hadn't talked this over with someone I could trust. I got off the exam table and put my clothes on because now I wasn't sure. After I was dressed the nurse came in and said, "Sorry about the wait, but one of our patients needed a bit more care than we expected. You can get undressed and we'll be right in." I knew I wasn't taking my clothes back off because I had changed my mind. After she left, I went to the receptionist, got my money, and told her if I changed my mind I knew their number.

By the time I got home I had changed my mind again so I called the center back to schedule another appointment. The receptionist suggested I speak with the counselor before making a decision, and after talking with her I was to come back in two days to start the procedure. When I went to meet the counselor I was met by a crowd of protestors. They were blocking me from gaining entrance to the center because they had their arms interlinked. And those who weren't forming the human chain had pictures of babies that had been aborted in the third trimester. At a glance, the images were excessively graphic, and once I laid my eyes upon the pictures of discolored, torn ligaments, underdeveloped, dead children, my stomach turned. One of the protesters came over to talk to me and I burst into tears. She hugged me and wiped my eyes while she talked about alternatives, such as adoption or getting help with taking care of my baby. A worker from the center came over and tried to get me to go with them. They had previously warned me about the potential of protesters, but I didn't think they were going to bring the entire women's movement to the front door. The representative from the center was aggressive and ready to make whatever move I wanted, but I wasn't sure. I couldn't look at those pictures and do that to my child. Besides, maybe leaving my appointment and then returning and being met by protestors wasn't coincidental. If I had received the first part of my procedure I would have had no other option but to finish the job, but now I had a choice to make. I stood there with two women telling me my rights, and one was fighting for my child's rights as if her life depended upon it.

Sometimes when you don't know what to do, a decision still has to be made, whether you make it or it's made for you. In my case, after seeing those pictures, it was clear to me that whether I wanted a baby or not, I couldn't live with myself if I aborted my child. At this point, in my eyes, I wasn't talking about an embryo but an actual life. So I went home and prepared to be a mother. I didn't want to be alone anymore, and I knew I needed to call Sandra because this was too hard for me. When I walked in the door I didn't have to call because she was already sitting in my living room. Instantly my load felt lighter. All this time I was under the impression I was on my own, but thankfully Jermaine kept Sandra informed about every little step I took.

As soon as we embraced I felt like a child who was in need of her mother. I spilled my guts to her, and remarkably Sandra wasn't disappointed in me nor did she judge me. She knew I had given Hercules the money, and she had news for me that at the moment I was unable to decipher as good or bad - he was home!

"I can't believe he's home...how?"

"Cops have to follow procedures too, and if they don't, they have to let the rooster out of the cock house."

"So he's home for good?"

"Yup."

"Did he snitch?"

"Now I don't like him, but one thing I know about him is he ain't one of those."

"Where is he?"

"Broke and tryin' to get back, but nobody will mess with him right now, he too hot."

"When did you talk to him?"

"I didn't. Jermaine did when he found out you were pregnant. You know how he is about dudes taking care of their seed."

"I know. I have to see him. He's probably mad at me though."

"Why you say that?"

"I didn't write, I didn't visit, I moved on him. I trashed him!"

"He's gonna be a daddy to your baby no matter what happened in the past. Now it's all about y'all future."

## Chapter XXXV

I moved back in with Sandra until I transferred all my belongings from NY and then quickly found a place in Bensalem. Now that Herc was back in my life, I felt safer staying in the suburbs instead of the city. Our reconnection occurred during a phone call. I didn't know how to apologize or if he'd forgive me, but he was so happy about the baby and wanting to rub my stomach that nothing else mattered. At first the reunion didn't sound tempting because I hadn't seen him in eight months and now I was showing. He had never seen me this fluffy, and though I should have been worried about leaving him in the dust, I was shallow and cared more about what I looked like. But I was easily persuaded once he used some choice words that reminded me of the days when he worked me in the bedroom like a professional. Being pregnant, my hormones were jumping off the wall and I often dreamed about dick, but I didn't react. The opportunity was there – many men told me they loved pregnant pussy and the added growth of my ass and tits may have added to their desires – but I wasn't about to lie down with any strangers.

Herc and I arranged to meet at his grandma's house. Luckily for me she wasn't there because he went straight in and handled his business. It's true what they say about pregnant pussy – its wetter and has its own vibrating pulse. I was leaking through my panties, and talk about soaking a bed sheet. I had forgotten I was pregnant, and my fears of having sex while I was expecting, thinking it would hurt the baby, were immediately dissolved because I was fucking. I think the baby was enjoying it too. Legs here, bend here, lift me up over there, stick it here, lick and suck there, and finally don't pull out just keep coming right in there. It was so good I hoped we'd never have to talk, but who was I kidding?
"You know I'm mad right?"
"I guess."
"What you mean you guess...shit you know!"
"I've been through a lot...You'll never understand."

"I understand we supposed to be a team and you don't cut a nigga off like that."

"I was running away from my problems…"

"So what Imma problem!"

"No I'm not saying that."

"What about my baby? Was you ever gonna tell me?"

"Yes."

"When?"

I couldn't answer his questions, but I could cry. I was a crybaby, and if you yelled at me or raised your voice in the slightest, I would cry. It was nasty, and I frowned at my behavior but I had no control of it. The doctor said it was a feature of my pregnancy, and I, along with the people in my life, would just have to deal with it until I delivered the baby. So for now Herc dealt with my tears and held me as I sobbed like a baby and endlessly asked him, "Why do you have to yell at me?"

We moved in together. He was very attentive to my needs and helped around the house. I never asked him about my money, although I still wanted it back, and he never brought it up. Money, for the moment, wasn't an issue because Jermaine was still giving me the same allowance, and Herc was making small moves but nothing that would get him caught up with the law. It was a good feeling to have a place to live, a few dollars in the bank, and because I wasn't in a rush to get a job until after I got the baby settled, I was tremendously thankful to Jermaine and Herc for helping me out.

Even if I wanted a job, I knew I couldn't because during the end of my pregnancy the ugly side had come out. I thought I had narcolepsy because I was falling asleep in the middle of eating, in mid-sentence, or while relaxing. My diet had turned from preferred, to all-you-can-eat and what's the closest? It had gotten so bad that one day I forced myself to stop eating because I had eaten fifteen chicken wings in less than fifteen minutes. If I hadn't stopped I would have finished all thirty because there wasn't a moment where I felt full. Since I didn't have any concern for what I put in my mouth, I only had myself to thank for my remarkable weight gain. In a matter of two months, I gained twenty-eight pounds, and a good majority of the weight had ballooned into my belly. I couldn't see over my tummy, and I was scared because I didn't want to have trouble getting rid of the baby weight. But my concerns couldn't stop me from eating. With all the negative things, such as the weight, the crying, the sleeping, the bad moods, the hot sweats, the chills, the swelling of the feet, and the ridiculous cravings, the positive things did outweigh the bad. The joy, the privilege, and the experience of a life growing inside of you is so powerful and truly can never be duplicated. Each time my baby kicked, that always brought silent laughter or a smile to my face, and now that he was a constant mover, Hercules and Sandra were never concerned with me. They just wanted to touch my stomach so they could feel the baby move.

The baby hype had my focus all screwed up, and I was unprepared for his homecoming. With my due date right around the corner, I called Sandra so we could go shopping at the mall. I didn't have a car seat, stroller, receiving blankets, clothes, pampers, bottles or pacifiers. She said she was coming, but it shouldn't have taken her two hours to come and get me. Since it was still early I tried to call her back and let her know I was going by myself, but as soon as I started dialing I heard Lil Jermaine in the hallway. When I opened the door I was pleasantly surprised to see Lil Bitts, Big and Little Jermaine, Sandra, Herc, Pastor Jordon, my brother, Shawn, and my mother. They had gifts, and most importantly food. I was hungry and the smell of fried chicken was definitely agreeing with my stomach, but I must admit it was good to see Lil Bitts, Shawn, and my mother again. My mom's boobs and butt were just a bit bigger than I would have expected them to be, and when I commented on them, she let me know that two weeks ago she had another set of twins. I was surprised but ecstatic. I wished my mother would have brought my new sisters, Sherell and Sharniece, but she left them with the Pastor's aunt. The old me might have been pissed off because I thought my mother had too many children and shouldn't have added any new additions, but I could care less. I was just thrilled to be around my family, and of course I missed my brother Shawn the most. Seeing him always lit up my soul, and today was no different. He was currently pursuing his BA in Business Management from Morehouse College, down in Atlanta, and I couldn't have been more proud. With the help of the pastor, he had followed the straight and narrow and avoided being another statistic. My brother was so handsome, and he was very articulate and behaved in a mature, professional manner. It had been a while since we last spoke, and I wanted to pull him to the side and just have a brother and sister day, but I was in the middle of my baby shower. However, I tried to spend as much time with him as I could because he had to go back to school the following day.

The shower was fun, and everybody wanted to see and feel on my belly. My favorite part came when it was time to open my gifts. They were good gifts, and nothing I had was cheesy. I got a stroller, a car seat, a swing, a crib, bottles and pacifiers, diapers, clothes and shoes, and an envelope with three thousand dollars from everyone. When we were growing up I might have thought somebody robbed a bank, but now my family had proven to be financially sound. My mom had since gone back to school, took her GED and was now working for the city as a phone operator, making thirty-two thousand a year (a far leap from her welfare days); the Pastor had money from an inheritance and his flock took good care of him; and as far as Sandra and Jermaine go, it was too hard to count how much money they had. He had houses and businesses all over that provided him with a hefty monthly profit. He still kept one foot in the streets – a concern for Sandra but an issue he wouldn't discuss. I couldn't judge, nor would I try. I was just happy to be in a position where my family wasn't scrambling, begging, or trying to make ends meet.

With all the goodies opened and my belly full, I couldn't help but do what came naturally – I fell asleep. As rude as it appeared, they understood that my narcoleptic pregnancy was the reason I nodded off. Everybody left except Lil Bitts who stayed and cleaned up. When I woke up, she and I had plenty of catching up to do. It was a good feeling to know she was my friend and was always loyal to our friendship. Whenever I needed her she was there, and even though we hadn't talked much because I moved and our lives were moving in different directions, she never stopped loving me or being my friend. I was so emotional that when she went home I cried until Herc told me, "Enough is enough."

Later that night while we were having sex, I felt as if I had to pee and this time I couldn't hold it. I rushed to the bathroom and when I wiped, I felt really uncomfortable. Next thing I knew, I was put on my ass by a pain that started as a sharp pinch and grew into a feeling like that of a rapid stabbing in my back by a butcher's knife. I screamed. Before I could touch my back to ease the pain, the feeling had jumped into my vagina. Herc ran into the bathroom and foolishly asked, "Did I hurt you?" I couldn't help but respond, "You wish," and then I yelled, "I'm having the baby!" Hercules was scared. It took him two minutes to understand everything I said. This pissed me off because each moment he delayed was another moment I wasn't at the hospital.

*Dead Silence*

## Chapter XXXVI

Sandra and Jermaine met us at the hospital, and I was relieved because Herc was getting on my nerves. I was in too much pain to put up with his nonsense questions, and he kept touching my back, even after I asked him to stop because it felt like someone poured acid on my spine. I never imagined the pain could be this intense. I mean, it felt as if the baby was ripping the mouth of a lion through my skin. I was ready to push because I wanted to get this monster out, but the nurses said I wasn't dilated enough. I was only two centimeters with more than a few to go, but I was ready now. With each contraction I wanted to push, but I didn't want to hurt myself or the baby so I dealt with what I could. The pain of labor was unbearable. All that shit I talked about going natural went out the window. I wanted the epidural. The more time they spent prolonging the needle, the more profanity I spilled into the hallways. Sandra asked me to keep my cool, but how could I? She kept laughing at me and telling me, "I told you so," but what the hell had she told me? Nothing. This pain was indescribable. She never said it would feel worse than death. And she thought it was oh so funny until I damn near ripped her scalp bald when I yanked her ponytail during one of my contractions. No matter how I turned, rocked, or shook, I was beyond repair. They had me laid on a bed with my stuff out for all the world to see with monitors hooked up to my heart, IVs in my arms, and I still hadn't gotten my epidural. I screamed for it, begged for it, and they kept saying, "We'll be there soon."

After using every curse word known to man because I hadn't gotten my epidural yet, the doctor came in to see how far I had dilated. I couldn't believe it but I was ten centimeters, and it was time to push! But now I wasn't ready! Herc was downstairs with Jermaine doing god knows what, and I was scared. I asked for the epidural but the doctor said I was too far. However I was still feeling pain and now tremendous pressure. The nurses began breaking down the bed. I looked at Sandra to find my strength. I knew I had to push, but I wanted Herc in the room too. She walked to the hallway to look for him, but I yelled for her to come back to my bedside. I wasn't about to be alone and if Herc missed this he would have hell to pay. The doctor was ready for me to go. "Push, Sunshine!"

"I have to wait for the father."

"Well the baby won't wait for him. Push!"

"Ten. Nine. Eight. Seven. Six. Five. Four. Three. Two. One…"

"Good job. When you're finished pushing I don't want you to inhale so much. Keep the breath in the push, you understand?"

"Not really."

"Just put all your energy in the push, you ready?"

"No."

"Well get ready. Here we go. Push!"

"Ten. Nine. Eight…"

"Okay, okay, I see the head crowning…keep pushing."

"Sandra help me. It hurts!"

"I can't help you, you just have to push." My cervix, uterus, and all those female gadgets wanted to explode. Why couldn't the doctor just go in and grab the baby out? I wish I could have scheduled a C-section because that probably would have been easier. I still hadn't seen Herc's face, and I started to get frustrated. When the doctor said, "Baby's almost here," I saw Herc walk into the room. I wanted to slap him, but I didn't have the time because now the pressure had turned into a burning sensation. I had to get this baby out. "One more big push and we'll have a baby. Ready Sunshine?"

"Yes! Ten. Nine. Eight…"

"Nurse call for Dr. Rogers!"

For a minute everything seemed fine, but I didn't hear the baby cry, and they hadn't brought him over to me. I wanted to hold him and see what he looked like, but when I heard the nurse say the umbilical cord was wrapped around his neck I panicked. They rushed the baby out of the room. When the doctor asked Herc, Jermaine, and Sandra to step outside, I knew it couldn't be good. I felt like my greatest fear was about to come true. "What the hell is going on?" I screamed to a room full of silent nurses. I was in full panic mode. I tried to pull out my IVs and get up so I could go see my baby, but they restrained me to the bed. My doctor came back in the room and told me the umbilical cord had wrapped around my baby's neck and a specialist was trying to resuscitate him.

The words were hard to swallow. I cried out for my baby, but nobody would respond. Sandra said what she could, but her words bounced off of me because the only thing I wanted to hear was that my baby was okay. Herc was in the hallway pacing with Jermaine trying his best to get him to relax. If he felt like me, then only knowing our baby was coming home would soothe us. I lay there motionless as the doctor took twenty minutes to remove the placenta and stitch me up with two stitches. I still hadn't gotten word. I tried to gather patience because no news is good news. At least that's what I tried to make myself believe.

Finally, damn near an hour later, the pediatric specialist came in my room and said, "Unfortunately, your baby choked on his umbilical cord while passing through the birth canal. We did everything we could to revive him, but...there's nothing else we can do." Nothing they could do. That's all I remember before collapsing within myself. I had been pregnant for almost ten months and now my baby was dead because the lifeline that kept him growing had suddenly cut off his air supply and damaged my heart. I blamed myself even though my doctor said it wasn't anyone's fault. I remembered falling off the bed and going to the abortion clinic. I never wanted to be pregnant, but after accepting my child, I wanted to be a mother.

The nurses had cleaned him off and brought him in to me, wrapped in a white hospital blanket. He was so handsome. He didn't look dead, but rather like he was sleeping. As I held him I kept waiting for him to open his eyes or cry, but that would never happen. He smelled so fresh and new, as babies do, and I didn't want to let him go. His skin was so soft and the smell of innocence crept up my nostrils with each sweet kiss I laid upon his calm, sleep-like face. It was hard for everyone to fathom what happened. I asked Herc,

Jermaine, and Sandra to hold him because I wanted to feel as normal as I could. My son was eight pounds, two ounces, sixteen inches, with a caramel complexion and a full head of wavy hair. I wanted his life to have a positive impact on the world so when they asked me to donate his small, beautiful, priceless organs, I signed the papers.

The hospital staff was very respectful of my situation and tried their best to comfort me. They sent in a priest who explained my options in regards to a ceremony, but I asked him to leave out any details in regards to a burial or cremation. I asked to have the ceremony on the same day because I could feel his body losing warmth, and I didn't want to wait much longer. Before the ceremony Herc and I had to name our child. It was hard for us to think, but we had to do it. I knew I didn't want him to be a junior and neither did Herc, so I asked Sandra and Jermaine if they had any suggestions. Neither one of them had a name in mind, and I could see from their eyes it was hard on them just trying to support us so I told them I'd come up with one.

I dressed Scott in the cutest, most adorable outfit. My mom had brought it to the baby shower. It was an all-white one-piece with detached angel wings on the back. The outfit was quite fitting for the small service we had in the hospital's chapel – a homecoming for a small, beautiful angel. My angel. It was peaceful, and the pastor said a few words and asked that we hold Scott for the last time before he took him away. It was hard for me to let him go, and I kept thinking maybe he's going to come back to me. I kissed him and felt he was much colder. It was then I realized he wasn't going to cry, he was never going to wake up.

After the service all I had to remember Scott by was a lock of his hair, two pictures, a birth and death certificate, and a home full of baby items that would surely add to my depression.

## Chapter XXXVII

Sandra contacted our State Senator, our Congressman, and the School Board because returning to school wasn't an option for me. Others may have dreamed of going on their prom or walking across the stage for graduation, but all I wanted was a diploma. The School Board requested a detailed report from my doctor and therapist in regards to the trauma I suffered as well as a written recommendation for the possibility of me testing out of school. My suicide attempt was more than enough to convince the School Board I met their criteria to test out.

My family was trying to deal with the idea of me trying to kill myself, but it shouldn't have come as a surprise. I had taken twenty of my depression pills, when the recommended dose was one 300 milligram pill a day. Within twenty minutes I began seeing colors, feeling woozy, and felt the urge to vomit, but I fought it. I didn't want to throw up any of the medicine because I wanted it to be over. I was tired of seeing Scott's face, tired of dreaming about being beaten to a state of unfamiliarity, tired of the abuse, the pain, and the fear. I wanted to hold my baby, to smell him, to hear him laugh, to change his diapers, to imagine the day he'd say, "Daddy," when all along I'd been trying to get him to say Mommy. But all I had were dreams and nightmares, and it was too much hurt. The pain was more than therapy, pills or family support could overcome.

Instead of falling asleep I became delusional. I went outside nude and began to urinate on the lawn. I found this out later from the neighbor who called the paramedics once I began to seize out. There wasn't too much I could remember besides the pain of having a tube running through my nose down into my throat, and having my stomach pumped. While I was in the hospital, I knew I wasn't getting right out because they had me in bed restraints. There was a nurse at my bedside twenty-four hours a day for two days. The first nurse asked me question after question about why I had tried to hurt myself and if they took off my arm restraints would I try to get away, but I never answered her. To tell the truth

I'm not sure what I would have done, especially since I wanted to die. I used to think that suicide was for weaklings, that nothing in the world could be so bad to make me hurt myself, but I stood corrected. Once the shift changed my other nurse did a better job at getting my attention because she didn't talk too much. She asked basic information about my pain level and explained to me what monitors I was hooked up to, and when I could expect to go home – which wasn't going to be soon. I talked to her about my son and how I missed him, and she told me she miscarried a year earlier. We were getting along fine until she started giving me needles in my stomach every six hours. They were supposed to prevent blood clots from forming, and since I was lying down and unable to move, the doctor felt they were necessary. I asked to get up so I didn't have to get another one of those shots because they hurt a great deal, but she said she couldn't unstrap me until the doctor said it was okay.

I wasn't able to get loose until they moved me to an in-patient facility in Fort Washington, PA. They kept me restrained the entire ride and didn't release me until I was inside my room. They put me in a co-op facility with crazy folks. The first thing I had to do was talk to someone about getting out of that hellhole because I wasn't crazy. But when I told the supervisor I didn't belong there because I wasn't crazy, her response was, "Everybody tells me that." Even though everyone there might have said that, most of them were lying. There was this one woman who had a wig on her head that was so matted, it looked like Mumia Abu Jamal locks, and she had a nerve to take the two longest pieces of the wig and tie them under her chin like a bow. Then she had this dress on that had some type of dark colored stain on it, and I didn't dare ask her what it was, and she didn't dare wash it. She had the same clothes on for my entire stay. There were other crazy people there that talked to themselves, wet themselves, or fought everyone, but no one was worse than my roommate. She was a very short female and didn't speak a word of English until she needed a cigarette. Her name was Monica. Monica walked around    in circles most of the day, and when I tried to sleep I woke up with her standing over my head chanting in Spanish. I slapped her the first night, and she quietly walked away, but I never slept after that because I didn't trust her.

I thought being in there was supposed to make me feel sane, recovered, and guilty about my actions, but it only made me angry, sick, and left me feeling isolated. During therapy, I participated and tried everything in my power to get out early, but once I realized I was staying whether I participated or not, I stopped talking. I tried to escape and even got into a no-win fight with the staff. I saw it as no-win because even if I hit hard or hurt them, they were only going to restrain me and dope me up. Code 100 was a regular term in there, and once it was used on me I knew I never wanted a Code 100 again. I'm not sure what medication they shot me up with, but I felt loopy, as if I would never get back in my right state of mind again.

After two weeks of group, restless nights, horrible meals, and no visits from my family, Sandra came to pick me up. I didn't feel embarrassed nor did I care to ask her why she hadn't come to see me. I was only worried about getting home. When I got there, my mom and the pastor were sitting on the couch, but I walked right past them, showered, and went to sleep. Later on that evening, Herc came home and looked at me as if I was the weakest link. Then he grabbed a few of his clothes and said, "I'll see you in the morning." I wasn't sure if I should've been upset, but to be spiteful I shouted, "You don't have to see me in the morning! Why don't you go see those guys who fucked me to death? And when you get a second, make sure you repay my money, plus interest because it's long overdue!" That didn't faze him. And when I heard the door slam, I knew he wasn't going to reply or repay me.

Once the School Board received all of my paperwork they agreed to grant me my high school diploma, as long as my scores on the G.E.D. exam ranked in the eightieth percentile in all subjects. The test was given on a Saturday. It was just me and the examiner, and I was given three hours to complete the entire exam. Luckily for me the test was a breeze, and I only took an hour and a half to finish. When they graded my exam I scored in the mastery percentile for every section, and with the letters of recommendations from my doctor, my former therapist, and the school counselor, I was awarded a high school diploma. The school offered me the option of walking with the graduating class, but I declined because it would have served no purpose. As long as I had that piece of paper the ceremony was meaningless to me.

I tried to move in the direction of being content, but Herc wasn't about to help me with that. He was cheating and didn't do much to cover her tracks. He'd come in the house at 3 a.m. or later at least four times a week, and as for the weekend, it would be a miracle if I saw him any day besides Sunday. We still had sex, which at first made me believe his alibi of being at his dad's house, but reality kicked in when he started getting calls all times of the night. The numbers were always private, and the ones that were visible, he made sure I never saw. If I even glanced over at his phone, he damn near broke his neck to cover up his caller-id screen. I don't know if cheating was his way of dealing with the loss of our son and my suicide attempt, but it wasn't a healthy way for either of us if we were going to stay together.

It got to the point where no alibis or lies were going to cover up the obvious because he infected me with Chlamydia three times, Trichomoniasis twice, and the flaming torch of Gonorrhea once. Each time I begged him to use a condom if he was going to step outside of our relationship, but instead of manning up, he blamed the infections on me. I know if I had infected him he would have taken those humongous hands and choked me out, so even though his lips were saying it was me, his heart knew the truth. I was weak from depression and didn't care about myself, which explains why I put up with his bullshit at first. But after realizing he could have killed me with HIV, I built up my strength and my commonsense. He wasn't paying my bills, he owed me money, his shot was dirty and infectious, my son died, and he wasn't helping me with that, so it was time for his broke, STD-infected, ignorant, nut ass to leave. I made it clear to his broke ass how badly I wanted my money by writing him a nice letter, which I left on the cracked windshield of his car that was parked in front of one of his girlfriend's house. Don't wonder how the windshield got broke – I stood on top of his car, took a brick, and slammed it into the windshield. Then I took out an icepick and jammed it into each tire, followed by quickly breaking his head lights, brake lights, and his windshield wipers. Normally I would have had Emo do my dirty work, but this was a job I felt I needed to do myself. I wasn't scared of him, and this fool had put my life at risk. Once the deed was done, the locks were changed. I was done with that scum. Fuck with fire, and they say you'll get burned. I felt firsthand the effects of getting torched. But now payback was a bitch.

I told Jermaine what I had done because if Herc was going to give me any problems, I wanted his punishment to be swift, hard, and just. If that meant a leg shot, head shot, back shot, ass shot, or major artery to the coffin shot, I wanted him to get it. I usually wouldn't have been s o intense, but I was tired of being used up and laid out to dry. Fortunately for me, Jermaine was tired of it too. He put the word in Herc's ear, eliminating a stalker-ex banging on my door or calling my phone. Now I had no strings attached to this fool. The money he owed me was a loss. He was a has- been, and I was a woman scorned on a new mission. Besides, he probably wasn't Scott's father anyway.

After getting my body completely cured from those pesky STDs and attending a few therapy sessions, my plan was clear. I wanted to go into business with Jermaine. He had asked before, but I wanted to do my own thing. However, now wasn't the time to let any opportunities pass me by. Jermaine had acquired a store-front down in Center City and wanted to open a fashion boutique. I was excited because I loved fashion, and being as though I had some experience in the field, he wanted me to head the store up. The money, of course, would be supplied by him while I would be the face of the boutique.

We had a detailed dinner meeting and my job description and expectations were laid on the table. I was responsible for the store layout, stock, clerks, security (if necessary), and luring the customers to our store. Getting clientele in Center City wasn't going to be a problem because a new, fresh face with a great product always equals sales. After going over our product sheets, it was clear our items were beautiful, different, creative, and more importantly, reasonably priced. We priced to sell, and our items wouldn't easily be found in the neighboring stores or shopping mall. Jermaine was connected with a fashion design teacher in New York. Many of our items would be detailed, one-of-a-kind, handmade pieces. I was very excited about this originality because my entire reason for shopping at consignment and thrift stores was to find an item that no one else would have, minus the Versace price tag.

Two added perks to the boutique were that I would have a personal designer, and I could choose the name of the store. The student designer whom I was assigned was a genius and had them faggot skills, no insult intended. Everyone who knows fashion knows when a gay guy put his thing down, no one can match it. This guy was no different. I lost all of my baby weight, and having the perfect hips and ass, he had my jeans fitting like a charm. The second part of my bonus package was flattering and that went to my head for like an hour. Being able to choose the name of a boutique I would be managing was mind blowing. It may have seemed shallow, but of course I wanted my name to filter in the store's name somewhere, but the final decision was Jermaine's. I came up with: A Touch of Sunshine, Sunshine's Boutique, Bask in the Sunshine, Sunful Flavors, Drops of Sunshine, and Sunshine's. All the possible names went over well with Jermaine, and since I couldn't tell him which was my favorite, he put them in a hat and pulled out A Touch of Sunshine. So that was the name. I was happy with it and now it was on to running the store.

It wasn't an easy task, even with the monetary help from Jermaine. Knowing how much and what to buy, how and when and where to advertise, and then carrying around the load of being personally responsible for the store's success, I needed to take a few breathers here and there. Fortunately the store was on the road to success. My best teacher was hands-on experience. I made a few mistakes of overbuying and of buying some out-of-season items, but the store had plenty of friends, and with the high-quality, diverse, affordable items, I wasn't afraid of us going out of business. The clothing business is a high-risk venture, but thankfully Jermaine is a good businessman, and thankfully I proved to be an excellent marketing and management coordinator.

Within a year, we had four members on board (two part-time clerks, one assistant manager, and a security guard), and the boutique was making good money. I encouraged Jermaine to have a customer appreciation party for our loyal clientele. The party planning, of course, was in my hands, and after getting the budget approved, I was ready to pull it off. From the food to the decorations I had it all covered. We had devoted customers, many of whom held events such as book signings, poetry readings, food tastings, and a single's night in our upstairs event area. Now it was time for repayment, along with the always needed exposure from the party.

The night of the party was beautiful. Club La Mushulu hosted, "A Night of Appreciation", presented by A Touch of Sunshine. I couldn't have asked for a better turnout. Many of our New York fans and designers came over the bridge and brought more product sheets. It seemed like it was always business, even when I called myself taking the day off. Jermaine was pleased and kept looking at me like I was his little prodigy. Sandra, who I rarely saw because I spent most of my days and nights at the store, managing, ordering, and nursing my boutique to success, was there with smiles and congratulations. I often wondered why she didn't want to get involved in Jermaine's businesses, but if the shoe was on the other foot where I could have plenty of money and not work, I might have decided to play homemaker as well.

With the party entering the final stages, I geared up for our fashion show and made my way to the model's changing quarters. I was scheduled to model three outfits, one being the finale dress. In that moment I took a deep breath and suddenly realized how happy I was. Working hard and making money had been two things that brought  happiness in my life, and I didn't want that feeling to end. I was proud of myself, of what I had accomplished in such a short time. To be young and successful is a feeling many ponder but few ever get to put their hands on it. My car and wardrobe had been upgraded, and I was living on the waterfront, single and not depending on anyone, including Jermaine's  allowance. All this without a college degree and with enduring a  tragic loss that included an abundance of pain and misery – I had surprised myself. I was a survivor and was excited about the future chapters in my life.

*The Sun Can't Shine Forever, Especially After the Shit Hits the Fan*

## Chapter XXXVIII

"I love you!"

"I love you too. I'll see you later on tonight."

I don't know how it came to this. I was in love with a man who wasn't mine. This wasn't my character, my style. This wasn't me, but at the same time this was me. It was everything I wanted, everything I desired. He was my man when he had time, when I needed him to be, and whatever the cost, I had to find a way to keep him. I felt I had it all until I tasted him. This forbidden fruit had to be mine. I can't remember when this started or how I allowed it to get this far. But I know now that one flirtatious glance followed by a seductive comment can lead to an unforgettable, unforgivable night – with a gift that doesn't belong to you. My conscience was in overdrive. I kept questioning my actions, trying to rationalize my choices, but never trying to find evil in my doings. This couldn't be wrong. If it was, there had to be a way to make it right.

Each passionate moment I spent with Jermaine was a moment I desired and longed for. He was the topping to my ice cream sundae, the cherry, the whipped cream, the peak to my climax, the perfect orgasmic flavor for my needs. I loved to please him. It came so natural. But I hadn't truly figured out if he was a guilty pleasure of mine or if it was love. I was leaning more towards love. I had gotten the idea of infatuation out of my mind because the money and the success weren't new for him, and to be honest they weren't new to me either. Although, before now, I hadn't always experienced them on an independent basis, I still had a taste of the comfy life. I had been running the boutique for two years, and we were still making money. I invested my money well. Jermaine helped me purchase two duplexes, and I was in talks with my designer about opening a boutique in New York in the fall. When my thoughts about our situation
- whether it was good, bad, rational or deplorable – subsided, all I thought about was being with him.

Sandra was an obstacle for me, but as much as I loved her, I had no intentions of leaving him. She had helped me, and at first I felt guilty, sick, and sorrowful, but that was before I realized he fell out of love with her a long time ago. She wasn't his type. Once he began moving up, she was simply happy with being an old maid, and he needed more. He needed a woman who would get involved with his business ventures and have his back, as well as fuck him like a man needed to be fucked. My sister was dull and needed a tune up, but she wasn't the type for change. She was too complacent. I was just what the doctored ordered. I made him happy, and he damn sure pleased me. He made love to my body and trust me when I say I know the difference. Each time he lay on my pillow, he was relaxed, thrilled, and satisfied, mentally and physically. I was able to be nasty, similar to the whore or the one-night-stand, and then sweet, like the submissive wife. He brought the beast and the queen out of me. We were able to talk about our deepest secrets, our goals, what we enjoyed and hated, and about having a life together. To think about it, he always had my back and my best interest at heart, so why shouldn't this have happened? We were made for each other, and I w a s n ' t letting go, but the sneaking around had to stop eventually.

I wanted him to tell Sandra. He promised he would, but he was taking too long. He had too many excuses, and even though it may have seemed like an unbearable secret for her and for my family, I know they would ultimately get over it. I wanted to live my life with him openly and freely, and I was determined to get this secret uncovered. Twice I tried calling her but her unsuspecting, lovable voice made me panic, and I quickly made up a reason why I had to call her back. Sometimes I believed she knew their relationship was over. She may not have known he was in love with me, but she knew he was sleeping around. Sandra was a pushover. I couldn't wait until she got a whiff of this, but for now it was quickies in my office, late nights at my condo, and weekend business trips to New York, Miami, and Las Vegas where we could openly be together.

The hardest part of all this was when he was home with her, when he and I knew he belonged in our bed. I didn't want it to be this way, and I would never have imagined myself being one of those people who indulged in her sister's closet. But how could I deny his or my feelings when they were so powerful? There was even a moment when I tried to leave him, but within a day I was calling him, and he was begging me to come back to him. I wanted to tell someone in order to get an unbiased opinion as to what I should do, but I knew no one would understand. For now I worked my hardest in the boutique, traveled with him on weekends, and continued carrying on an affair with my sister's man.

## Chapter XXXIX

Our relationship began to bring up tension. For some reason, Sandra was popping up more than usual, and it wasn't sitting well with me. Whenever he came to the store, she followed, and she was sticking her nose in business she normally didn't care about. She had so many questions to ask about the business - where money was going for this, for that – and she pushed the limit when she asked me how much I was getting paid. I started to blurt out, "I get paid for fucking the boss, so ask him how much that pays," but I was trying to remain professional and respect his wishes. Jermaine did his best to put her in her place, but there was a clear case of miscommunication as well as a battle for authority. I decided to take an early lunch but as soon as I got up Sandra demanded I sit down, and I did.

"Sunshine I need to talk with you."

"Whatever we have to discuss can wait until I come back from lunch."

"No it can't."

"Okay, so what's up?"

"I don't like the way business is being run around here. And more importantly you're not in charge."

"Damn it if I'm not. I run this okay, and if you have any problems you can take it up with my boss."

"Your boss…I think you got the game twisted. First and foremost, you wouldn't be in this position if it wasn't for me."

"Wasn't for you? I come in here and work every day. I hire, I fire, I buy stock, I design the layout, I make sure shit runs smoothly, and you want to come in here with this nonsense. If you wanted to be the boss, why didn't you run the boutique three years ago? Let me guess, you too busy playing house maid, lying on your ass, and watching TV."

"Sunshine I'm let you take a walk because I'm five minutes from…"

"Five minutes from what! We ain't little kids no more!"

I stormed out of there and left the store in his hands. If he didn't have the balls to tell her what was up, I hoped he   had the sense to know he or she needed to run the store today. I went home. He was constantly calling my phone but I was too busy trying to make myself busy. I hated delayed comments, and we could have talked about plenty at the store. Whatever he was saying now I didn't care to hear. And Sandra was so out of the loop she just embarrassed herself. I wasn't getting special favors from fucking the boss. I worked my ass off and made the store what it was. She knew the boutique was just one of his successful businesses, so I wished she would have said what she came there to say. Within the hour Jermaine had stopped over, but I gave him the silent treatment. He was trying to explain that Sandra was upset because she thinks he's seeing somebody, and I exploded. "What the fuck do you mean seeing somebody? You are! You're seeing her goddamn sister. How long do you think I am going to put up with your shit!"

"Baby I'm just asking you to understand my situation."

"Your situation?"

"I have a son with her, and she's a joint owner of my businesses."

"Don't try to school me on y'all situation. I know what's going on. So your hesitation to tell her about us is about some money! You got plenty. Give her what she wants, but let me know what's up with us or get the fuck out!"

I really didn't want him to get out, and when he started walking to the door I swiftly followed him and pleaded with him to stay. It quickly turned into one of those times when anger turns into lust and gets confused with love. I wanted to fuck him, and I could see from the imprint in his pants so did he. I let him strip me by the door and pushed him to the ground so he could cater to my needs. He was aggressive, yet gentle, and his tongue had me stuttering.

"So you wanna leave me…"

"Uh-uh...no...no…"

"What? I can't hear you?"

"No, dddaaddy...Please donn't sstopp." The longer he ate, the more I wanted him, but he was teasing me. I didn't want him to stop, but I wanted him to pound it. I began to grab for his dick, but he kept pushing my hands away and    continued

to eat me out. I was calling out his name at the top of my lungs. I wanted every part of him. Still I was upset, and I showed him by forcefully grabbing his dick. But it didn't bother him, it only turned him on more. Once I had taken off all his clothes and he was seated in the chair, I put on our favorite song,
"Sunshine" by Babyface.

*"Last night I laid with you...Twas like a dream come true...I never felt so right...No...Want you for the rest of my life...Maybe we should settle down and raise a family, a girl for you and maybe a boy for me...that is how much, how much I love you girl...Noo, ohh..Sunshine, you brighten my life...Sunshine, you make me feel alright...Sunshine, you turn my darkness to light and you brighten up the corners of my heart..."*

Then I started to ride him. It was slow on the way up and swift on the way down. The motion was just right and with each call of my name, "Sunshine, oh Sunshine," I could feel my orgasm peering to a head. I loved being with him and enjoyed each moment we shared. Was I asking for too much? I was in love with a man that wasn't mine, but I couldn't stop and neither could he. He couldn't deny his desire to be with me or the power our sexual intimacy held. Right before he was about to cum, he stood up and turned me over so he could fuck me doggy style. This was my favorite position, and since I started taking birth control I loved it even more because he could cum in me. He is the only man who showed me the ultimate moment of intimacy
– cumming together in unison. There's nothing like two people having an orgasm at the same time. "Oh my god. Oh shit. Oh shit, Imma about to cum..."
"Me too!"
I couldn't believe what I just heard, or what I saw. He was bleeding. He had been shot. Sandra was standing there holding a 45mm with tears rolling down her face. I didn't know what to do, what to say, or where to go. She had the gun pointed at me and I was scared. I couldn't think. He was

standing up for a moment before he fell to the ground. Sandra didn't speak. She only stood there. All of a sudden I remembered giving her a spare key when I first moved in, and I started thinking about why I hadn't changed the locks or gotten my spare back, but none of that mattered now. She suddenly spoke. "I knew he was, but I had to see it for myself. Sunshine how could you do this to me?"

"Sandra..."

"Bitch don't say nothing. Did he tell you he knew the guys who raped you! Did he tell you that? Huh, Jermaine, did you tell her that? Or did you think your money would be enough to cover that up?" I couldn't believe it. Was she telling the truth, and if he knew, how did she know? How long had she known? What had I gotten myself into? Sandra started walking over to us and I started panicking. "Don't cry now because you're gonna get everything you deserve. Here all this time I thought you were the victim, that you needed protection, but today you're gonna get all that and more!"

"Sandra I'm so sorry."

"Shut the fuck up! That depression medication must have really fucked you up, but for you to do this, to me! And Jermaine what do you have to say for yourself? I went against the grain. You sent those guys to get your money from Herc, and you begged me to forgive you. Didn't you?"

"Sandra, I'm sorry."

"Shut up! I'm the sorry one."

"Sandra please get me some help..."

"Jermaine all the help you need is right here."

She fired another shot into his head. I stood there not fully capable of making out the image of splattered brains. I was scared because she didn't put the gun down after she shot him. Instead she was pointing it back at me. She was quiet for a while as if she was contemplating her next move, and since I didn't want to encourage her to shoot me, I kept quiet and held my head down. I knew the mere visual of my face along with my naked body was enough for her to snap, so I shook and trembled but kept my mouth shut. It was only seconds before she began speaking again. "I bet you want to know how long I've known. I found out last year. He never wanted you to get hurt. They were never supposed to touch you, and he made sure he dealt with them. Jermaine and his need to protect his reputation, he couldn't let Herc mess up his money, no matter how much he had...I thought I could forgive myself for staying with a man who was responsible for taking away your shine. Somehow I think this is my punishment. He loved you, did you know that? Sunshine do you love me? Answer me!"

"Of course..." I knew what I was going to say to her, but the loud bang and the sudden jolt of my body sent my words in another direction. I knew I had fallen, but I couldn't feel much more than that. I began to see the sun but it was all different colors. At one point it was extremely bright but then it started to fade and then I heard another loud bang, then...

## Chapter XL

"I stand here today only with the help and grace of my Lord and savior. I lost two beautiful gifts that were sent to me from the Lord above…for reasons I may never understand. Today I lay both of my daughters to rest. But truth be told, I lost one of my daughters quite some time ago. I lost my baby when her innocence was snatched from her, when I allowed my addiction to be greater than the love I had for her. Love can be painful. Today and forever I will bear the scars of lost love. Words will never be enough for you to understand what I feel, how much I mourn…Today I read a poem from one of my daughters. In her own words of how she viewed life, how deep she hurt, and how much she desired the pain to evaporate. My daughters…Dear God, help me through this…"

*The sun, a sign of power, strength, beauty*
*A great energy, a dynamic force of nature*
*The name given to me*
*So strong I would never be able to live up to its expectations*
*I know my sun will not shine forever*
*Because my wounds no longer heal and my pain seems more like pleasure*
*Somebody took my shine a long time ago*
*He took this child to a valley where children aren't supposed to go*
*And every time I tried to recover*
*I dealt with a new loss, a different pain, or another trauma*
*Will the world end if my sun stops shining, will they remember, will they care*
*I wonder about this so hard that I pray for the sun to fall,*
*Because I know they'll never shed a tear*
*My world is filled with hurt and pain*
*A world filled with more rain and too little sunshine*
*Should I shine, Shall I Fall?*
*They say the sun never sets, that the moon just hides it at times*

*Tiona Pathenia Brown*

*But I say it's time for the sun to set, No more hiding*
*Today I decide my sun no longer shines*

R.I.P…Sunshine

*To the reader*

*I hope you enjoyed this read and got a message from this story. The sun can shine as long as you want it to, but you have to make positive choices, even in the face of disaster or after taking a walk with trauma. Life is always what you make it, even when others make it hard for you. Although this tale had a tragic ending, it doesn't have to be your story. I have had the firsthand opportunity to live with devils, walk with snakes, and drink from the same glass as demons, but I remember first that I shine bright, and that I come from a strong tree, which was planted in a million gallons of cement and shall never be moved.*

*I enjoyed writing this story and hope you enjoyed reading it. If we ever meet, let me know who your favorite character is, what's your favorite chapter, and what you most enjoyed or didn't enjoy about the book. I am open-minded and always open to suggestions so I may better please my readers in the future.*

*Peace, Love, and Strength to All*

*Tiona*

Coming Soon

# M & M Suites

## Success Now, Then, & Always...

**Growing** up I was the ugly duckling; the bony dark-skinned nigga with the unmolded head. I knew I would need a little help getting the ladies but I never imagined my cup would be spilling over. But when a hustler is bred, raised up by a true gangster, and given the charm from the best hoe that ever did it, the swagger is one no one will deny. I kept it real, they kept it grimy, and still I managed to get crowned. I'm still rising. I'm a CEO and not by chance or choice but by **breed.**

Visit www.tiona.net for information and updates.

# Who?

*It never mattered to me how or why; I only want to know Who?*

Available Now!!!
Visit www.tiona.net to purchase.